THE PEACOCK STONE

The Stone Collection

NICK HAWKES

The Peacock Stone

First edition published in 2019
by Hawkesflight Media

The characters in this novel are purely fictional.
Any resemblance to people who have existed, or are existing, is coincidental.

ISBN 978-0-6481103-3-0

www.author-nick.com

Cover Design by Karri Klawiter

The Peacock Stone

A novel

by Nick Hawkes

To Mary, who shared the adventures of India

Chapter 1

The beggar tapped with his stick, feeling his way through the crowd, toward his usual squat. As he did, the madness of India waking to a new day assailed him. It was the sound of ordered chaos; of fifteen million people fighting to survive.

Delhi was not an easy city to live in, particularly if you were blind, but occasionally, kindness came between the curses. Rough hands would sometimes reach out and steer him safely past the stalls of the market traders. Their carts were set up in the open area opposite the entrance to Delhi's main railway station on the west side of Chelmsford Road. They sold everything: bananas, pomegranates, pineapples, paratha bread, curries, and, of course, hot chai. If your taste was for something cooler, you could buy the sweet liquid that came from men turning the wheels of sugar-cane crushers.

He paused to listen. The noise of the Delhi traffic was at its normal level of drama, just a smidge shy of mayhem. Horns beeped continuously. The asthmatic squawk of rubber balloon-operated horns on auto-rickshaws competed with the indignant blare of the buses and the hooting of cars.

The noise was comforting.

The beggar stank. He knew he did. A dog had urinated on him during the night as he slept in his usual laneway. The pungent warm stream had woken him. He'd cursed the dog, causing it to skip a few paces sideways, and then he'd gone back to sleep. It was not an uncommon experience.

His smell did, however, make the prospect of being given breakfast by a stall owner less likely.

An impatient hand reached out and jerked him sideways. He could hear the hiss of a gas cooker and the bubble of boiling oil nearby. He was probably being pulled away from someone cooking puri. The Indian puff bread would be ballooning spectacularly into the size of a football in a pan of boiling oil before it burst and collapsed into a crisp bubbly pancake.

That was the trouble with going blind late in life—you remembered.

"Pah. You stink, old man."

He lowered his head, held out his hand and dared to ask, "Food?"

"Piss off."

He moved on again, tapping left and right with his stick—seeking kindness elsewhere. Unless someone gave him breakfast before he arrived at his squat, he would not eat until he tried his luck again when he walked back to the food carts at lunchtime. He would dearly love someone to hand him a samosa wrapped in newspaper. Surely the gods would smile at such an act of charity.

The prospects did not look good for he was now nearly at his squat. The gods were not smiling.

He'd chosen the squat carefully. It was among the stalls operated primarily by the barbers. There was a spot where he could sit on a slab of broken masonry that had once covered the sewer underneath. The hole it had left in the pavement was treacherous. He'd discovered it painfully two years ago, and it had taken months for the wound in his leg to heal. In fact, he would probably have died if the nuns had not found him.

They were from the Missionaries of Charity, the order founded by Mother Teresa, and they'd been keeping an eye out for him over many years. In a city of two hundred thousand beggars, he knew he was fortunate to have their attention. Sister Rosalind normally found him some time during the week in order to tend his sores and give him food.

Aah. He was at his squat now. Bending down, he swept the area in front of him with his left hand to check it was free of feces. It was wise to do so. Cows, dogs, donkeys, and goats wandered freely amid the traffic and the street stalls.

Around him, he could pick out the murmur of conversation between the barbers and their clients. The morning commuters would be sitting in chairs on the barber's platforms having a shave before they went to work. Some of them were having their faces slapped enthusiastically to cause their skin to glow.

It was a good spot for a squat. Shaving put customers in a positive mood, and they had to open their wallets to pay for their shave or haircut. However, there was one particular reason why he came here. It was the place she could always find him.

He squatted down, pushed his begging bowl in front of him, and waited.

Being a beggar required you to have well-practiced plaintiff cries and routines designed to attract attention. It needed a delicate balance to be bold enough to attract attention, but not so bold as to offend the sensibilities of potential benefactors. It was important to lower your head humbly and not look people in the face when they spoke to you. *Let them know you are less than they are.*

He squared his shoulders. He had not always been less. Once he'd been a gifted craftsman, honored for his skills—before he had needed to hide, and before he'd gone blind. His shoulders slumped down again.

He could hear raised voices from the women who gathered with their plastic containers at the public tap. They were arguing. It was little wonder. The women of the district only had a short while to collect water before it stopped flowing. They had to fight.

Water was a constant source of irritation in Delhi. Although eighty percent of houses had access to piped water, it was only available for two hours a day, usually in the morning. To make matters worse, the quality of the water had fallen over the years so that it was even beyond the abilities of carbon filters to make safe. A quarter of Delhi's population now had to rely on water tankers. The beggar scowled. The water crisis in Delhi had been orchestrated by the notoriously inept Delhi Jal Board. They promised every year that things would be improved. It was now 2009, and things were as bad as ever. Word was that the Jal Board was clogged up by under performing, unsackable bureaucrats. He spat on the ground.

Light feet walking quickly. He thought he recognized them. Was it the sound of her feet?

He waited.

The footsteps stopped in front of him.

He was almost sure.

"Rohit, Uncle…oh dear, dear. You smell really bad."

The beggar smiled. Her fourteen-year-old voice was full of concern.

"Aah, Jayanti, my dear; the dogs have taken a liking to me even if the gods have not."

"I've brought you your water." She tapped his arm with a plastic bottle.

Wordlessly, he exchanged it for an empty one he pulled from the bag hidden under his *chadar*, his shawl.

He could hear her sniffing him, working out where the offensive smell came from.

"Uncle, give me your *chadar*. I'll wash it and bring it back this afternoon."

He sighed and unwrapped it reluctantly from his thin shoulders. Rohit hated parting with it. He lived in his shawl. It was the only security he had.

He felt water being poured over his shoulders and small hands sluicing him clean. He bowed over and surrendered to Jayanti's ministrations. His only protest was to say, "You're wasting your water, you know. You will have to queue again to get some, and it will probably have run out by the time you reach the tap."

"Never mind. Auntie will just scold me, and I will be told to go to a neighbor and beg some water from her roof top tank. I will

4

probably have to pay for it by doing her washing, but that is no matter. You can't stink like this. No one will come near you."

He blew the water away from his mouth. "May you be blessed by the gods."

"There," she said. "That's better." She rested a hand on his shoulder. "I'll see you this afternoon."

"*Accha.*"[1]

Jayanti pattered away on her bare feet, leaving him feeling vulnerable, dressed only in his lungi.

He was just deciding to surrender to self-pity when he heard coarse laughter coming from a group of young men behind him.

"I wouldn't mind her hands over me washing me clean."

Laughter.

"I think we'd both get nicely wet."

Another voice: "Yes, I've been noticing her. Her fruit will be worth plucking any day now."

The initial man: "I saw her first. You can have her after me."

Ribald laughter.

"She's a pretty thing, right enough. You know, I think I'll come back here this afternoon—so I can get to know her."

"Know her! So you can slide between her petals, more like."

More laughter.

It was chilling, dirty, and demeaning talk which might have been dismissed as bravado had this not been Kaseru Walan—a none too salubrious area of Delhi. In this context, their words presaged real danger. Jayanti was frighteningly vulnerable as she had not grown up locally. She was a 'blow in', a southerner who did not have the protection of any significant person locally.

The beggar wanted to scream; to flail at the men and damn them to hell. He wanted to cut them into pieces—very small pieces; pieces that were so small, they were worthless.

Instead he bowed his head and said nothing, allowing his long hair to hide his face.

But he thought. Oh yes, he thought hard.

Around him, Delhi tooted and bustled impatiently, careless of his angst.

He rocked backward and forward. Life was cruel, and he was weak. What could he do? Jayanti was the most precious person in the world to him. What could he do to protect her?

He thought back to the time when he'd first met her. She'd come with Sister Rosalind. The nun had explained that Jayanti was from Kerala. Her parents had died so she'd been sent to Delhi to live with her great aunt. The young girl had asked to accompany the nun and the new sister who was with her as they walked the streets and lanes of Kaseru Walan.

Ever since that time, Jayanti walked with the sisters on a good many mornings, helping them by carrying their food sacks. It became apparent to Rohit over the months that Jayanti idolized Sister Rosalind, so when the nun asked her to keep an eye on him, she'd accepted the responsibility immediately.

She'd cared for him faithfully for years, bringing water, some-times food—and a friendship, even love, had grown between them. Jayanti had come to call him 'Rohit Uncle'…a term that delighted him—even though it was not his real name. It was wonderful to be of significance to someone.

He put his hands together and offered a perfunctory *puja*, a prayer to *Ganesh* for Rosalind. The elephant-headed god was thought to be particularly kindhearted. However, Rohit had never experienced much kindness, so he didn't place much faith in his prayer. Maybe in another life, when he was a better person, *Ganesh* might take more notice of him. As it was…*Ach shpput*. He spat again. *Life was a bitch.*

For on top of his weight of concerns for Jayanti, was the knowl-edge that he himself was being hunted. A man very much wanted him dead.

Chapter 2

R ahul held the knife against the throat of his friend as he
    pushed him against the wall.

Kumar yelped with alarm and froze, pressing against the bricks
in submission.

"Just who did you say I was in love with?" cooed Rahul.

"Ah, ah," spluttered Kumar.

His friend, Arjun, leaned back against the door and grinned. "I
think you said that our mighty captain and fearless leader, Rahul
Khatri, was in love with Clueless, the little schoolteacher."

"Damn lie; damn lie," protested Kumar.

"Rahul, be kind to Kumar," said Arjun with a sigh. "He might
be forgiven for thinking such a thing. You spend an hour with her
outside her Auntie's house most afternoons…practicing your
English."

"I go there to escape the smell of you guys," said Rahul taking
the knife away from the throat of his stricken friend. With a fluid
motion, he sheathed it in a scabbard tucked behind his waist. "And
to learn enough English to teach a *gaandu*[1] like you to work the
tourists at the train station."

"Which we are doing with good results," Arjun pointed out.

Rahul acknowledged the truth of the statement with a nod and patted Kumar on the cheek. "You should see your face, Kumar. You just about shat yourself."

"*Hey Ram!*" expostulated Kumar as he sank onto a chair in front of a small table. A carrom board was placed on top of it. The fourth member of Rahul's team, Malick, sat on the other side of it—silent, as usual.

Rahul looked at his friends. All were of a similar age to himself, about sixteen—as far as any of them could tell, and all of them came from the alleyways. Arjun was the witty one. He was stick thin and sought to cover his gawky frame in western clothes he thought were trendy. Kumar, on the other hand, loved his food, was strong as an elephant, and passionate about cricket. Malick was the odd one out. He was a Muslim, the son, paradoxically, of an alcoholic father. He was silent, brooding, and dangerous. His trouble was that he remembered too much of his childhood.

Rahul rubbed the back of his neck. He remembered nothing of his. All memory of it had been wiped clean.

"Whose go is it?" muttered Kumar.

Malick pointed a finger at him.

Kumar took the small wooden disc, set it behind a line painted on the carrom board, and flicked it at a black disc causing it to skid into one of the pockets in the corner of the board. Both were addicted to the game and had become very good at it.

Rahul looked at his watch. It was a cheap imitation, but it worked. The overcrowded commuter trains full of locals would have all arrived by now. Tourists rarely caught these trains, preferring to come later. They would start to arrive any time now. "Time for work," he said.

They trooped out of the laneways, crossed Chelmsford Road and began to work among the tourists at the station. Rahul was soon busy assessing the tourists and using his primitive English phrases on likely customers.

To those getting on the trains, his stock phrases were: "Where you go? Show me ticket. I will take bags to your very fine carriage."

However, the most profit came from tourists getting off trains at the station. For them, he had a different stock of phrases.

He'd grab the luggage from startled passengers and say, "I am carrying your good self's luggages."

After hefting the luggage onto his head, he'd pad along in front of them and ask, "What is your good name, Sir?"

It was all about getting them to engage in conversation.

"You have hotel for your very good selves?"

At this point, the tourist would tell him the name of the hotel.

Rahul would grimace and say, "Hotel no good. Very dirty."

Sometimes he'd use a variant. "Hotel burned down. But no problems. You are wanting cheap and excellent hotels, isn't it? I take you." He'd lead them through the dust toward the shoe-cleaning boys.

"You are wanting shoes cleaning isn't it. Look, shoes are dirty. See boy here. He number one at shoes cleaning. Very cheap. Your great self must look good."

When they arrived at the hotel, he'd drop the bags in the foyer and be paid. The hotel receptionist would treat him disdainfully and call the hotel porter to carry his customer's bags to their room. Rahul would be paid his kickback later from the kitchen door.

Some of the more accommodating hotels allowed him to carry his customer's bags to their rooms. This was where real money could be made.

"What is it you are wanting sirs? I know best food places. Very cheap. Best foods."

If the tourists were carrying back-packs and had the right demeanor, he could be bolder. "You wanting sexy business, or maybe hashish—very good, or *garad*[2], maybe *chandu*[3]? I buy for you. Can smoke it in this hotel. No problems."

Money was to be made at every stage.

But there was stiff opposition. Rahul and his team were a rising force in a fiercely competitive market. There were scores and scores of 'station flies' engaged in the same business. There was only one answer to this.

Violence.

Intimidation by those older and already established in the trade could only be met by violence. It was the language they understood. This was never meted out in public at the train station—that would attract the attention of station security. Violence happened in the laneways, usually at night. That was why Rahul needed his team.

The day wore on, and Rahul did not succeed in doing very much business. He felt distracted, and his heart wasn't in it. As the time grew near for the evening commuters to begin arriving, he headed over to the food stalls across the road, kicking his way through the dust and rubbish. He ordered a potato curry, squatted down on the pavement, and began eating it, scooping the food into his mouth with the fingers of his right hand.

His eyes scanned the passing throng. It was a reflex habit —*always look for opportunities.*

Across the other side of the square, he caught sight of Clueless. She was behind the barber's stalls talking to a beggar. He watched her as he mopped up the curry gravy, and shook his head. She was being clueless as usual. You don't speak to beggars. You don't display naïveté if you live in the laneways; you don't help Christian missionaries without financial reward; and you don't look so...he searched for the right word: 'disturbing', he decided—not in Kaseru Walan. You keep a low profile.

He wiped his hands on a piece of newspaper he tore off from a bundle threaded onto a string hanging from the side of the food cart, and nodded his thanks to its owner. No money had changed hands. The food seller was an outlet for some of Rahul's hashish.

He continued to watch Clueless covertly. She was not, he conceded, hard to watch. Her long black hair was plaited down her back. She had given it sheen and luster with coconut oil—and decorated it with tiny flowers. He hadn't got the words to describe why her face was striking, just that it reminded him of the Bollywood actresses who stared down at him from garish posters on almost every corner in Delhi. However, her face was also different. It had a serenity, a guilelessness about it.

Her dress was modest, but it did not hide the woman's body that was blossoming underneath it. This was also betrayed by the way she now walked. She swayed at the hips—and was probably completely unaware she was doing it. Clueless: that's what she was.

Bloody hell.

A frisson of alarm ran down ran down the back of Rahul's neck.

He recognized the young man who was accosting Clueless as she walked away from the beggar. He was a member of a gang of older boys that had laid claim to a good section of the alleyways. His approach looked friendly—initially. He pointed to a food cart.

She shook her head and pulled her arm away.

More conversation followed.

Clueless then did the worst thing possible. She lowered her head and stood stock-still; meek as a sacrificial chicken. *Fight, you stupid woman. Scream, scratch.*

Clueless's aggressor began to walk around her flicking her shoulder and hair in a derisory way, talking all the time, sneering, establishing his superiority.

"What's got your interest?"

Rahul jerked his head around to see Kumar's familiar bulk approaching. He was scratching his crotch absentmindedly. Rahul didn't answer but returned his attention to the scene being played out. Kumar followed his gaze.

Clueless's tormentor went to grab her arm, but she shook it free. Then she turned, lifted her head, and began to walk into the laneways.

Her assailant trailed behind her until she entered the alleyway, then he ran forward, took her by the arm, and propelled her forward.

Kumar chuckled. "I doubt that she will be a maid by this time tomorrow."

Rahul shot him a dark look. "You forget, Kumar. We need her to teach English. She is an asset of ours. If we allow these bastards to ruin her, or anything else of ours, they'll be all over us."

It wasn't quite as clear-cut as he sought to portray it, but he was in no mood to quibble about detail.

Kumar looked at Rahul speculatively. "Are you suggesting that we should rescue Miss Clueless? Have you thought of the implications?"

Rahul's answer was to set off toward the laneway at a brisk walk.

"It'll get physical," warned Kumar jogging behind him to keep him company."

"I hope so."

Violence did happen in the laneways, but it was considered bad manners. It broke the unwritten code of live-and-let-live. The most brutal violence usually took place in dark, lonely places. This was not to say that the streets were without drama. Arguments over prices and quarreling between husbands and wives broke out all the time. So, no one would raise a glance at a girl being marched along by the arm by a young man. She was probably being forced home for a thrashing by a brother for some misdemeanor or other.

Rahul and Kumar made up ground on Clueless and her captor as they threaded their way deeper into the laneways, pushing their way past women carrying pots on their heads heading home to begin cooking the evening meal. Their men were demanding and fussy about their food, for it, more than anything else, represented security.

If the women weren't cooking at home, they were sweeping with brushes made of bundles of reeds. Rahul had once wondered about the fetish of cleanliness at the immediate frontage of each house. The center of the laneway was in stark contrast. Vegetable waste, excrement, and torn paper cluttered the streets to be picked over by dogs, cows, and rats.

Rahul barely saw any of it. His focus was on Clueless, and he was waiting for the inevitable move.

It wasn't long before it came.

Clueless's aggressor suddenly clamped his other hand over her mouth, pulled her across his chest, and backed into a doorway.

Almost immediately, an older woman was pushed through the

same door out into the alley. She held her hands to her cheek and looked around her, terrified and bewildered as the door slammed shut behind her.

Rahul snatched up a piece of metal piping from outside a cycle repair shop and ran forward. He stopped beside the door and nodded to Kumar.

Kumar hit the door with his shoulder at a run.

The door didn't even begin to open normally. It flew off the hinges and fell backward on top of two bodies sprawled underneath it.

Rahul ran straight over the door and hit the male head protruding from under it with the steel pipe.

Clueless screamed.

Rahul hissed to Kumar. "Get Clueless outside and tell the old woman to take her home. Quick, quick."

Rahul ducked into the back room so he wouldn't be identified as Kumar dragged Clueless from under the door and led her outside.

A few moments later, Kumar returned. "All good," he said.

Rahul was grateful. The old woman could have screamed until a crowd of locals, armed with sticks, assembled to mete out summary justice. As it was, they had some time. He walked over to the flattened door and stood it back up in order to ensure privacy. The latch on the locking mechanism still worked, so he was able to secure it shut—after a fashion. Then he knelt down and rifled through the comatose man's pockets. He pulled out a wad of money and handed it Kumar. "Take half and leave the other half for the woman to pay for the damaged door."

Kumar nodded, peeled off some notes, and put them in a cooking pot beside the stove. He pocketed the rest and stood with his hands on his hips. "Now what?"

"Pull down his pants."

"What?"

"Pull down his pants."

"I suppose it's no use me saying that what I think you're going to do might be extreme?"

Rahul found a ball of twine on the bench and cut two pieces from it. He then held the blade of his knife in the flame of the stove.

Moments later, the would-be rapist was rendered incapable of fathering a child.

"Right, pull his pants up and let's get him out of here."

A rickshaw was squeezing its way down the alleyway as they carried the man outside. Rahul stopped the driver and helped Kumar lift the unconscious man into the seat.

"Pay the rickshaw-wallah well" he ordered.

Kumar took some of his newly acquired money and paid the driver, explaining cheerfully that his friend was drunk. "Just take him to Main Bazaar Road and leave him where he won't be a nuisance." Taking acceptance for granted, Kumar turned, placed an arm around Rahul and led him down the laneway. "Have you calmed down yet?" he inquired.

Chapter 3

The morning sun tried to fight its way through the window shutters. Thin pencil-lines of light patterned the parquet flooring—too few to dispel the gloom. The dark paneling around the walls of the dining room failed to add any comfort.

Ravi stood to attention before the figure seated at the end of the table. He could not see his father's face as it remained hidden behind a newspaper. Ravi was again being reminded of his place. His father's authority eloquently voiced by his posture of belligerent indifference.

Its malevolence caused Ravi to take an involuntary step back so that he bumped into the massive figure of Aakar Singh standing behind him. The huge Sikh put out a hand to steady him. Aakar was part bodyguard, gatekeeper, and personal driver. Ravi sometimes felt that the role of 'prison warder' could be added to the list.

The Sikh's hand was surprisingly gentle.

"Please father. May I have a dog? My friend Aarav's dog has had puppies. May I have one? It's an Alsatian." He hurried on. "It would be a good guard dog."

A voice came from behind the paper. "No. We have guards

enough. We have Aakar. I'll have no dog messes in my house." The man paused, then added. "You may leave."

Ravi remembered the softness of the puppies. They were full of life, lunging at his face, trying to lick him…and completely trusting, rolling over to expose a stomach to stroke.

"Please father."

The paper fell away and his father's fist banged on the table. "I said no; and that's an end to it."

The verdict was crushing. Ravi ached for the companionship and joy a dog might bring him. He wanted to feel its ears; he wanted to care; he needed to experience its love. He was desperate.

Before he could stop himself, he blurted out, "Why do you dislike me so much, father? I try to please you. I am a good student. Why do I disappoint you so much?"

Ravi again felt the Sikh's hand rest on his shoulder. It was a warning.

His father did not reply.

Ravi was beyond care. "Why?" he repeated.

The Sikh's hand tightened.

His father began picking up the newspaper but then dropped it back onto his lap. "You are too much like your mother. You're too soft."

"But I have never known my mother."

His father gave no impression that he'd heard him. "Goodness gets you nowhere! It is money you need." The fist crashed down again on the table. "Do you hear! Money is your only security. Let the poor chase their gods. They have no option." He pointed at Ravi. "You don't have any lust for power. You are too gentle."

Ravi dropped his head, and failed to understand what was being said. "I, I'm sorry father."

His father looked at him for a long while before wiping a hand over his face, causing it to distort.

"Get out!" he roared.

Aakar turned him round and steered him out of the room.

Outside in the entrance hall, Ravi held onto the pillar beside the marble staircase and wept.

Aakar Singh remained silent.

Eventually, the giant Sikh, cleared his throat and said. "Follow me to the kitchen, Ravi, I have something to show you."

Ravi began to get himself back under control. It was one thing to cry in front of Aakar, and quite another to be seen crying by the kitchen staff.

"Why?" he asked.

"Come," ordered Aakar.

The Sikh led him down the corridor that led to the kitchen. Staff stiffened as they passed the cooking benches and sinks to the back door. Ravi had very rarely been to the kitchens. Its alien world of sweat and steam was intimidating. The people who worked there were part of a wider community of servants whose social hub was the patio outside the kitchen door. He didn't understand them at all.

They passed through the back door to the covered area. Dish-cloths hung from lines tied between the supporting posts.

The giant Sikh bent down and picked up a shoebox from a trestle table and handed it to Ravi.

Ravi took it cautiously and lifted the lid.

Inside was a bird. It immediately tried to flutter and shuffle into a corner of the box, but Ravi could see that the bird was badly hurt. One wing, at least, was broken.

Aakar spoke gruffly. "The bird will die soon. It flew into a window." He shrugged. "If you don't take it into the house and you look after it here, it may live for a while." He glanced at Ravi. "Would you like to care for it?"

Ravi looked at the terrified bird. It was so vulnerable and helpless.

"Yes," he said. "Will you show me what to do?"

The giant nodded.

An hour later, Ravi emerged from the hallway to the kitchen into the grand entrance foyer. As he began to climb the stairs, his father crossed the hall behind him. His accusing voice reached him from behind.

"Did you just come from the kitchens? You know the kitchens are no place for you."

Ravi's mind whirled. "Yes father, I went there to scold one of the servants."

"Really. Which one?"

Oh no! Outside, Ravi could hear the sounds of normality, of sanity—the hum of the traffic, the toots of their horns, and cries of vendors advertising their wares. These sounds mixed with the chattering buzz of a lawnmower outside.

Ravi hurried on, "Oh, I can't remember his name." He affected a dismissive wave. "One of the gardeners. The grass was getting too long for me to play on."

"I'll sack him."

Acid rose in the back of Ravi's throat. "No, no," the mower was broken. It's been fixed and, as you can hear, the man is now mowing the grass. It wasn't his fault."

His father frowned.

Ravi rushed on. "But I gave him a dressing down all the same."

His father nodded. "Good. If you want power, you must continually reassert it." He walked to the front door and said over his shoulder, "Maybe you are less like your mother than I thought."

"Aakar, will you teach me to fire a gun?"

The Sikh opened the drawer to his desk and put away the oiled cloth he was using to wipe his pistol. He placed his hands on either side of the gun. "Why?"

"It is a new skill, and might help me to feel less…" he wanted to say 'useless' but couldn't bring himself to.

The giant looked at him for a long time.

Ravi dropped his head.

Finally Aakar nodded. "I will check with your father. If he says yes, I will do so."

Ravi brightened. "Excellent."

Aakar stood up and slipped the pistol into the shoulder holster inside his coat. "I had planned to go to the pistol club today to practice. Then I was going to come back and take you to your tennis coaching. If your father says "Yes", be ready to come with me after lunch so we can go to the firing range?"

Ravi nodded.

After bolting down his lunch, Ravi waited impatiently for Aakar in the entrance hall. When the Sikh finally arrived, Ravi was relieved to learn that permission had been granted. When they arrived at the pistol club, little was visible from the outside. Aakar explained that it had once been an ammunition bunker, which explained why it was covered in earth. The bunker had been cleaned out and modified into a firing range.

After a lengthy safety briefing, Aakar began instructing him in how to fire a gun.

"Pull back the cocking slide, then let it go. Let it spring back by itself. Don't try and hang on to it as it goes back into position."

"Why?"

"Because there is a chance it might fire. If it does, the slide will bang open and damage your hand."

"Oh."

"The bullet is now in the chamber ready to fire. Now, watch what I do. Brace your feet and hold the gun with two hands like this—very firm. Keep the gun upright and aim through the sights."

Ravi gulped. "Is there a bullet in there now?"

"No. I haven't put the magazine in yet. It's safe to hold."

Ravi took the gun, and was shocked by its weight. This wasn't what Hollywood and Bollywood had led him to expect. He felt sweat in the palm of his hands and began to breathe in shallow pants. His sense of adventure at firing a pistol now gave way to a sense of dread.

Guns killed. It was sobering.

"Relax. Switch off the safety catch then squeeze the trigger gradually, little by little. Take your time... and hold your breath. You will feel the trigger harden. Keep pushing past that pressure point until it hardens again. This is when the gun will fire. Try it."

Ravi fired, and was rewarded by a benign click.

"Good. Now we do it for real. Put on these earmuffs. But first, watch me as I shoot so you know how big the recoil is. You will need to hold your firing wrist firmly. Yes?"

Ravi nodded.

The noise and energy of Aakar's shot was shocking.

"Your turn now."

Ravi took the gun, sighted on the target… then lowered it to the ground. "I can't fire it," he sobbed.

Aakar took the gun from him. "Why not?"

"Because the target is a silhouette of a person."

"Is that the only reason?"

Ravi nodded.

"Then we'll change the target to a round bullseye. Would that be satisfactory?"

"I…I, think so."

A few minutes later, Ravi fired his first shot.

Chapter 4

Sister Elizabeth already loved the people of India. They had the ability to make-do in any situation and exhibited extraordinary grace. However, she was not yet sure she loved India. She'd been in the country three months and the assault on her senses was unrelenting. Tragedy, triumph, greed, poverty, desperation, demons, and gods—the whole panoply of India's culture assailed her from every direction. It was all so different from her native Australia.

She scurried after Sister Rosalind who was threading her way past a bullock cart, narrowly missing an auto-rickshaw (or 'auto' as they were known locally), which was being overtaken by a motorbike with an entire family aboard. How on earth did Sister Rosalind do it? Was it because she was Indian, or was it her trust in God? She seemed to move with an unhurried grace exhibiting a level of faith Elizabeth could only hope she might attain herself one day. She cowered back and coughed in the diesel smoke of a luridly painted Tata truck that lurched by. Their drivers needed to make a living on the hazardous roads of India each day, often driving long distances. She'd been told that they sought to make life more bearable by smoking hash or availing themselves of the 'truck prostitutes' who were readily available.

The heat was oppressive. However, despite her discomfort, she reveled in her work and had learned to be grateful for the regulated nature of each day. The ordered routine of the Missionaries of Charity gave her a safe foundation from which she could push out into the madness of India.

The day began with mass and a time of meditation, followed by breakfast. From there, the sisters sallied forth in pairs to the homes for the destitute, to schools, or with hessian shoulder bags of food for the poor. After lunch, the routine would be repeated except that aspirants, such as herself, would have classes. Only the professed sisters would go back to work.

One of her favorite times of the day was the recreation time after dinner. All the sisters would talk like crazy for half an hour before they headed off to chapel. The evening service signaled the end of the day.

That morning, they'd caught a bus from their convent at Timarpur not far from the Yamuna River where Krishna was said to have played on the banks and enjoyed sex with a milkmaid.

Their morning mission was to give books, pencils, and slates to a tiny school that operated in Kaseru Walan. This was an area of dense housing bounded by the Gupta flyover to the north, Chelmsford Road to the east and Basant Road to the south. It was a poor area that had evolved haphazardly over the centuries. A few hotels clung optimistically to the main roads, but the real activity happened in the maze of laneways behind them.

Elizabeth pulled at the front of her white sari to encourage some airflow, and flicked another bead on her rosary. She wrinkled her nose. That prayer had become disjointed by the demands of crossing the road. Elizabeth risked talking with Sister Rosalind. Technically, it was discouraged as it was seen as a distraction from prayer, but Sister Rosalind never seemed to mind.

"How do you ever get used to it?" she asked, stepping around a man urinating into the gutter. Whilst men generally tried to hide behind something when relieving themselves into the drains, urination was done with a great deal less modesty.

Sister Rosalind smiled. *"Mor nach raha hai."*

"What did you say?"

"It's a local phrase used to describe men peeing in the streets. It means, 'the peacock is dancing'."

Elizabeth giggled. Any notion that the nuns might be prudish had been quickly dispelled in the first week of her stay with them. They were earthy pragmatists, which she thought was fabulous— and probably not surprising. The nuns saw more of the harsh realities of life in a month than most people saw in a lifetime.

"How long have you been a nun?"

"I trained for six years and began my tertianship nine years ago."

Elizabeth stole a quick look at her companion. Sister Rosalind was a woman of contradictions. She was pious and afforded herself no privileges at all. Yet, although dressed in the humble white sari of the Missionaries of Charity, she still managed to look beautiful. Both her face and her figure were stunning, and she walked with a languid grace that was lovely to see.

This, she reflected, was in sharp contrast to her own body that was pale, freckled, and in every way unremarkable—except for her auburn hair, now demurely hidden under her headscarf.

"You haven't always been a nun, have you?"

"No."

"What did you do?"

Sister Rosalind glanced at her.

Elizabeth hurried on quickly. "I mean: how did you make the transition, you know, from ordinary life to that of being a nun?"

"Every journey is different. God will call you down your own path." Sister Rosalind smiled. "Don't worry. He won't run out of ways of inviting you to follow him."

"Hmm." Elizabeth looked up at the sky. It was a dirty, pale haze —so different from the blue skies of home. "Where are we going, today?"

"To the home of a widow. Technically, she's a retired teacher, but she still runs a class for low caste children, teaching English from her home for an hour or so in the late afternoon." She smiled sadly.

"It's the time when children can be spared from whatever manual work they're engaged in."

"Oh. How many students does she teach?"

"It varies. Typically, about forty. They can't fit into her house, so she sits on the front step with a blackboard, and the children sit in the laneway."

"Wow! And she does all this by herself?"

"She's had the help of an orphaned relative for the last two years—a great niece, from Kerala. Bright. She speaks English well. We're visiting them today to give out reading resources."

Elizabeth reflected on the harsh reality of the caste system that still held India in its thrall—and required special classes for low caste children. She struggled to understand it.

"Tell me again about the caste system and how it works?"

Rosalind shot her a glance. "It is...not easy to explain to a Westerner."

Elizabeth persisted. "Does it really stop children from being educated?"

"Yes. That, and poverty."

"How?"

Sister Rosalind sighed. "You need to understand that caste discrimination and rural feudalism are the bedrock of Indian life. Both have stubbornly resisted any political initiatives aimed at dismantling them."

"But how does it actually work?"

"The caste system has four tiers. On the top are the Brahmin priests. You've seen them. They can be identified by the 'sacred thread', the *yajñopavītam*, worn diagonally across their bare chest."

Elizabeth nodded.

"Next come the warrior caste. They often become policemen or soldiers."

"And they always seem to be scowling with disapproval or impatience," laughed Elizabeth.

Rosalind shrugged. "It is just their way. She paused. "The next level is the merchant class...and these are followed by the *Sudra*, the servant class. But what you must remember is that twenty percent of

India's population don't even rate a position in the caste system. These are the Dalits, or the *Harijans* as Gandhi preferred to call them. They are India's compliant work force and they do all the nasty, menial jobs." She sighed. "So you can understand why many high caste Indians think that educating Dalits is dangerously destructive of our social order."

Elizabeth shivered. "Their old name was 'the untouchables' wasn't it?"

"Yes. But it is not used now—and you must never use it."

"Of course." Elizabeth knew that most of the people she had already met were Dalits. She could tell. Their dark faces had a haunted, desperate look that broke her heart.

She trailed after Sister Rosalind as she led the way into a maze of laneways where industry lived cheek by jowl with houses. To the left, she could see a sweatshop of tailors through a ground-level basement window. There was no glass in the window, just metal bars. Boys sat cross-legged in front of hand-propelled sewing machines. None of them spoke. Only their machines made a noise: *tickety, tickety, tickety*.

The buildings, no more than three or four stories high, crowded closer together the deeper they went in among them. The laneways quickly became too narrow for cars to proceed, then too narrow for motorized autos and hand pulled carts. Finally, you were forced to push past people and interrupt the dialogues taking place between shadows in the doorways.

No cottage industry appeared to need a sign in these alleyways. Everyone apparently knew—or was it that nobody was welcome who didn't know?

As Elizabeth walked along the alleyway, she had a sense that she was trespassing. The locals, engaged in cottage industry or domestic chores, seemed to be happy and at ease with each other— but they stopped to stare when they saw the nuns approach. As a Caucasian, Elizabeth not only felt watched but resented. Dark eyes smoldered, betraying feelings that ran deep. It was as if they were saying: 'This is our place. What right do you have to walk through our community here? Have you come to wonder at our poverty, or are you here to exploit us? This is not your place. Our rules apply here.'

She shivered. Indians seemed able to say a thousand things with their eyes. Resentment, anger, fear, disdain, carping subservience, friendship (feigned and real), and love—could all be expressed without words. In a country of a thousand languages, it was probably fairly useful.

Sister Rosalind stopped at the door of a house that seemed to be better kept than most of those around it and knocked.

An elderly woman with wisps of gray hair escaping from under her headscarf opened the door and invited them in.

Both nuns kicked off their sandals and followed her into the gloom.

The woman sat her visitors down on a bed and went off to fetch them a glass of Limca, the local fizzy drink.

Elizabeth glanced around the room. A shrine of some sort was perched in an alcove on the far wall. The rest of the walls were covered with calendars, faded old family photographs of people looking stiffly formal, and pictures of Hindu gods. She was surprised to see that among them was a portrait of Jesus and his bleeding heart. In a nation with over a million gods, Elizabeth supposed that one more was neither here nor there—it was good to hedge your bets.

Sister Rosalind and the old schoolteacher were soon engaged in conversation. It was in Hindi, so she understood none of it. Elizabeth was trying to learn the language but had not progressed very far. She contented herself with unpacking their two hessian shoulder bags. They contained writing slates and books, both of which had proved heavy to carry. As she did, she saw a girl appear in the rear doorway of the room and remain in the shadows. The girl was was wearing a yellow sari.

"Hello," said Elizabeth instinctively.

The girl smiled and lowered her head.

Sister Rosalind saw the girl, held a hand out toward her and said in English, "Jayanti: it is good to see you."

The young girl stepped across the room, knelt down, and kissed the nun's feet. Then she laid her head on the nun's lap. Sister Rosalind stroked her hair and spoke gently to her in Hindi.

Rather surprisingly, the girl started to cry.

A conversation of sorts followed, punctuated by more tears that verged on the edge of hysteria, as if the young girl was re-living a nightmare.

Sister Rosalind frowned with concern. She took hold of the girl's shoulders, lifted her up, and hugged her, rocking her back and forward. It was the instinctive act of a mother.

Eventually, emotions were controlled, and the girl stood to her feet. Sister Rosalind kept hold of her hand and fingered the yellow sari with the other. "And what's this, Jayanti: you are wearing a sari now, not a long skirt *langa* and *choli* any more?"

The girl again dropped her head and said nothing.

The old school teacher answered for her. "Jayanti has been a woman for some time now. It was time her dress proclaimed it."

Sister Rosalind nodded and stood up. She placed a hand on the girl's head and prayed a blessing on her.

"May God your heavenly Father bless you with an understanding of his love and bless you with knowledge of your purpose."

Chapter 5

Elizabeth and Sister Rosalind threaded their way back through the laneways toward Chelmsford Road. Both were silent. Sister Rosalind seemed preoccupied, and Elizabeth was taking in the scenes that unfolded at every corner, her prayer beads forgotten.

They passed a man at a handcart doing ironing for the local hotels. His flat iron was ornate, its metal decorated to look like lace. It was heated on a charcoal fire that was burning beside him. She had seen a number of such men in Delhi. Somehow, each of the million items ironed by them found their way back to the right person in the right hotel.

Sister Rosalind brought her mind back to their mission. "Sister Elizabeth."

"Er…yes."

"There is a beggar I would like to check up on not far from the bus stop before we return for lunch."

Elizabeth heard the *tring* of a cycle bell behind her and stepped aside to let a tinker go by on his pushbike. So many large metal pots had been tied behind him onto the bike that they towered above his head. "Ah, um…is the beggar sick?"

"No. He is blind and doesn't find life easy."

Elizabeth could well imagine it, particularly in a city like Delhi. His life would be terrifying.

His situation caused her to reflect on a question that had been gnawing at her for some weeks. "Why is it that in this land where so many gods are worshiped, that beggars can be so uncared for?"

Sister Rosalind smiled sadly. "I'm afraid the Hindu culture is not very kind to beggars. Good Hindus do occasionally give alms to the poor as it is considered a spiritually meritorious thing to do, but at the heart of Hinduism, there is a different value system."

"Really," she said.

"You don't understand, do you?"

"No, I'm afraid not."

"If a Hindu priest saw a beggar, he could reasonably say three things to him. First, he could say: 'The Vedas teach that your pain is an illusion.' Second, he might say: 'Your low status is your own fault, the result of poor behavior in a past life.' And thirdly, he might say: 'You must live out your karma, your situation, faithfully and not try to improve it.'"

Elizabeth shook her head. "What can we say...or do, for that matter? It's all so overwhelming."

Sister Rosalind put a hand on her arm and stopped her walking. She turned and faced her. "Think. Tell me what three things you could say to the beggar."

"Ah." She thought furiously. "Um...'Your pain is real.'"

"Good; and..."

"Er, 'Your situation is caused by humanity's brokenness, for which we are all partly responsible.'"

"And finally...?"

Elizabeth couldn't think of very much at all. In the end, she shrugged and said, "It's just that God has given me a compassion for them and compels me to help them."

"Bravo, Elizabeth. This is why you will do well in India."

"But there is so much suffering. How can we hope to make a significant difference?"

Sister Rosalind readjusted the bag over her shoulder and

continued walking down the laneway. "God has not called us to be successful, Elizabeth, only faithful."

They walked past the shop fronts of the soapstone carvers making statues of Hindu gods, out into the open area where the market barrows were.

With unhurried grace, Sister Rosalind headed toward the barber stalls where she stopped in front of an old man sitting with his legs crossed on a slab of concrete. He had his head lifted up as if praying to the heavens. His gray hair, long and unkempt, tumbled over the shawl he'd wrapped around his torso. Both eyes were open and both were clouded white. It was a disturbing sight, one calculated to elicit compassion from the passers by.

Sister Rosalind spoke to him in Hindi. Almost instantly, the old man became animated. He beat his breast and wailed so much that the nun put a hand on his shoulder to steady him. The only word Elizabeth recognized him saying was 'Jayanti...Jayanti'.

Elizabeth felt she was intruding on the beggar's personal grief and looked away. She found herself staring at a telegraph pole. The haphazard tangle of wires at the top was absurd. But somehow, it all worked. Plastic bags and other unidentified litter hung from many of the wires, blown in by the wind—like so many of the poor of Delhi.

She turned back to see Sister Rosalind squatting down, listening and nodding to the old man as she wrote notes with a pencil on a notepad. As the nun stood up, the beggar beckoned her to come close again as he fumbled with his other hand under his shawl. A moment later, he held out what looked like a large soapstone pendant. Elizabeth watched as Sister Rosalind turned it over in her hand. On one side, a six-pronged star had been etched into the stone. On the other was a peacock—the native bird of India.

As they left, the old man put his hands together and bowed the classic Indian salutation—'I worship the god within you.' He seemed more at peace.

Later, as they traveled by bus along the Outer Ring Road to Timarpur and their convent, Elizabeth asked what had happened... and what the meaning of the pendant was.

Sister Rosalind didn't answer directly. Instead she said, "Elizabeth, I am going to ask the Reverend Mother if you can be excused classes this afternoon to accompany me back to town so we can deliver a letter—and escort the young girl, Jayanti, to what may be her new home. Would you be amenable to that?"

Elizabeth nodded. "Of course."

The aged schoolteacher and Sister Rosalind again sat on the bed in the old woman's home, engaged in earnest conversation. Elizabeth felt left out. She really should get a move on and make better progress in learning the language. It was late afternoon and the children had all scampered home after their language studies, some clutching their new writing slates. *Oh to have minds like theirs, so open to new skills.*

Elizabeth sat herself in the only chair in the room. It was the one the schoolteacher had moved inside after using it to teach from. As she sat down, she heard snatches of a conversation outside. Jayanti was sitting on the step talking to an older boy who was slouched against a wall on the other side of the alleyway.

"You teach me wrong thing," said the boy in heavily accented English.

"I did not," retorted Jayanti. The girl had certainly got spirit.

"Yes you did."

"What?"

"I say good things to this man, just like you teach. I say, 'Your very good self is an impotent man, isn't it?'"…and he smack me on the head."

Jayanti laughed.

"What?" demanded the boy.

"You say it wrong."

"What?"

"Ahee. Impotent means his, er…man's thing doesn't work. You need to say, 'important', not 'impotent'."

"What man's thing?"

"*Shishan.*"

The boy laughed. "It funny, school teacher girl use that word."

The girl snorted. "You call me 'Clueless' and then complain when I know too much. Pah! Men!"

"Jayanti," called the schoolteacher.

Jayanti came inside and stood demurely before her. She was dressed in her old blouse and skirt. Elizabeth suspected that she had quickly changed into the sari earlier that morning in honor of Sister Rosalind's visit. Her daily dress was still the modest dress of a little girl.

The old woman sniffed and began to speak. "It has become too dangerous for you to live here in Kaseru Walan with me. Sister Rosalind and I think it better you live in a better place—a safer place."

The girl's response was instantaneous. "No Aunty." She flung herself at the schoolteacher and clung to her. "I will be a better girl. I'll work harder. Let me stay. Please." Her terror was evident.

The old woman stroked her hair and spoke gently to her in Hindi.

Eventually, the tears subsided, and Jayanti knelt in front of her great aunt with her head bowed, looking forlorn. Elizabeth sympathized with her. For a young girl who was orphaned two years ago and had to travel to the other end of India to live with a relative, another move would be traumatizing.

The old woman startled Elizabeth by yelling out, "Rahul Khatri, come in here."

A boy's face appeared around the edge of the front door. Elizabeth suspected that he'd been eavesdropping.

He was a well-built boy dressed in a white lungi and a loose shirt. His expression was simultaneously wary and defiant. "How you know my name?" he demanded.

The schoolteacher waved her hand dismissively. "You think I not know. Stupid boy."

Silence hung between them.

She continued. "Come in here."

The boy stepped into the entrance and stayed there, a silhouette.

"It is too dangerous for Jayanti to stay here with me. The nuns may have found a new place for her—in a rich man's house with big walls that will protect her." She waved toward Elizabeth.

"Elizabeth Sister can take her, but she's new in Delhi and doesn't know the way. She needs a clever man who knows...and a strong man to protect her. Can you be that man?"

"Clever?" he glanced at Jayanti seeking understanding.

She rattled off an explanation in Hindi.

He nodded, apparently mollified. "Where?"

To Rajaji Marg road, in the Vijay Chowk area. Not far away.

"Big-shot place."

"Yes."

The boy shook his head. "Jayanti no go. I keeping her safe, isn't it?"

The schoolteacher put her hands on her hips. "Jayanti was attacked today. You cannot watch her all the time."

The boy looked at her impassively.

Elizabeth held her breath, wondering how the stand off would resolve.

The schoolteacher continued in a softer tone. "And Jayanti will not be far away if you want to see her. But right now, she needs your help."

Silence.

The schoolteacher pressed on. "She needs your help, Rahul. Take an auto. I'll pay."

More silence.

Finally, the boy gave a curt nod.

The transaction was done.

The old woman turned to Jayanti. "Go pack your things."

Jayanti, trailed out of the room. She paused at the door and asked, "Aunty, can I take my sari?"

"Of course."

Elizabeth watched Jayanti leave, then turned a puzzled frown to Sister Rosalind.

"Forgive me, Elizabeth. I am needed here. A woman along the alley believes she is being troubled with evil spirits and wants me to pray them away." She smiled. "I've suggested that it would require coming under the lordship of Jesus, but she and her husband said they can't afford to be Christians yet. He needs to cheat in his business for a while longer. He's said he'll become a Christian when he's rich." She sighed. "So I think there's a bit of talking to do." She nodded toward Rahul and smiled. "Rahul will take good care of you. When you arrive, knock on the door of this address." She handed Elizabeth a piece of paper. "It is the house of a very rich man, a businessman, Mr. Gokul Panwar. Mention that Jayanti is under the care of the Missionaries of Charity and give him this letter. It contains information that I learned from Rohit."

Elizabeth furrowed her brow. "The beggar?"

"Yes, but please forget that you know anything about Rohit." She paused before continuing. "If this businessman agrees to take Jayanti into his home: well and good. If not, bring her back here. I'll be waiting for you."

Sister Rosalind pointed to the letter. "If you are asked where the information in that letter came from, say you have no idea—for that is the simple truth. Mention only that Jayanti is under the watchful care of the Missionaries of Charity." She handed Elizabeth the letter. "God go with you."

Sister Rosalind turned and squatted down in front of Jayanti. "Jayanti, I understand that you are feeling very scared at the moment."

The girl said nothing.

The nun reached out and took the child's hands in her own. "You are very special, Jayanti. You are intelligent, and you have a beautiful heart. My concern is to keep you safe and to see that you prosper."

"Can't I go home to my village in Kerala? I...I can cook for my brother," the child pleaded.

The older nun moved her hands to the girl's shoulders and searched her face until eye contact was made. Then she tapped her heart. "Jayanti, do you feel you belong in my heart?"

Jayanti nodded, almost imperceptibly.

Sister Rosalind drew the child into an embrace. "If you feel you belong in my love, I will never be far away." She moved her head back and stroked the girl's hair. "Now, let me pass on to you a small gift, something that will remind you that you are loved, not only by me, but also by Rohit."

Half an hour later, Elizabeth, Rahul and Jayanti were in the back of a green and yellow auto, spluttering down Rajaji Marg. Impressive houses lined both sides of the street. One of them, Elizabeth noted, was the British High Commission.

Rahul barked an order to the driver who responded by swinging the auto into the curb. Elizabeth peered at the imposing wall and the roof of the house behind it.

Rahul nodded toward the house but remained where he was, seated in the auto. The young girl kept her eyes down. She had been silent during the ride, clutching the sack that contained all her worldly belongings.

With some misgivings, Elizabeth stepped down from the auto and walked to the wrought iron gate. She pushed the electronic buzzer beside it and waited. The house was now visible. It was built in the Victorian-colonial style, although the presence of air conditioners on the roof indicated it had been modernized. Security cameras mounted on posts had been installed in the gardens.

The front door of the house opened, and the largest man Elizabeth had ever seen began to walk down the gravel driveway toward her. He was a Sikh. The man was dressed in a belted, gold tunic and wore a crimson turban that had a gold spray on its side. None of his bulk appeared to be fat. A handlebar mustache and beard added to his intimidating presence.

Elizabeth swallowed. She was not surprised that a Sikh guarded the gate. Sikhs seemed to gravitate to roles where there was the risk of a fight. She'd seen them outside moneychangers with shotguns across their knees, in hotel foyers, and, of course, in army and police uniforms.

The giant walked up to the gate with his dark eyes glittering. His military boots were shined to perfection. He ran his eyes over Elizabeth's white sari and spoke with a voice that was surprisingly soft.

"What do you want, Memsahib?"

"I have a letter for Mr. Gokul Panwar. If he would be kind enough to read it and give me a response, I'd be grateful."

"Sahib Panwar is a busy man. If this is a begging request, please give it to his business office."

"Oh no. This is a personal letter and important." Elizabeth rushed on. "And I am happy to wait here for a reply." She thrust the letter through the bars of the gate.

The giant paused, took the letter and held it up to inspect it. "Wait," he said. With that, he turned and marched back up the gravel path to the house. He might have been on parade.

It proved to be a long wait. But if there was anything that the Missionaries of Charity had taught her, it was how to be patient. She had learned that it was not possible to waste time when you could retreat to that private inner place where you were known and could be known. When she arrived at that place, she prayed for Jayanti.

Dusk was beginning to fall, and Elizabeth had a feeling that she was being watched. She glanced at the house and saw the face of a boy in an upstairs window. She was tempted to wave to him but at that moment the giant came marching back down the driveway. He looked severe.

Elizabeth suppressed an involuntary shudder.

The Sikh stopped at the gates and pushed a button on a remote control.

The gate opened, leaving nothing between Elizabeth and one hundred and fifty kilograms of Sikh warrior.

"Tell the girl to come in. She shall work in the laundry," he said.

Elizabeth felt constrained to say, "Jayanti is very bright and educated. You will find she can do a great deal more."

"She will work in the laundry," he said impassively.

Elizabeth called for Jayanti to come to her.

She came tentatively, clutching her sack.

Rahul got out of the auto behind her and walked beside her.

The Sikh's eyes narrowed when he saw Rahul.

Rahul returned the gaze and did not blanch. Elizabeth had the impression of something primitive going on that she did not fully understand. The giant sniffed and turned to Jayanti.

"Come," he said, beckoning to her in that upside down way Indians do, to avoid giving offense.

Jayanti did not move.

"Come," he said again, beckoning impatiently.

Elizabeth knelt beside her and gave her a hug. "Go, Jayanti. We will come back whenever we can to check you are well."

The girl hugged Elizabeth fiercely, then walked to the giant with her head down. The Sikh turned and led her to the house as the gate closed.

All the time, the boy in the top window continued to watch.

Chapter 6

The man stood with his back to her next to the drinks cabinet in the corner of the room. The room was magnificent and utterly unlike anything Jayanti had ever experienced before. The walls were paneled, the ceiling was decorated, and a side-wall was composed entirely of bookshelves containing more books than she'd ever seen. Many books were in sets, as was evident by their similar covers. Everything was neat and in order—nothing like the untidy collection of books at her great aunt's house. There, every book was different. Their dog-eared state was all they had in common. She'd read every one.

In the center of the room was a heavy, ornately carved desk.

Still clutching her sack, she waited in fear. The terror of the day showed no signs of abating. Earlier, a boy had tried to rape her. Terror at the memory stabbed at her heart. It had all been so vicious. Memory of its brutality remained clear even though she could recall little of what had actually happened. She'd been bundled out of someone's house by a stranger...and then a woman had taken her to her great-aunty's place. Only Sister Rosalind's steadying hand had calmed her. The nun was always able to. Now Jayanti was standing in a house—a place of strangers—and who knows what might happen to her. She wanted to cry, but was too terrified to do so. The Sikh's hand resting on her shoulder was all that prevented her from fleeing.

The man put down a crystal glass and turned. He was middle aged, middle height, and running to fat. His dark hair was slicked back over his head and rested on his collar. One end of his pencil mustache lifted as his lips curled in distaste. Hostile eyes swept over her.

Jayanti recoiled in fear and dropped the sack she was holding.

"Pick it up," snapped the man in English.

Terrified, she bundled up the sack and held it in front of her again.

The man flicked the edge of a letter with a finger. "It says here that someone gave this letter to the nun who brought you here."

Jayanti said nothing.

"Do you know who that messenger was? Did you see him?"

"N…no, sir."

"What do you know about this letter?"

"I don't know anything about it, sir. I've never seen it before."

"Where do you come from?"

"I've been living with my great aunt in Kaseru Walan."

"By the railway station?"

"Y, Yes, sir."

He sniffed, walked to the desk, and sat down. The man was wearing a jacket of a type she'd never seen before. It was made of soft royal blue silk, embroidered with gold.

Blue smoke from a cheroot drifted lazily toward the ceiling from an ashtray on the desk.

"There's an implied threat in this letter," said the man.

Jayanti, stammered, "I…I don't know anything about the letter sir…or what it says."

Silence.

"You're to be kept safe, evidently." He reached for the cheroot. "The Missionaries of Charity have been asked to check on you from time to time."

She had no idea what he was talking about, so she kept quiet.

"Well, another brat to feed is neither here nor there. But you will work for your stay. Just keep out of my way. I don't expect to see you again." The man pointed to the Sikh. "Aakar Singh will take responsibility for you. He's in charge of security," he laughed, "so that should keep you safe enough."

He dismissed her with a wave, swiveled around in his chair, and drew on his cigar.

Aakar bowed and marched Jayanti out of the room.

They crossed the marble-floored entrance hall with its majestic staircase, down a corridor to the kitchens.

Preparations for the evening meal were in full swing. Steam and smoke billowed up into the extraction hoods and two people were hard at work.

"What's your full name?" demanded the giant.

"Jayanti Panikkar, sir."

"Stay here," he ordered.

Aakar marched through the kitchen to the back door and yelled.

Presently, an assortment of servants, cleaners, and gardeners had joined the cooks in the kitchen.

He pointed to Jayanti. "This is Jayanti Panikkar. She will help Shiika and Atul with the laundry and perhaps do some cleaning." He placed his hand on her shoulder. "She is to be kept safe. No harm is to come to her; she is under my protection."

Dark eyes darted in her direction, some curious, others resentful.

Aakar continued. "Where can she sleep? Shiika, where do you suggest?"

Querulous servants immediately began complaining to each other and shaking their heads.

"Enough!" barked the Sikh.

There was instant silence.

Shiika, a middle-aged woman dressed in a lilac Punjabi suit, shrugged. "There is no room in the servants' quarters outside. All the servants' rooms are occupied. She could sleep with me but I sleep with my husband, Atul."

Aakar scowled and glared at the assembled staff.

"*Tatti*," he swore, and wheeled Jayanti out of the kitchen door.

He marched her along the corridor and down some stone steps that led off to the right. At the bottom, was a wooden door. Aakar unlocked it with a key from his waistband and switched on a light.

It was a large storage cellar. Cobwebs hung everywhere high-lighted by the dust. The edges of stacked pieces of furniture could be seen peeping out from dust covers. High on the end wall was a small ground-level ventilation window.

"The servants' bell will ring at 6am each morning. When you hear it, get up immediately, wash, and have breakfast at the table outside the kitchen with the rest of the staff. You will be told what to do from there."

"Am...am I to live in here?" she asked, aghast.

"Yes. It is safe."

"Alone?"

"Yes."

"But...where do I...toilet?"

The giant put his fingers to his forehead and closed his eyes for a moment. Then he said. "Follow me."

She trailed after him up the stairs and followed him along the corridor. Just before the entrance hall, the giant opened a door to the left. It led into a beautiful bathroom containing a Western toilet, sink, and shower room. "I'm going to give you a special privilege. This toilet is for downstairs visitors. It almost never gets used. You can use it, but you clean it perfectly so it is ready for visitors by 8am. This bathroom will be your responsibility. Is that clear? I shall inspect it."

Jayanti nodded.

He returned her to the top of the steps going down to the cellar. "The door to my quarters is behind the stairs in the entrance hall. Call me, but only in an emergency. Otherwise, do not enter the main house except to do your work."

Aakar began to march off toward the entrance hall. Jayanti called out after him, "What do I sleep on?"

"Use a dust cover."

Jayanti began laying out her belongings on the stone floor of the cellar. She glanced at them—they didn't amount to much.

Her thoughts turned to her childhood village hugging the banks of Kerala's inland waterways. How she wished she could go back in time, back there with her parents: back to a time when it was safe—back when she could dance with her mother.

She sniffed. But her parents were dead. Her brother now lived in their house. She wondered what he was doing at this moment? Probably having tea with her aunt and uncle next door—he hated the bother of cooking. Jayanti felt in her pocket. She always kept his last letter there. He rarely wrote, so each one was precious. Each was a lifeline. Each was a reminder of a life that was simpler...and kinder. *Would the people in this terrifying house allow her to continue writing to him?*

She shuddered, and reached out to take hold of her most recent possession—a large soapstone pendant. It was a gift from Rohit. Evidently, he'd asked Sister Rosalind to give it to her. Jayanti pressed it against her cheek. Whilst it wasn't particularly beautiful, the pendant was from someone who cared for her—and right now, she desperately needed to feel that care.

Then she slid down the wall, drew up her feet...and wept.

Jayanti woke next morning to the sound of geckos calling to each other. *Chuck, chuck, chuck.* She could see three of the tiny lizards clinging to the cellar walls near the window. Their calls were interrupted almost immediately by the sound of a Muslim cleric who began to wail his morning prayers from a loudspeaker on a minaret somewhere.

She'd only slept a few hours. Sleeping on a folded dust cover hadn't bothered her at all. She had only ever slept on a mat. What troubled her was how quiet it was at night. She was used to the noise and drama of the laneways. However, on the plus side, the cellar had kept her deliciously cool throughout the night.

She breakfasted with the staff on the long table set under the patio that separated the servants' quarters from the main house. The food was good, but she had no heart for it. Afterward, she presented herself to the couple in charge of the laundry, Shiika and Atul. They seemed at a loss as to what to do with her. Jayanti suspected that they had their routines well in place. Either that, or they felt that she might represent a challenge to their indispensability and therefore their job security.

"Come with me and learn where to collect the laundry from Mister Panwar and Master Ravi," said Shiika through crooked front teeth.

Jayanti followed Shiika up the wooden servant stairs to the first floor and made her way along a beautiful wide landing. Shiika pointed to a door at the end. "That is Master Ravi's bedroom suite. If you pull the handle in the panel beside the door, it opens the laundry chute. Collect the clothes from there and take them to Atul. Mister Panwar's suite is at the other end of the landing. I'll collect his."

Jayanti hesitated. "Is there a Missus Panwar?"

"No. You ask too many questions. Now go."

She found the laundry shoot easily enough and pulled out its contents. It included Western clothes of excellent quality and some sheets that the maid had probably put in there. As she bundled them up in her arms, the door beside the chute opened. Jayanti stared over the bundled sheets in fear.

A boy, dressed in a crisp white shirt, tie, and long trousers, stared at her. She guessed he was about her age. He was tall and gangly—a boy growing into a man's body. She gaped at him. Although his deep brown eyes and aquiline nose looked pleasing enough, there was a bleakness in his countenance—in the compression of his lips, that Jayanti found alarming.

He reached out and pressed down the top of the sheet that half-obscured her face, and inspected her more closely.

She lowered her head, appalled at his actions.

He stepped back and dropped a pair of pajamas he was holding on the floor in front of her.

She struggled down to her knees and fished for the pajamas with one hand. It was difficult. When she found them, she staggered back to her feet.

He watched her. Then without a word, he went back into his bedroom and shut the door.

Jayanti walked downstairs with her burden and made her way outside, trying not to trail the ends of the sheet on the ground. Atul saw her and pointed to a basket. She dropped the clothes into it and waited to be told what to do next. Atul ignored her and after wetting the clothes, began rubbing a bar of soap over them. Once he'd done this, he twisted and bashed them over a piece of flat stone set on a concrete plinth.

"Find something to do," he said, eventually.

"Mr. Aakar says I must clean the downstairs toilet."

Atul nodded over his shoulder. "See the cleaning lady over there. She'll show you where the cleaning materials are. Come back after lunch and help get the washing off the line."

This set the rhythm for the rest of the week.

Jayanti's favorite job was cleaning the bathroom. She did it meticulously. As she cleaned, she had the delicious feeling that she was cleaning it for herself. It was her special place. Feeling slightly guilty at her self-indulgence, she set up a vase beside the wash basin and filled it with flowers she'd picked from the garden.

At the end of the week, Jayanti was delighted to have a visit from Sister Elizabeth. They sat at the end of the staff dining table behind the kitchen and talked. There were tears, assurances, and questions.

One question had been puzzling Jayanti all week.

"Aunty," she said, shyly, unconsciously adopting the idiom of intimacy and respect, "How do Western people use the toilet? It is a Western bowl, not a hole; and there's a roll of paper but no cup."

"A cup? How do you use a cup?"

"You, know. You pour it in front of you into your left hand… which, sort of…directs it."

"Oh."

When Jayanti learned how Western toilets worked, she was appalled and thought that Westerners could not be nearly as clean as Indians.

44

Elizabeth glanced at Jayanti from under her shawl. "Rahul wants you to keep teaching him English."

"I don't think that's possible. He won't be allowed in here."

"He's got an idea of how it might work."

"How?"

"There's a monsoon drain that flows through the front wall near the corner of the garden. Evidently, it goes under a small archway through a barred grill. He says he can sit on the outside, and you can talk to him from the inside without attracting anyone's attention."

"When?" she asked, tentatively.

Elizabeth blew a strand of hair from her face. "You decide. Scratch on a stone the time and day and leave it there for him to find. Then he'll know." She smiled. "He says he won't always be able to come. Maybe once a fortnight."

"Why are you helping him?"

Elizabeth reached out and put a hand over hers. "Because it is another way you can get a message to me or Sister Rosalind. She sends her love, by the way, and apologizes that she can't come here. Her duties have taken her elsewhere."

Jayanti nodded. "I think Sister Rosalind is lovely."

"I agree."

All too soon, Elizabeth rose from the bench and walked with her through the kitchen and down the corridor toward the entrance hall.

Aakar Singh had an office on the far side of the hall that had both an inside and outside window. On seeing them, he rose to escort Elizabeth to the front gate.

Jayanti hugged Elizabeth and watched sadly as she walked away from her down the driveway beside Aakar.

Jayanti had seen almost nothing of the giant Sikh since the evening she arrived so she resolved, with some trepidation, to wait for him to return in order to speak with him.

Aakar marched back and stopped before her with his hands on his hips.

She flinched, thinking that he was about to strike her.

"You have something to say?" he asked.

"Please, Mister Aakar. Sorry sir."

"What do you want? Quick," he said, pursing his lips.

"There is some furniture in the cellar, and I have nowhere to put my things. May I use a cupboard?"

The giant's dark eyes glittered, and he looked at her sternly.

"Whatever you use, you clean and polish. You must leave them better than you found them."

"Yes sir."

Chapter 7

The auto was tipped up on its side at forty-five degrees resting on two wheels. A man was squatting on his haunches underneath it holding a spanner. Rahul sat on a toolbox on the pavement knowing that the auto did not need repairing and that the man underneath was not a mechanic.

Night had fallen, but the road outside the hotel was still busy. Rahul pushed a kerosene lamp closer to his companion with his foot. They were playing out a scene that occurred all the time on Delhi streets. No one would notice…which was entirely the idea.

He glanced sideways as a dumpy black Ambassador taxi drew up to the front steps of the hotel. Three women got out and climbed the steps. The doorkeeper, dressed in a white jacket, trousers, and turban, opened the door for them without a word.

Rahul nodded to himself. They were prostitutes. *Good*. This was another hotel ripe for business. Drugs and prostitutes went together as surely as the left and right bank of the Yamuna River.

They'd scoped out a good number of the less prestigious hotels in Delhi Central. The more luxurious ones were already catered for by powerful drug rings, so they left these alone. But the smaller ones were fair game. Rahul and his team were often able to displace the existing supplier or introduce the hotel management to a regular supply arrangement if he didn't already have one.

The hotel they were watching tonight was a fairly good one, right at the top of their bracket. Having established the moral climate of the hotel, Rahul knew he now needed to engage the doorkeeper. He'd already be selling drugs, of course—just small-time stuff to individuals, so he would need his cut in any new arrangement. The doorkeeper would then go to a manager, who would come outside and sit at a café where either Rahul or Arjun would put a business proposal to him. Both were adept at negotiation.

Kumar and Malick's role was to deliver the drugs. Their intimidating presence was usually enough to ensure the level of cheating was kept to a minimum.

Rahul was about to get up from the toolbox and begin proceedings when a black Humvee with silver wheels pulled in alongside the front steps of the hotel. The doorkeeper hurried down the steps to open the door of the vehicle but was waved aside by a burly figure who got out of the front seat. Rahul recognized him instantly. It was the huge Sikh who guarded the house where Clueless was living.

The Sikh opened the door for a man Rahul did not recognize. He was dressed in expensively casual Western clothes. The Sikh followed him up the steps and entered the hotel lobby with him.

Rahul watched him covertly. The man had to be the master of the house where Clueless lived. *Well, well, well.* He certainly didn't need a hotel with his own home less than ten minutes away. He could only be here for one purpose.

Twenty minutes later, negotiations were going well. The hotel's manager was an ambitious man from Mumbai. Although he'd been newly appointed to the position, he was well used to the ways of the world.

The manager smoothed his hair with both hands. "I need some *garad* and *charas* hashish straight away. But the hashish must be good."

Rahul wobbled his head. "It is good."

"It will be shithouse."

"My *charas* is from Himachal Pradesh. It is the best."

The man lifted up his nose to signal his disbelief.

Rahul was familiar with the pantomime—mere protocol. "I'll give you some to try."

"You have a *chillum* pipe?"

Rahul nodded.

"Bring it in through the kitchen. One of the staff there will take you to my back office."

Five minutes after the manager left, Rahul returned to the auto. "Arjun, I'm going to the hotel."

Arjun gave a long-suffering sigh. "I want to get out of these stinking clothes as soon as I can. So don't stay to savor the local delights."

Rahul picked up the toolbox and walked down the service driveway of the hotel.

Fifteen minutes later, his drug samples had been inspected and most of the arrangements for supply had been made. Rahul was packing up his toolbox when there was a tap on the door.

"Wait," barked the manager. He swept Rahul's free samples into a top drawer of his desk and closed it. "Come," he ordered.

A man dressed in a receptionist's uniform came in, bobbing up and down obsequiously. "Please sir. Sorry sir. Very sorry, but there's been screaming; too much screaming. It's beginning to upset some of the patrons."

The manager placed both hands on the edge of the table and sighed in resignation. "The Butcher?"

"Er, yes. Can you advise him to be, er…more moderate."

"No. I'm busy. Just knock on his door and ask if all is well. That should do it."

The man left, bowing as he went.

Rahul's interest was piqued. He raised an eyebrow. "The Butcher?"

"Yes, one of our less inhibited guests; he's not happy unless he draws blood." The manager shook his head. "He has strange sexual appetites. The staff nicknamed him The Butcher."

Rahul experienced a rising sense of concern. "Ah yes. I think I saw him arrive in a black Humvee with a Sikh. Mr...aah..."

"Yes, Mr. Panwar; Mr. Gokul Panwar. Rich, but..."

"A bastard."

The manager nodded.

"Why do the girls put up with him?"

"They don't; the word's out for women to avoid him. We've had to go further afield and use the services..." the manager smiled at his own cleverness..."of those less able to be choosy."

There was another bang on the door—this time, louder and more urgent.

"Come."

The same hotel receptionist came in. This time, his bows were more like jerks. "Please sir. Mr. Panwar has left...but the woman... she's unconscious on the floor, and there is much blood. Please come, please to come."

The manager slapped the desk and swore. "*Kutte ka aulad.*" He glanced at Rahul.

Rahul could guess his predicament. He was thinking. *I can't leave him in my office unattended.*

"Come with me," the manager ordered and marched out of the office toward the stairs.

They found the woman splayed out on the floor. She was completely naked. Much of her body was covered in ugly red welts and blood was pooling on the floor tiles from between her legs.

"Damn," said the manager. "We've got to get her out of here and dump her somewhere."

Rahul said nothing. He went into the bathroom, grabbed a towel, and folded it between the woman's legs. The manager started to object but kept quiet when Rahul shot him a dark look. He ripped the woman's scarf along its length and used a strip of it to tie the padding in place.

They dressed the girl as best they could—no easy task, and carried her down the service stairs to the delivery entrance at the back of the hotel.

Rahul went back inside with the manager to retrieve his toolbox and, after confirming when the first delivery would occur, was escorted to the rear of the hotel. The manager paused and looked with distaste at the woman propped up against the rubbish bins. "What am I going to do with her?" he asked querulously.

Rahul glanced at the woman. She was young, but her face, once pretty, now wore the severity, hardness, and disillusionment of the streets. Her head lolled to one side and rested against the filth spilling down from an industrial rubbish bin. *Abused and abandoned.* He shook his head. It could so easily have been Jayanti's fate. Indeed, he thought savagely, it could still be. Anger began to rise up within him. "I shall take her," he said.

The manager looked at him in disbelief, shrugged, and went back inside.

Rahul walked around to the front of the hotel where Arjun was still under the auto. Arjun gave him a reproachful look and immediately began to complain. "You know, there are only so many things you can do with a spanner under an auto when you haven't a clue what you are doing."

Together, they pushed the auto back upright onto its three wheels. "Was your visit successful?" inquired Arjun.

"Yeah. But we've got a job to do."

"What's that?"

"We're taking a woman to those lunatic Christian nuns."

"What! To Timarpur?"

"Yes."

"Now?"

"Yes."

"My father says we have to put petrol back into his auto...and that I'm to remind you that I'm not licensed to drive it."

"Are we licensed to sell drugs?"

Arjun inclined his head. "No we're not. Fair point." He chuckled. "Only the police are licensed to do that."

Rahul gave no indication that he enjoyed the joke.

Jayanti could hear music. She was on the wide landing outside Ravi Panwar's room about to collect the laundry from the laundry bin. Someone was playing a *sitar* to the accompaniment of *tabla* drums. It was beautiful. She could hear a woman begin to sing a *thumri* of a girl's love for Krishna.

Instinctively, Jayanti started to dance. She danced as she'd done with her mother in Kerala. With neck held high and arms held out sideways lifting and falling like the waves of the sea, she dipped to the left and then to the right. Soon she was twirling, bowing, and skipping, lost to the world. The music was heavenly. She stood with knees akimbo, holding her palms together above her and danced her head from side to side, then bowed to the left and bowed to the right…and froze—appalled.

Ravi was standing at his door. He'd opened it barely a hand's breath and was watching her. Jayanti pulled herself upright and lowered her head.

Ravi opened the door fully and walked over to her. For a long time, he simply looked at her.

Jayanti kept her eyes downcast, wondering what he would say.

"It's a recording by Lakshmi Shankar," he said.

She darted a glance at him. "With Ravi Shankar playing?"

"Yes."

Silence.

He cleared his throat. "What is your name?"

"Jayanti Panikkar."

He nodded. "A southern name."

"From Kerala. I came to live in Delhi when my parents died."

More silence.

"You dance well."

Jayanti didn't know what to say. She stammered, "May I go now, sir?"

He paused before saying, "Yes."

She turned and walked quickly down the landing.

"Jayanti," he called after her.

She stopped in her tracks, keeping her back to him.

"Don't forget the washing."

Jayanti pulled on the dustsheet that covered the wardrobe and chest of drawers. It started to come off but then snagged.

She gave another tug then looked to see where it was caught. When she saw where, she groaned. It had snagged on the cornice at the top of the wardrobe. How on earth could she reach it?

She laid her sleeping mat on the chest of drawers in order to protect it, then climbed up on top. From there, she was able to reach up and unhook the dustsheet. As it came away she could hear voices. She paused to listen.

"…square of the hypotenuse. Any questions?"

It was a voice she'd not heard before. An English voice. This was followed by a voice she did recognize. It was that of the boy, Ravi Panwar.

"But only of a right-angled triangle?"

"Correct."

The conversation seemed to come from above her, from the top of the cellar wall. She glanced up and saw a recess above her with a piece of wood wedged into it. By standing on her toes, she could just reach it. She took hold of it and pulled it away. As she did, a thin stream of light came through the hole.

Jayanti reached down and lifted a chair on top of the dresser. Tentatively, she stood on the chair and peered through the recess. She found herself looking through a patterned grate into some sort of classroom. Jayanti realized that she was seeing through a ventilation grate set into the skirting board of the room above her. She could see a blackboard very clearly. A man with blond hair dressed in a navy blazer was writing on it. He must be the teacher. To the right, she could just see the leg of a desk where Ravi Panwar must be seated.

The boy was having his school lessons. It appeared that he was being tutored at home.

Jayanti looked wistfully at the scene before her. How she would love to be at school, to learn more. She and her brother had been well educated in Kerala…and her great aunt had continued to teach her in Kaseru Walan, so she'd been very fortunate in her education. However, schooling had come to an abrupt end when she'd come to this house.

Then a realization dawned on her. If she collected the laundry and cleaned the bathroom early, she could eavesdrop on what was being taught all morning. She was not required to do any any more work until after lunch, by which time schooling would probably have ended anyway.

Could it be done?

She glanced about her.

If she could move the wardrobe back from the wall, she could sit on its top with her legs over its back edge where there wasn't a cornice. That would make it easy to see. She glanced down. A chair would give her easy access to the top of the dresser...and another chair on the dresser would enable her to get on top of the wardrobe.

A wave of excitement flooded through her. She resolved to move the furniture that night when nobody could hear. In the mean time, she would borrow a pencil from the cook and collect some old newspapers to write on. That would do until she could beg an exercise book from Elizabeth...or maybe Rahul could get her one. She would be meeting him in few days time. He'd be rude to her, of course. He always was...but she found herself looking forward to seeing him again.

Chapter 8

"How is she?" asked Elizabeth.

"She's been damaged but will recover."

"How damaged?"

Sister Rosalind stepped close to Elizabeth in order to confide. "The doctor has sewn up a tear in her vagina and given her antibiotics to prevent infection in the anus. Her bruises and bite marks are not serious, although she is suffering mild concussion from being knocked unconscious."

Elizabeth was appalled. "Is...is this...a normal experience for an Indian prostitute?"

"It is too often an occupational hazard for a Dalit prostitute. They are not valued."

The two nuns were walking the *galis*, the laneways, of Shahjahanabad. Shahjahanabad was the name for Old Delhi—and it was a place that Elizabeth had come to love. The *galis* were colorful. Each alleyway specialized in selling different products. There were alleyways for bolts of cotton, others for vegetables, and yet others for car parts.

Sister Rosalind bent down to pray a blessing on an old woman squatting on a low wooden platform the size of a doormat. In front of her was a similar platform on which she'd arranged piles of fruit and nuts. The display represented the woman's livelihood—and it looked pathetically meager.

The old woman picked up a handful of fruit and placed it in the sack Sister Rosalind was carrying.

Elizabeth felt humbled that charity should come from someone so poor.

India was full of contradictions. She'd learned enough to know that the apparent easygoing attitude of India was an illusion. Under the surface, the intensity of greed, need, and scheming was extreme. *So, thank you Lord for acts of grace like this.*

She was momentarily distracted by a fabric shop. Rich colors assaulted her senses with their variety and vibrancy. Customers were sitting on a bench in front of a raised platform on which male shop assistants sat cross-legged displaying bolts of fabric. They got up occasionally to pull another from the shelves that lined the shop from floor to ceiling. She glanced at her plain white sari edged with blue. Did she regret having to wear it?

She mulled the question over in her mind.

No, she decided. She was content with what she wore. It said all she wanted to say. But that didn't stop her enjoying the colors of a fabric shop.

Sister Rosalind nodded. "I think we've got all the food we can carry." She hefted the sack over her shoulder. "It's time we caught a bus and took it to the children's home."

They returned to the main road and ran the gauntlet of road-side vendors who had set up near the bus stop, selling salty snacks, plastic sachets of artificial mango juice and bottles of water— usually from non-health regulated sources.

The bus took them over the Greeta Colony Bridge across the Yamuna River and headed south down the Noida Link Road. Elizabeth wanted to question Sister Rosalind more about the woman Rahul had brought to them the night before—and share a disturbing revelation.

She chose to wait for the bus conductor to finish yelling abuse through the open door at a cart driver who was holding up the bus' progress. The cart driver didn't even flinch. The two doe-eyed oxen that pulled his cart seemed to exude the infinite patience of India. Their horns had been painted blue and had brass bangles attached to their ends that chinked as the animals plodded down the road. Elizabeth had learned that many of the cart drivers refused to carry lights at night, making them a real hazard. Evidently, their drivers reasoned that they had been in existence well before cars and trucks, and so it was up to cars and trucks to avoid them. Most times, they did. Traffic traveled fairly slowly in India. The exception, of course, was buses. They had a schedule to keep.

Elizabeth began circumspectly. "Sister Rosalind, you stayed up most of the night with the woman Rahul brought in; did you learn anything of her story?"

Sister Rosalind turned from looking out the window. "Her name is Durgamma. She is a devodasi prostitute who has run away from her temple."

"A what?"

"A devodasi." Sister Rosalind sighed. "A devodasi is a temple prostitute. They are usually daughters of the very poor, the Dalits. Their parents give them to the temple so they don't have to pay for the girl's dowry." She shrugged. "A daughter's sacrifice is a small price to pay compared to the alternative—starvation."

"But surely that's illegal."

"It was banned in 1982, but it is still a common occurrence. The devodasis have been in existence for about five thousand years, so it is not something that can change overnight. India..." Sister Rosalind seemed to search for the right words..."takes time."

"What sort of god requires a girl to be a prostitute?" said Elizabeth hotly.

"Usually, the goddess Yellamma. The girl effectively gets married to Yellamma, so that when men have sex with her, they believe they are giving pleasure to Yellamma." She smiled sadly. "Not so different from us, really. We are brides of Christ."

"But people experience him through our charity, not...not..." Elizabeth was lost for words. Eventually she spluttered, "Why does all this...happen?"

Sister Rosalind looked at her, as if weighing up how much to say. She breathed in and said, "The American Declaration of Independence proclaims that people have equal worth and an equal right to life, liberty and happiness. It says: '*We hold these truths to be self-evident.*' The fact is, however, that in many parts of the world—particularly those which lack a Judeo-Christian heritage—these truths are not at all evident; they are actually quite foreign."

"But even so, how does a girl become a…" she shook her head in disbelief.

"Well, as I understand it: The girl's parents bring a goat to the temple for the priest to sacrifice. Her female relatives apply a sandalwood paste to her body, then wash her and dress her in a white sari. A priest chants a prayer in Sanskrit, then she's processed to the temple. There, a string of beads is placed around her neck and she's sprinkled with turmeric." Sister Rosalind shrugged. "It's a simple as that."

"But how old…?"

"Durgamma became a devodasi temple prostitute at the age of twelve."

Elizabeth shuddered. "But she ran away."

"Yes. She ran away and became a street prostitute two years ago."

"How old is she now?"

"Eighteen, she tells me."

The bus revved hard as it lurched its way down the freeway.

Elizabeth stared out the open window. The wind was causing both of their headscarves to flutter. As the bus slowed down for a roundabout she could see women dressed in saris and punjabis working on a building site. They had a pad on top of their headdress on which balanced a single brick. Four pairs of bricks were balanced on top of it. *And they carried bricks for the bricklayers all day long.* Elizabeth shook her head. *Will I ever understand the women of India?*

Sister Rosalind pointed out the window.

Elizabeth could see a formal garden at the end of which stood a huge, multi-domed temple with intricately carved pillars and roofs. "Wow!" she exclaimed.

"That's the Akshardham Hindu temple complex." Elizabeth tapped on the window strut. "The Delhi Development Authority had to bulldoze the slum tenement homes of 140,000 people in order to build it. You should go and see it. It contains a Hindu theme park, an IMAX cinema, and 20,000 idols. The complex presents Hindu history and culture from a more positive perspective." The beginning of a sad smile played around her lips. "You won't find any devodasis there."

This comment returned Elizabeth to the issue that had been troubling her since the previous evening. "Sister Rosalind."

"Yes."

"Rahul spoke to me briefly before he left last night."

"And...?"

"He...he told me that the person who had so abused Durgamma was Gokul Panwar, the man who owns the house where Jayanti lives. Rahul is concerned that she could be in danger."

Sister Rosalind nodded to herself. "He was concerned?"

"Yes."

"He needn't be."

"Why?"

Sister Rosalind looked back out of the window and said nothing.

Elizabeth furrowed her brow. "Sister Rosalind, what was in the letter I gave to Gokul Panwar?"

Jayanti first saw the book three days before. It had fallen behind a carved camphor wood chest at the top of the landing. She had left the book lying where it was because her arms were full of dirty laundry.

But Ravi's laundry bin was empty today. She walked back toward the servant's stairs, past the head of the grand staircase, and saw that the book was still there—only just visible.

A book...a whole book. *Oh, to read again*, she thought longingly.

She looked around her to check that no one was watching then squatted down to pull the book out.

It was written in English: 'David Copperfield by Charles Dickens'.

She fingered the pages, caressing them and turning them over. Her eyes read snatches of text from the different pages.

'Whether I shall turn out to be the hero of my own life, or whether that station will be held by anybody else, these pages must show...'

'New thoughts and hopes were whirling through my mind, and all the colors of my life were changing...'

'It was a long and gloomy night that gathered on me, haunted by the ghosts of many hopes, of many dear remembrances, many errors, many unavailing sorrows and regrets...'

Wonderful words. Beautiful writing.

She clutched the book to her chest appalled at herself as a temptation began to take shape.

The book had been there, unwanted, unfound, for three days. Surely no one would miss it for the next few days—which would give her a chance to read it during the nights.

She tucked the book under her sari and fled with her demons of guilt to her sanctuary in the cellar.

That afternoon, she made her way to the corner of the garden, pausing only to pluck a zinnia from a flowerbed and tuck it into her hair. She arrived at the low archway through the bottom of the wall where the monsoon drain flowed. The drain was dry, as it would be for most of the year. The monsoons would fill it only between July and September. It was now October and Delhi was beginning to edge toward winter. October was the marriage season, a time when it was not uncommon to see *barats*, bridegrooms, dressed smartly in their high-collared Nehru jackets and *zara* turbans, being paraded to their wedding on a white horse. *What would it be like to...*

"Hey, Clueless."

It was Rahul.

"If you call me Clueless one more time, I shall leave you to stew in your own ignorance and rudeness."

He laughed.

She continued. "And speak English. How will your English improve if you don't?"

Rahul was lounging on the ground where he could see Jayanti through the grill. Debris from the monsoons was still wrapped around the bars that separated them. Jayanti wished she had thought to clear it away.

Rahul picked a piece of grass and began to chew the end. He said in English, "You are good, yes? No jolly bad rascal hurt you or frighten you?"

"No, I am safe here."

Rahul spat and looked around him, giving every impression that he was already bored by her conversation.

"This, your prison, yes?"

She lapsed into Hindi. "It is not a prison," she said hotly. "I get a small allowance and I can go shopping with some of the servants once a week. They need me to help carry the groceries."

"You're a big-shot now, eh?"

"Yes. I have my very own bathroom."

Rahul nodded, then rolled over and forced a fart. "Can I use your bathroom?"

"You are disgusting."

He looked at her. "You look ugly in your yellow sari. It makes you look like a wrinkled banana."

She straightened her back and re-adjusted her scarf—secretly pleased. He had noticed how she was looking. Good.

"What do you know about the big-shot fellow who owns this place?"

Jayanti was surprised at this twist in the conversation. "What? Mr. Panwar?"

"Yes."

"I know very little. The servants say he is very rich. His family had been rich, but he was doing poorly until he came into great wealth some time ago." She shrugged. "The servants say he trades in gemstones and has investments."

"Does he speak to you?"

"No, not since I first arrived. He was...not very nice."

"He is not nice. People say very bad things about him."

She tipped her head sideways. "Oh yes, and you would know, I suppose," she said with as much sarcasm as she could muster.

"Seriously, Jayanti. He is a very bad man. He hurts women. He's a very bad man. Don't let him near you."

Jayanti blinked, chastened by Rahul's concern. In fact, she was so surprised that it took a moment for her to realize that he'd called her Jayanti for the very first time.

"I...I think we should...speak English now," she said, "so you can practice."

Chapter 9

Three days later, Jayanti was perched on top of the wardrobe with her legs dangling over the back. She'd placed a pencil and a piece of paper beside her and eagerly awaited her fourth day of school. Her sense of wellbeing was heightened by the knowledge that today was her birthday. She was fifteen.

Of course, no one knew, and she could expect no favors during the day but nonetheless, she allowed herself to enjoy the knowledge. There would be time enough later in the day for the sense of desolation and loneliness to catch up with her. But for now, her optimism was as fresh as the flowers she'd put in the downstairs bathroom.

She'd learned that Ravi's tutor was called Mr. Hodges. He was English and had only been appointed at the start of the year. His academic skills were excellent, although the servant responsible for attending him during the mornings spoke of his breath smelling of alcohol. Jayanti thought she could see the beginnings of the ravages of it on Mr. Hodges' face. His face was red and frequently flushed. Even from the back of the room, she could make out spidery red venations on his face.

She'd seen Ravi enter the room and make his way to his desk. A few minutes later, Mr. Hodges came in. He did not look well.

"Morning, Ravi."

"Good morning, Sir."

Mr. Hodges leaned on his desk with one hand and rubbed his forehead with the other. He sighed and stood up. "Today, you will do the English comprehension test I told you about two weeks ago."

"But Sir, I haven't been able to find…"

Mr. Hodges interrupted him and slapped the desk with his hand. "I don't want to hear any excuses. You will find that life is full of unalterable deadlines. You have to work to them or suffer the consequences." He walked toward Ravi.

Jayanti instinctively leaned backward. She could hear Mr. Hodges put a piece of paper on Ravi's desk and then make his way to the door. He said over his shoulder. "That's the exam on David Copperfield. I will be back in twenty minutes to collect it."

Jayanti was appalled…and stricken with fear. What should she do? She had taken Ravi's book. There was no way he could do the exam. Should she creep upstairs and place it back behind the chest on the landing and pretend all innocence?

No, that would be cowardly. The fact that he did not have the book was entirely her own fault.

She should take the book to him? Yes. That was it. He might have time to flick through it and do at least some of the questions.

Jayanti climbed down from the top of the wardrobe as quietly as possible. She picked up the book and fled up the stairs to the corridor.

"Quick," she said to the startled cook in the kitchen. "I need to take a glass of lemonade to Mr. Ravi."

Three minutes later, she made her way to the grand entrance hall, knocked on the schoolroom door, and opened it.

Affecting a normalcy she did not feel, she carried in a small silver tray with a glass of lemonade on it…and the missing book.

Ravi, who had had his head in his hands, looked up with a puzzled frown. "What are you doing here?" he demanded.

"I thought you might like a drink, sir…and I came to report that a book that may belong to you has been found behind the chest on top of the landing, where it must have fallen." She placed the glass and the book in front of him. "Here it is."

Ravi put his head back in his hands and groaned. "Too late. I've got to do an exam on its contents, and I haven't been able to read it."

Guilt and remorse began to stab at her. "I'm so sorry sir."

He grunted and looked up. "You speak English very well." It was more of an accusation than a question.

"Yes sir. I've had a good education." She turned to go.

"I don't suppose its good enough to do a literary exam on this book?"

Jayanti froze in mid stride—struck by a pang of guilt. This was one of those defining moments. If she owned up to knowing most of the story, he would know she'd taken the book. But if she didn't, Ravi would face humiliation…all because she'd not been strictly honest.

"What's the first question?" she asked without turning around.

"Ravi rustled the paper behind her. "I have to put in the missing words in a list of sentences."

She turned around. "The first?"

Ravi looked at her speculatively, drew in a deep breath and read, "'I have encountered some fine ladies and gentlemen who might as well have been born…' I have to fill in…"

"Caterpillars," she interrupted.

Ravi's jaw dropped open. "Seriously?"

"Seriously."

He wrote down the word then read again, "'Yes. He is quite a good fellow – nobody's enemy…'" he looked up. "What's next?"

"But his own."

Ravi scribbled quickly. Jayanti noticed that he had a neat quick hand. After a moment he read again: "'What is the message Mr. Barkis tells David Copperfield to give to his nurse?'"

Jayanti smiled. "Barkis is willing."

Ravi looked up. "No, it can't be. That sounds ridiculous. It doesn't make sense."

"It does," she insisted, stabbing the desk with her finger. "It's his way of asking Peggoty to marry him."

"Oh." He began to write…then glanced up at her.

Jayanti became apprehensive.

Ravi put down his pen, leaned back, and folded his arms in front of him. "You've read my book, haven't you. You took it."

"No sir. I did find it behind the chest. I really did. It's just that I took a few days to work out how to get it to you."

He stared at her. "Can you help me with the rest of the questions?"

She hesitated. "I…I haven't quite finished the book, but I should be able to help a bit."

He picked up the exam paper. "Then, let's conspire together." He read the next question. "'What was the phrase Uriah Heep used repeatedly to describe himself?'"

"I'm ever so humble."

"And who was he?"

"He was a scheming, dishonest, hypocrite."

"Oh." He picked up the book and riffled through its pages. "Perhaps I'll have to read it. It sounds interesting."

"You should. It's wonderful."

Ravi sniffed, glanced across to the exam paper, and read again. "'Why doesn't David Copperfield marry Agnes first?'" He looked up. "Agnes is the heroine, I take it."

"Yes, she's lovely."

"Then, why doesn't he marry her?"

Jayanti leaned on the desk and said, "Mr. Copperfield can't see his love for Agnes because he has mentally locked her into the childhood status of being a friend."

Shafts of morning light through the window highlighted panes on Ravi's face. Even though his expression was grim, he looked good. She could see the man beginning to appear in the spare frame of the boy. She continued. "Mr. Copperfield is sometimes quite blind to the obvious."

"Slow down," complained Ravi as he scribbled with his pen.

When he finished. He looked up and gave half a smile. "Next

question." He picked up the exam paper. "'What does Charles Dickens use James Steerforth for in this commentary on English life?'"

Jayanti sniffed derisively. "James Steerforth represents the cruelty and abuse of the privileged class toward those less able and less rich than themselves. He preys on the vulnerable but parades himself as a fine fellow."

Ravi raised his eyes and said slowly. "I'm not sure I will like this book."

"Oh no," she protested, bending down to bring her head level with his. "It is a good book. Reading it will grow your compassion and understanding of life."

"Pah! He leaned back and put his hands behind his head. "You think I need compassion and understanding?"

Before she could stop herself, she heard herself say, "You threw your laundry on the floor for me to pick up when I had my hands full."

Silence hung in the room.

"You are a servant."

"I am a human being."

"My father tells me servants are inferior…and that they should be kept in their place."

"Sister Rosalind says that all people are sacred and equally valued by God."

"That's rubbish," he snorted.

She stood up, put her hands on her hips, and glared at Ravi. "What I can tell you is that we have feelings just like you. So, no one should do anything to anyone they wouldn't like being done to them."

"Ho, ho. And who is this, then?"

Jayanti spun around in shock. Mr. Hodges had entered the room behind her.

Ravi sat himself upright and shot a warning glance at Jayanti.

She gulped and elected to take the initiative. "Please sir; sorry sir. Mr. Ravi was using me to explore the nature of the social message in the book he's been reading."

"'Nature of the social message...' Who are you? Where did you learn about social messages in Charles Dickens?"

"Reading it was part of my education sir."

"Well, if you are a friend of Ravi's, you need to come back this afternoon. He has schooling in the morning. What's your name?"

"Her name is Jayanti Panikkar," said Ravi.

Jayanti was amazed that he remembered.

"She works in the house...as a servant."

Did he exaggerate the word 'servant'? Jayanti bristled. She set her jaw and said, "Mr. Ravi was in need, so I came with a glass of lemonade—to steady his thinking."

Mr. Hodges nodded and sat on his desk. "And what were you arguing about?"

"Mr. Ravi was insisting that the sort of abuses by the upper caste of the lower castes detailed in this book still happen in India—causing a lot of people to be hurt."

"Class, not caste. The English have class distinction, not caste distinction." Mr. Hodges continued. "And what did you say?"

"I said that servants have no feelings, and it doesn't matter if high class people abuse them and make them fearful."

Mr. Hodges frowned. "But you are a servant. Don't you have feelings?"

"Oh yes, sir. Very much sir. But we are not permitted to let high-class people know. It is our secret."

Mr. Hodges laughed. "Well, Miss Jayanti, you'd best be about your business."

Jayanti hurried to the door. As she opened it, Hodges called to her, "What exactly is your business? You didn't say."

Jayanti held the edge of the door and looked at the floor, "I help with..."

"She helps with...any bookwork that needs to be done," said Ravi.

Jayanti nodded and slipped out of the door before anything more could be said.

Jayanti paused on the landing in order to look out of the window. She could see over the garden wall to the street in front. It was already busy with activity. Men were walking to work carrying their 'tiffins,' stacked stainless steel containers holding their lunchtime meal of curry. A dirty haze from the traffic was already in the air. In the distance, she could hear the banging drums and the clashing cymbals of a religious procession that was taking place—probably a funeral. The busyness of life and death was already in full swing.

She watched a man pushing his rickshaw along. The rickshaw had a large metal box on it with windows cut in the sides. It was the school bus. She thought she could count eight or nine schoolboys sitting inside, all dressed smartly in white shirts and blue shorts. It was little wonder the man was pushing rather than pedaling.

There was so much going on—but it was all outside the garden walls. Had this house become her prison? Was Rahul right?

She returned her gaze to the landing and the doors along its length. All the doors were shut. She had no idea what was behind most of them. It occurred to her that the house was, in many respects, a house of secrets. She glanced down to the entrance hall below. Ancient curved swords hung in patterns on the wooden paneling like fish-bones. It was all very masculine. Another notable feature of the house was that there were no photos or portraits to be seen anywhere. This was most unusual. Photos featured prominently in almost every Indian home. This house seemed to have nothing personal in it at all. It was as if it had been built as a film set.

Jayanti made her way to the end of the landing and opened the door to the laundry bin. It was empty…except that a book lay in the bottom of it: 'David Copperfield by Charles Dickens.'

She picked it up, tentatively. Ravi had meant her to have it, presumably so she could finish reading it. That surprised her. She didn't think he would care.

She walked slowly down the landing as she leafed through the book to the place she'd reached in the story. *Ah yes.* Ham had just died during a storm in the process of rescuing a sailor who was none other than the despicable James Steerforth. Without thinking, she sat on the top step of the grand staircase and began to read.

He was ten paces away before she realized he was there.

Ravi Panwar had a wry expression on his face as if he were trying not to smile. Jayanti jumped to her feet. As she did, the front door opened below them. She glanced down and saw that Mr. Hodges had arrived for the morning's tutoring session.

Ravi looked over the banister and said matter-of-factly, "I passed the exam even though I didn't do the last two questions. I blamed you for distracting me and using up my time."

"I'm glad…you passed. I'm so sorry…"

Ravi waved his hand dismissively. "Give the book back when you've finished it. I'd like to read it…" He glanced at her, "to grow my compassion and understanding of life."

She stood before him, mute, with eyes downcast.

"Come with me down the stairs."

"Oh no, sir. I have to use the servants stairs."

"Come," he ordered.

Side by side, they walked down the sweeping staircase to the entrance hall.

Mr. Hodges waited for them, watching them descend. "Well…I must say," he said, smiling genially, "you both make a fine picture." He seemed to be in good spirits today.

"Good morning, sir," said Ravi. He then surprised Jayanti by adding, "I have a request to make, sir."

Mr. Hodges swept back his hair. "And what's that, Ravi?"

"You've mentioned before your concern that I don't have enough interaction with people my own age…and in view of how helpful it was to me to discuss the last book with Miss Panikkar, I wondered if she could sit in with me during the morning lessons." He turned to Jayanti. "You'd be amenable to that, I take it? I've cleared it with my father."

Jayanti opened her mouth in shock, then realized that she must be looking foolish. She nodded—not trusting herself to words.

"Splendid idea," said Mr. Hodges. "Absolutely splendid." He slapped Ravi on the back. "Let's get to it, then."

That evening, Jayanti had the unexpected task of replacing the wardrobe and chest of drawers to their original position in the cellar. It would not be an easy task. The wardrobe, in particular, was very heavy. She looked behind the wardrobe to check that it could slide freely back up against the wall. As she did, she noticed the edge of a pattern carved into the stonework low on the wall. Most of the carving was hidden in shadow. Curious, she bent down and traced its shape with her fingers. The carving was small, about the size of the palm of her hand.

There was no mistaking its form. It was a six-pronged star— exactly the same pattern as that carved on her stone pendant: the one on the back of the peacock stone.

Three years later

Chapter 10

Some alleyways were worse than others, and the one Kumar was leading Rahul down now was not one he liked. Not that Rahul was frightened; he'd long since ceased to be frightened of any man or any place in Kaseru Walan. Kumar steered him down the laneway. Rahul tried to shake off the muscular arm around his shoulders, but his friend would have none of it.

"You're like a lion with a thorn in its paw. And you're like this every time. You need a drink," insisted Kumar.

Rahul grumbled but allowed that he was not his usual self. He never was after he came back from visiting Jayanti. He only went every few months now, not like the early days. They still met in the same place, by the monsoon drain. It was probably not necessary as she left the house often enough for shopping expeditions. They could have easily met in a café. He certainly had plenty of money these days. The truth was, he appreciated the quiet of the place... and had come to see it as 'their' particular spot.

Shops that sold alcohol were always down the worst and least salubrious streets. They were not convivial places where people met to socialize. Brash young men, full of hubris, would front up to the counter and order a drink. After being given it, they would drink it on the spot in a few gulps, then leave. The drunks, however, lingered in doorways up and down the alley, desperate, quarrelsome, and ruined.

It was not a place that women came near.

Women.

His life had changed three years ago because of them. He lived with Kumar in a house run by his widowed mother who suffered badly from arthritis. She and Kumar lived in the two front rooms. The kitchen and bathroom courtyard were behind that. Steps led up from the tiny courtyard to the flat roof on which a crude corrugated iron addition had been built. This was where Rahul slept. It was, of course, stinking hot for most of the year but things had improved a great deal recently. He had paid for builders to rebuild the room in brick and put a tiled roof on which he kept shaded with a tarpaulin.

Kumar handed him a glass of Indian whisky. "And how was the lovely Jayanti today?"

How on earth could he describe Jayanti? She was tall, elegant, and in the full flush of womanhood. In truth, he was slightly in awe of her. The saris she chose to wear were quite often multi-colored—usually slashes of fresh pastel colors. It was an unusual choice for an Indian woman. But there again, Jayanti was anything but usual. She was highly intelligent and loved to teach. She would do so demurely until he goaded her, then her spirit would flare and she would fly at him. It was fabulous…and terrifying.

Her role in the house had changed over the years. From what Rahul could gather, she had become Ravi Panwar's school assistant.

She also wrote letters for the servants when needed and was responsible for much of the house's organization.

Rahul's relationship with Jayanti had settled down to one of a teasing, easy friendship. He was no longer overtly rude to her—and even called her by her right name most of the time.

Rahul was suspicious of Ravi, of course, and often caught himself asking Jayanti about him. She always scoffed at the idea that there might be a relationship. Rahul shook his head and refused to believe it. How could Ravi, or anyone else, for that matter, be indifferent about Jayanti? It defied belief.

He blamed Sister Rosalind for the other woman in his life—not that he minded very much. It definitely had its perks. The sister had instructed him to pick up Durgamma, the woman who had been so badly abused, from the convent's medical ward and take her home. The trouble was, she had no home to return to. The upshot was, she'd ended up in Kumar's mother's house.

In truth, Kumar's mother was in need of help. She was a superb cook, something which probably helped explain Kumar's size, but her arthritic hands were able to do less and less.

She'd been scandalized by Durgamma, of course, and treated her very badly.

Durgamma had retaliated by sweeping the house and scouring all the pots and pans until they shone. She kept doing this in the face of rudeness and the occasional beating until Kumar's mother gave in to her own good nature and began to teach Durgamma to cook. A mother and daughter relationship soon developed.

What had alarmed Rahul was that he had awoken on the first morning to find Durgamma curled up in her shawl fast asleep in front of his door. The place she was sleeping was precarious. The ledge was only one pace wide before it fell down to the courtyard. She stayed there night after night in the open, refusing to sleep anywhere else.

Then, one night, Rahul was having one of his childhood nightmares. He hated them. They caused him to spasm and scream. White foam would froth in his mouth as disturbing images from the past screeched at him before being lost again in oblivion.

He had woken to find Durgamma mopping his brow with a damp cloth. After the terrors had past, he'd gone back to sleep. Durgamma had curled up behind him and held him.

In the morning, they'd had sex.

They'd been having sex most mornings ever since. Rahul's lovemaking was quick and passionate, and he soon reached a climax. Durgamma was generous and instructive…and she never reached a climax. He'd asked her about it once. She'd said that it had never happened. No man had ever been able to fully pleasure the goddess, Yellamma, whom she embodied, only themselves.

Nonetheless, she seemed to enjoy the act of coupling…and legitimately enjoyed his pleasure.

"Come down from the clouds," said Kumar, tapping his empty glass on the rough wooden bench.

"Oh, yeah. Jayanti. She's okay, I suppose. Seems to be doing well."

Kumar raised an eyebrow. "And just why do you keep seeing her? We don't work the rail station any more, so we don't need English." His statement was true enough. He, with Kumar, Arjun, and Malik had chosen to specialize in the more lucrative hotel trade. They were also beginning to break into the false passport business by introducing clients to the right people. Their interests were increasingly expanding beyond Kaseru Walan.

"Good English is a handy thing to have."

"Bullshit."

Rahul gave a lopsided smile to concede that it wasn't the truth. "I suppose she represents something that's different from my shitty world." He shrugged. "She intrigues me. Jayanti represents things that…" he struggled to find the right word: "give hope," he said.

It wasn't the whole truth, but it would do. He winced and gasped as he swallowed the fiery liquid in his glass. "I also want to keep an eye on her. She's still way too clueless for her own good."

"Do you have any reasons to worry?"

Rahul toyed with his glass, rocking it around on its base. "Until today, not really."

Kumar leaned against the side of the bar and waited for him to elaborate.

A man was hovering just out of earshot in the laneway waiting to gain access to the counter. Kumar let him wait.

"A car was parked in front of Jayanti's house yesterday morning —a fairly flash one. It had a CH number plate."

"From Chandigarh."

Rahul nodded.

"So what?"

"The bloke inside it was using a camera with a telephoto to check out the house. I saw the reflection off the lens."

"Do you think he was scoping it out for a break-in?"

Rahul shook his head. "No. You'd be mad to break in there. The security is terrifying."

"Then why?"

Rahul shrugged. "No idea. But I think I'll drop by to see if anyone's doing the same tomorrow."

Rahul sat on an upturned bucket and watched Kumar train. Kumar chose to keep fit by using two huge clubs shaped like skittles. He'd done it ever since seeing Parsee devotees twirl them in their hands to build their strength. He was twirling them now and looking very impressive with his bare chest. Having Durgamma in the house had given him a fresh incentive to exercise in the narrow confines of the rear courtyard. The kitchen looked onto it. Rahul suspected that Kumar was more than a little in love with her.

His own exercise regime was different. He, like Malick, used a knife. His favorite was the Indian made F-S commando knife. It had a heavily ridged cast handle, a steel pommel, and was twin edged. A fighting knife needed to be twin edged—you couldn't afford to restrict any option for cutting.

Knife fights were brutal and quick—so he practiced over and over again: straight thrust; reverse thrust; reverse flip cut; inward side slash; outward side slash; the tiger claw; and the coiled cobra thrust.

Durgamma didn't watch him train. She'd seen him do it only once, and it had taken her some time to recover from the experience.

Rahul threw a towel at Kumar when he'd finished stacking his clubs against the wall. Kumar began rubbing himself vigorously. "So, was your little friend with a camera there again today?"

"Yes. He wasn't there when I arrived, so I waited." Rahul rubbed the back of his neck. "The bastard turned up at 9:30 am but didn't stay long. He drove off after photographing Ravi Panwar getting in to his flash new sports car."

Kumar buttoned up his shirt. "Nothing to do with Jayanti then? You can leave it alone?"

Rahul nodded.

However, the truth was, he hadn't left it alone. Rahul had crouched down by the man's car and waited for a truck to thunder past, at which point he'd driven his knife into the car's back tire. A moment later, he'd got up and knocked on the driver's side window.

The window had slid down, and a Western man inside had spoken to him in English. He'd told Rahul, in no uncertain way, to get lost.

"But sir, you have flat tire. I am number one at changing tires, isn't it. I change your tire for your good self? Very cheap."

"Piss off."

He had—but not before he'd noticed a hotel key in the car's center compartment. Rahul recognized the fob and knew the hotel.

Chapter 11

"Happy birthday, Ravi." Jayanti glanced at him covertly from under her shawl...and wondered if she'd gone too far.

He was slumped on the bench with his elbows on the table, apparently deep in thought.

She smiled to herself. The fact that he was able to sit with her at the staff dining table behind the kitchen was one of the big changes that had occurred over the last few years. Ravi was now able to greet the staff by their first names and had found polite, if wary, acceptance at their table. This had been greatly facilitated by Ravi joining in with their games of cricket in the back yard. He'd even organized for a set of metal cricket stumps to be made. These had been welded on to a stand enabling them to be set up anywhere on the back patio or on the lawn.

"Thanks, George," he muttered to the servant standing beside him. George was pouring a glass of chai for him from a great height, showing off his ability to create a layer of froth across the surface of the tea.

Ravi cupped his hands around the glass. "That was definitely not your standard birthday present."

"It gave you a chance to drive your car."

He grunted, apparently careless of fact that he'd been given a BMW sports car for his eighteenth birthday.

Both of them had just completed their HSC exams and were now awaiting the results due out at the end of November. With her mornings now free, Jayanti had organized with Elizabeth for them both to visit the Missionaries of Charity home for the destitute.

The experience had a profound effect on Ravi. He'd remarked on the extraordinary peace he experienced in the ward, even commenting on the quality of light that filtered through the windows. Ravi watched transfixed, as a beggar with arms too thin and emaciated to hold anything, was spoon-fed. He'd been shocked that some of those dying were young. He'd stood behind the doctor on duty and watched him re-bandage an emaciated girl's twisted leg. Ravi then shadowed the medic around the ward, helping him in whatever way he could whenever he could.

The morning was particularly special because Sister Rosalind was able to be present with them. Jayanti had not seen her as often as she would have liked over the last three years; only occasionally at some pre-arranged location in the city. But the nun always had a warm embrace for her and never failed to question her closely about her well-being. The sister had spent most of the morning with Ravi and the doctor as they made their way around the ward.

Jayanti had watched them from the bedside of just one man; it was that of Rohit, the blind beggar. He was now very weak, but even in his feeble state, he smiled with delight at being in her company again.

She'd held his hand and talked for over an hour.

"I don't think I'm going to forget that in a hurry," said Ravi, sweeping his hair back from his forehead.

"Would you want to?"

He seemed to consider the question before answering, "No."

"You've changed a good deal over the years, Ravi Panwar."

Ravi glanced at her. "I don't think I had much option with you around."

His comment caused her to lapse into silence. Had she really had an influence on Ravi? She shook her head.

Ravi folded his arms on the table and rested his head on them. "My father's organized a birthday bash for me at a hotel tonight—and promised me another surprise. God knows what that's all about."

"That should be nice."

"Hmph. You can't come, I'm afraid. Wish you could."

"I never expected…"

"The guys from the tennis club will be there, and a few friends from St Columba's School." He sighed. "But, to be honest, I'm not looking forward to it."

"Why? It should be lovely." She poked him on the arm. "You can been too serious, you know."

"Hmph. Heavy drinking; forced gaiety—not quite my thing. I'll be aching for anything authentic and genuine by the time I come back."

Jayanti was adjusting the scarf around her shoulders and only half listening.

"Will you wait up for me?"

"What!" She jerked herself upright.

"We can sit on the stairway in the hall. We always talk well there. I want to talk about this morning."

She laughed. "That's crazy. It will be past midnight."

He grinned, "So what. School's over."

"Well, I…I suppose so. But you'd better let Mr. Singh know."

"Aakar? Oh, all right."

That was another thing that had changed. Ravi's relationship with Aakar Singh had grown closer. The two of them often went to the pistol range and trained together.

Jayanti shivered. She didn't like guns.

Jayanti was sitting on an ornate marble bench outside Mr. Singh's office when they came in.

Aakar Singh held the door open for them as they all but fell inside the entrance hall.

Gokul Panwar had his arm around a woman and was shouting loudly. "Tonight, you will become a man." He tripped, but his partner held him up. He bent over and giggled, hanging on to her waist. The woman also laughed.

Another woman was hanging on to Ravi's arm. She was dressed in a floral-print salwar kameez and had dark kohl around her eyes. The woman had looped her scarf around Ravi's neck and was holding it, and his arm, tight.

Gokul Panwar didn't see Jayanti as he lurched toward the stairs. He roared, "I have paid for you to have a good night. So, by God, you're going to have one. Be a man. Show her you can be a man."

Ravi, however, did see Jayanti. He darted a stricken look at her and half raised an arm to her as if to implore her help, before his partner towed him to the stairs.

"Father, I don't want…" began Ravi.

His father bellowed. "Nonsense. Your woman is one of the best." He laughed. "I should know, I've tried her out. So I don't want to hear any more whining." Gokul reached back and pinched the bottom of Ravi's partner. "Get him to bed, woman and make a man of him."

Gokul took one of Ravi's arms, and the woman took the other. Together, they towed him up the sweeping stairs.

Jayanti got up from the bench and stood beside Aakar Singh at the foot of the stairs as the party stumbled onto the landing.

Moments later, the giggling and yelling coming from the landing was muffled by closed doors.

Jayanti was holding her arms stiffly by her side. Slowly, she unclenched her fists and looked up at Aakar Singh. He was scowling.

"I believe Mr. Ravi is not happy and feels he is being coerced. He is likely to be traumatized." She expressed the conviction of her heart before she remembered to be frightened of the giant standing beside her.

To her surprise, he nodded and said, "Bad business."

Silence followed. Neither of them moved.

"Perhaps," she said diffidently, "we should be ready, and stand guard against anything…unpleasant happening."

Aakar Singh looked down at her.

She pointed to the landing. "From up there."

"I shall guard," he said and made for the stairs.

"I will come too."

He glanced back at her. Deep furrows creased his brow.

She lifted her chin, not quite in defiance, but enough to show her resolve.

He nodded.

Jayanti followed him up the stairs and along the landing to the door into Ravi's room. The Sikh stood two paces back from the door and folded his arms in front of him. He looked as if he would need little excuse to barge through it.

Jayanti stepped around him and pulled open the laundry shoot. Then, reaching through, she pushed open the flap to the bin on the other side of the wall. She squatted down and listened through the laundry cavity.

"Now, Mr. Ravi, let me show you what you can look forward to."

Rustling sound.

"Why don't you come here and take a closer look. I'll even turn around and bend over. Tell me what you like the look of, and what you'd like to do."

"No! Er…um: can we talk? This is my Father's idea…"

A yelp.

"Shall we just take these off you... My, my, you are not yet ready for action, are you? I shall just have to fix that…and see what you taste like."

Another yelp—louder this time.

"No, no." It was almost a sob.

Jayanti pulled her head back and nodded to Aakar Singh.

The Sikh lunged forward, threw open the door and marched through.

Some yells and scuffles followed and in remarkably short order, he returned to the door behind the naked woman. He had her clothes under one arm and was holding the woman's arm behind her back with the other.

He paused.

Jayanti said, "If you take care of her. I'll check Mr. Ravi is okay."

Aakar Singh nodded and propelled the woman along the landing.

Taking a deep breath, she entered Ravi's bedroom suite.

Ravi was sitting on the bed, bent over, holding his head in his hands. He was dressed in his underpants and an open shirt.

She stood in front of him, and said nothing.

He glanced at her between his fingers then put his head down. "I…I'm not a man. I…I…couldn't. I hated…" He gave a shuddering sigh.

Silence.

"You are every bit a man, Ravi Panwar. What you were made to do tonight is not the measure of a man."

Ravi lifted his head and sniffed. Then he leaned back on his arms and stared at Jayanti. Light from a bedside table lamp highlighted the muscular planes of his chest and the definition of his thighs. Tennis had made him very fit. Ravi shook his head. "No, I'm not."

"I have read enough to know that sex, the best sex, the sex that really is the mark of a man, happens between a man and the women he loves."

He snorted. "That's not what my father says." He dropped his head. "I…I just don't know what to do."

"Stand up, Ravi Panwar. I will tell you how a woman thinks, and show you that you know more than you believe."

Jayanti lifted her head and waited for him to stand before her. She was wearing her favorite sari, aqua blue, edged with silver thread. Very deliberately, she rested her hand on her chest, paused, and adjusted her scarf.

"A woman will signal her affection for her man by looking alluring. We have tricks to do this. She squared her shoulders so that her breasts lifted slightly. We do this to show you our heart—it is not hidden. A woman in love wants to be looked at; wants to be cherished."

Ravi looked at her with a pained expression. He began to reach out a hand.

She forestalled him by holding up her own hand. "It may take a little time for the heart to see. So be careful that she knows your love before anything happens."

"And then...?" he said, hoarsely.

"Then, there is touch—the feeling of the object of love; the marveling at it."

She took the fingers of his hand and placed them on the side of her neck.

Jayanti's chest rose and fell quickly with her breathing.

Ravi trailed three fingers down her neck, then across her lips.

She picked up his fingers and placed his hand on her waist.

"And when he does, she will signal her approval and love." She stepped close to him, laid a hand on his chest and brushed against him, allowing Ravi to feel the gentle pressure of her body against his thigh.

He whimpered.

Jayanti, stepped back smartly, keeping him at bay with a hand on his shoulder.

"And that's what you will do when you find a woman you love and want to have sex with."

He fell to his knees and reached for her.

Jayanti allowed herself to be caught around her thighs.

He buried his cheek against her stomach and held her.

She toyed with his hair and stroked his cheek, just once, then pulled away from him.

Ravi let his arms fall down beside him and looked forlornly at the floor. "How do you know...these things?"

Jayanti swallowed. "I know, Ravi, because I am a woman." She did not mention the many remarkably frank discussions she'd had with Sister Elizabeth.

He reached out to her.

She backed away to the door, again holding out a hand to still any instinct of his to follow her.

"Trust me, Ravi; what I have told you will make the best sex. You will love it and be very good at it."

She turned and opened the door.

Chapter 12

R ahul did not like the look of any of them. Three men were
waiting for the lift when he and Durgamma stepped out of it
on the fourth floor. All had hard faces. When you worked on the
streets, you learned to recognize the demeanor instantly.

Rahul didn't want anyone to recognize him, so he buried his
face in Durgamma's neck in an apparent show of affection as he
steered her past them. When the lift doors closed, he stopped the
charade and leaned against the wall to wait for Kumar and Malick.

Both of them came up in the next lift. The four of them had
agreed to split up, to avoid attracting attention. Moments later, they
were standing either side of the door to room forty-six.

Rahul nodded to Durgamma.

She knocked on the door.

A male voice called from inside in English, "Who is it?"

"Service," said Durgamma.

The door opened, but was kept on the security latch. A man
spoke through the gap. "What do you want?"

"Hotel say you want girl for sexy business. Is this right room?"

There was a pause.

"Well, well. Perhaps it is. Let's have a look at you."

The door came off the latch.

Kumar and Malick immediately barged through.

Rahul gave them a few moments to sort things out.

They didn't take long. He knew things were under control when Durgamma came out from the room and headed toward the lifts. She left without saying a word. Rahul flexed his fingers and entered the room, shutting the door behind him.

The man was now flat on the floor on his face. Malick had artfully placed a knife under his nose like an extended mustache. Kumar had the man's arms pulled behind him and was pushing a knee into his back.

Malick handed Rahul the man's wallet and mobile phone. Rahul opened the wallet and inspected the driver's license.

"Mr. Walker; from Mumbai, eh?"

Rahul pulled up a chair, sat down, and said conversationally. "Maybe you die. Maybe not. I don't care."

"Bastards. You don't know who you are messing with," came the muffled reply.

An instant later, Malick had lifted the man's head by his hair, taken the knife, and split the end of the man's nose. He banged the man's head back down and slid the knife back into position under his face.

Blood spilled out over the white tiled floor.

Rahul yawned, apparently indifferent to what had happened. "My friend...very bad man—rascal fellow. Next, he take pants off and cut. *Samajho?*"

The man stiffened instantly.

"One question: "Why you watch Gokul Panwar place?"

Kumar pushed the man's arms up his back.

The man screamed. "No, no. Stop."

"Talk."

"He has something..." he gasped, "I want."

"What?"

Silence.

Another push.

He screamed again. "Jewels. Jewels. He has jewels."

"Jewels?"

"Yes," the man sobbed. "They're not his. His great, great grand-father stole them…years ago."

"From your family?"

Silence.

Rahul repeated the question. "From your family?"

"No."

"So: jewels not yours."

Silence.

"Ahh." Rahul nodded his understanding, and changed tack with his questioning. "Why watch Ravi Panwar?"

Kumar adjusted his weight on the man's back.

"Kidnap, kidnap…" he said quickly, "so the father gives us what's left."

Rahul inclined his head. "Good plan. You very crafty fellow, isn't it. Very crafty." He sighed. "But very sad. I must stop you."

The man laughed, nastily. "It's too late."

"Why too late?"

"My men have just gone to get him."

Jayanti folded up the cord around the peacock stone and put it into her shoulder bag. For some reason, Sister Rosalind had asked her to bring it with her. Jayanti and Ravi had agreed to meet her inside the famous Red Fort in Old Delhi. She'd never been there before, so she was looking forward to seeing it.

In the last week, Ravi had gone back twice to the home for the destitute and dying. Jayanti hadn't questioned him about it, and he didn't volunteer any reasons for doing so.

Jayanti walked round the side of the house from the kitchen to the front drive. She found Ravi lounging against his car. He sprang up and opened the door for her.

Jayanti looked at him—interrogating him with a puzzled frown.

"Don't protest." He said. "I'm learning to be a gentleman...and enjoying it, rather surprisingly.

"I'm a servant, remember."

"Yeah, yeah. Get in."

He closed her door and walked around the car. A moment later they set off down the drive. The gate opened to let them through and shut behind them as they passed.

Suddenly, a car parked by the curb revved hard and speared forward. Jayanti screamed as it swerved into the driveway and smashed into the front of the sports car spinning it around. Almost immediately, another car swung in front of them and skidded to a halt. A man jumped out from each car and ran toward them. Jayanti thought for a fleeting moment they were coming to help— but people coming to help don't wear clown masks. She started to yell a warning. "Ravi."

Ravi was shaking his head and seemed half dazed. Jayanti grabbed his arm just as one of the two men sliced his seat belt free with a knife. The other jammed some sort of stun gun against Ravi's shoulder causing him to spasm. They hauled him from the car and began dragging him backward toward the second vehicle.

In the horror of what was unfolding, she was dimly aware of the spluttering revving of an auto coming to a halt. Three men erupted from the back of it. One leaped toward the driver of the second car. Jayanti could see the glint of a knife in his hand.

Another large man ran at the men dragging Ravi. He was carrying a cricket bat. The third man ran over the top of the car jumping up onto the boot, then over the roof, to land in front of the men holding Ravi. With a shock, she realized it was Rahul.

One of the masked men put a knife to Ravi's throat. "Get out of the way, or I'll kill him," he screamed.

Rahul didn't move. "Here's how this is going to play out if you're going to escape prison. Your driver has a knife in his throat, so you're not going anywhere. I'm certainly not going anywhere. And I don't greatly care what you do to this bastard."

"I'll kill him," the man yelled.

Rahul shook his head. "As I said, that doesn't impress me. But some friends of mine want him alive. So, you let him go, and we'll let you go. Simple." Rahul turned his head and called, "Malick."

A man with the darkest eyes Jayanti had ever seen walked around to Rahul. He was gripping the driver to his chest whilst holding a knife low into the man's kidney.

For a moment, no one said anything.

Rahul nodded and said, "Let him go, Malik."

The driver fled back to his car.

Instantly, the other men realized they risked the driver escaping without them. They dropped Ravi on the ground and sprinted after him.

Rahul laughed, walked over to Ravi and hauled him to his feet. He paused as he did, to glance down the driveway.

Jayanti turned and was relieved to see Aakar Singh running toward them.

"Come," ordered Rahul. "We've all got to go."

"No!" protested Jayanti. We need to go back to the house to make sure Ravi is not hurt and ring the police."

Rahul shook his head. "No. It's not safe. There are things I have to tell you."

"No, no, no," screamed Jayanti, and she began to flail at Rahul.

The man who'd been holding the cricket bat wrapped his arms around her and lifted her off the ground. She yelped and punched him on the arm.

Rahul, snarled at her. "Trust me, okay?"

The gate was opening, and Aakar was nearly upon them.

Jayanti and Ravi were pushed at a stumbling run toward the auto and bundled inside. The young man at the controls had it moving as Aakar came panting up behind it.

The auto was soon lost in the traffic making its way into the city.

Jayanti twisted round and lifted Ravi's chin up to inspect the cut left by the knife. Mercifully, it was superficial. "Are you all right?" she asked.

Ravi nodded. "I'm fine."

Rahul rolled his eyes at her concern. "Bloody hell," he said.

Indian autos could technically carry two passengers. They were, however, routinely abused, and it was not uncommon to see them carrying huge numbers of people. There were five adults in the one Jayanti was squeezed into, and one of them was very large. No one could move. She was wedged between the big man and Ravi on the seat. The other two were crouched on the floor.

"Who are you and where are you taking us?" asked Ravi, stiffly.

His question was enough to return Jayanti's thoughts to their immediate future. "Don't worry, Ravi. Rahul is a friend of mine. She glanced around at the others—the big man, who looked oddly familiar—and his colleague with the dangerous, brooding eyes. "The others are his friends, I think."

"What just happened back there? And where are you taking us?" Ravi continued.

"We have just saved your sorry ass from being kidnapped—that's what's happened," said Rahul. As to where we're going—that's pretty much up to you. But you probably shouldn't be going home until we've told you a few things that might concern you."

"What are you talking about?" demanded Ravi.

"Panwar, you're starting to irritate me. A 'thank you' might be nice."

"What are you talking about?" repeated Ravi.

"Well, as it turns out, a bloody relative of yours stole a lot of jewels years ago, and there are enough of them still around to persuade some very bad men to kidnap you in order to force your dad to hand the rest over to them."

"Rubbish!"

"Rahul shrugged. "Suit yourself. We can drop you off here if you like. "I'll probably read about you in tomorrow's papers." He looked grimly at Ravi. "But I won't let you put Jayanti in danger."

"Ravi," said Jayanti, laying a placating hand on his arm. "I think we should at least talk and discover what is happening, but we need to do it somewhere safe."

"At last," said Rahul, "some common sense. Where do you suggest?"

She turned to Ravi. "Why not go where we intended to go, to

meet Sister Rosalind at the Red Fort? We'll be safe enough there, and I'd very much value her wisdom right now."

"What: the crazy nun?" said Rahul.

"Yes."

He shrugged, turned and yelled to the driver, "Hey Arjun, drop Malick and Kumar at Kaseru Walan, then go on to the Red Fort."

Chapter 13

Jayanti stepped out of the auto and looked up at the majestic west front of the Red Fort. She'd read so much about it but, until today, had never seen it. However, the drama of the morning meant that she only half noticed the grandeur around her. She was dimly aware of giant red sandstone walls, surmounted with flame-shaped battlements.

Ravi paid the entrance fee for the three of them, and they walked through the Lahore Gate into the high, vaulted arcade of the Chatta Chowk bazaar. The sides of the arcade were lined with shops selling anything tourists might buy. They looked to be doing a busy trade.

Sister Rosalind and Elizabeth were waiting for them near its far end. Jayanti ran through the groups of tourists and hugged them both, barely able to suppress her tears of relief. "Oh, I'm sorry," she stammered, "but there's been an attempt to kidnap Ravi and we don't know what to do."

Sister Rosalind wrapped an arm around her, stroked the back of her hair and kissed her forehead. "Cush, cush, child. You are safe. You are safe." When Jayanti had her emotions back under control

Sister Rosalind held her at arms length and said, "Now, tell me what happened."

Jayanti and Rahul told the two nuns everything that had occurred. In the process, Jayanti learned how Rahul had noticed someone spying on the house, and then discovered where the observer was staying. He'd paid him a visit and somehow persuaded the spy, a Mr. Walker, to tell him why he was watching the house. Rahul was vague on the details.

When Rahul finished speaking, Jayanti put a hand on his arm. "Thank you, Rahul for caring, and for your courage…" she couldn't finish the sentence.

He laid his hand on top of hers and held it for a second.

Ravi nodded. "I'm in your debt, Rahul. Thank you," he said formally.

Sister Rosalind broke in to the conversation. "I think you should ring home, Ravi, and assure your father that all is well so that the police are not sent out to look for you."

Ravi rubbed his forehead. "But what about this other…er, allegation…against my father?"

"Best not mention that at this stage."

When Ravi finished making his call, Sister Rosalind looked out across the gardens and said. "Come, let us walk. I need time to process this." She gestured with her hand. "Let's enjoy this glorious place. It has an amazing history."

As they started to walk she began to talk about what they were seeing.

"This was built by the Turkish Mughals who claimed direct descent from Genghis Khan. Their empire reached its peak in the seventeenth century by which time it controlled all but the very tip of India." Sister Rosalind adjusted her shawl. "Shah Jahan, the fifth emperor, presided over the golden period of Mughal architecture. He built the Taj Mahal at Agra and the Red Fort here when he moved his administration to Delhi."

They walked down the wide path through to the Drum House, a massive three-story building that sat astride the processional path. Its red sandstone walls had been carved into floral designs.

"Music was played here five times a day. It must have made for a wonderful sense of arrival." She pointed to the archway. "This was where everyone, except royalty, had to dismount from their elephants."

Sister Rosalind led them through and along the path toward the Hall of Public Audience.

Despite her traumatized state, the beauty of the hall took Jayanti's breath away. It was built with three rows of scalloped arches, supported by pillars topped with floral corbels.

"This was where the emperor sat on his throne to deal with day-to-day matters. But come, let me take you to the Hall of Private Audience." She smiled. "That's probably the appropriate spot for us to sit and talk about jewels."

They made their way through a formal garden to a magnificent hall of white marble with domed pavilions on each corner of its roof.

Jayanti didn't think she'd ever seen anything so beautiful. The building was a pillared hall, with a flat ceiling supported by ornate arches. Floral inlaid marble panels were set into the base of the pillars. Tourists were filing through it, photographing everything they saw. Jayanti stepped back to make way for a group of school children being shepherded along by their teacher.

Sister Rosalind smiled at the children. Once they'd all scampered past, she pointed to the roof. "The ceiling was originally inlaid with silver and gold, but it was looted a long time ago."

"How did it all end?" asked Elizabeth.

"Tragically, I'm afraid. The Mughal Empire was invaded by the Persian emperor, Nader Shah. He was victorious even though the Mughal army was five times bigger."

Elizabeth showed surprise. "How did he manage that?"

"Nader Shah was wise enough not to fight all the Mughal army at once, but in sections. He also slung platforms between pairs of camels on which naphtha combustibles were placed. He set fire to it during the battle causing the Mughal war elephants to flee."

The conversations had been carried out in English, and Jayanti had been helping Rahul understand by translating when it was needed. He had his head next to Jayanti's and was nodding appreciatively. "Tricky fellow, eh."

"But the real tragedy came later. Nader massacred thirty thousand of the inhabitants of Delhi in six hours, after its merchants refused to accept the artificially low prices imposed by the Persians."

"Good grief," exclaimed Elizabeth.

"That was not the end of it. The Persians then levied a heavy fine and looted this fort of its wealth—in particular the legendary peacock throne and the Koh-i-Nor diamond."

"Isn't that the diamond in the British crown jewels?" asked Jayanti.

"Yes. It was put in queen Alexandra's crown. She was King Edward VII's queen."

Elizabeth nodded and began tracing the shape of a flower inlaid into the marble beside her. "What was the peacock throne?" she asked.

"It was a jewel-encrusted throne built by the Mughal emperor to impress those who had a private audience with him. Evidently, it cost more to build than the Taj Mahal." Sister Rosalind pointed to a raised dais. "That's where it once sat."

Elizabeth turned to look. "Wow! The Persians got a lot of plunder, then."

"Yes. So much that all taxes in Persia were suspended for three years." Sister Rosalind gestured to the paving beside a pillar. "Let's sit down and talk. I have something I need to share."

Once they were settled, she continued. "Jayanti, my dear, have you brought the stone pendant?"

Jayanti nodded, took it out of her shoulder bag, and handed it to Sister Rosalind.

The nun took it and turned it over in her hands with a look of infinite sadness. "Jayanti, as you know, this soapstone pendant came from Rohit, the beggar you helped care for. He asked me to give it to you, but to keep its story a secret until the time was right to share it. I think that time is now." She held the pendant out to Jayanti. "Do you see this mark on the stone?" She pointed to the six-armed star engraved on one side. "That mark is the 'star of India'. Evidently it occurs on some Indian sapphires. It's the symbol of the guild of Indian gem-cutters in Jaipur. Jaipur, as you may know, is the center for gem-cutting in India."

Jayanti nodded and asked, "Do you know the meaning of the peacock on the other side of the stone?"

Sister Rosalind shook her head. "No. But I can tell you that Rohit was a gem-cutter from Jaipur. He told me that he was one of three employed secretly by your father, Ravi, twenty-two years ago. Your father apparently came into great wealth at that time, a wealth founded on jewels."

"But how did he get them?" asked Elizabeth. "What happened twenty two years ago?"

"The..." Rahul turned to Jayanti and asked how to say the words he wanted to say in English. After listening, he nodded and continued on. "The jewels were stolen by Mr. Panwar's great, great grandfather." Rahul smiled. "I know. Mr. Walker—bad fellow, tell me. He wants the stones."

Elizabeth stabbed the marble floor with a finger. "But what happened twenty-two years ago? How did Mr. Panwar get hold of the jewels?" She turned to Ravi. "Any idea?"

Ravi was looking grim. He began to shake his head, paused and said, "The only thing that happened then was that my grandfather died. He'd been dying for a long time, almost ten years, I understand."

The five of them sat in silence under the arches that carried the terrible burden of history.

Elizabeth said slowly. "Ravi, could it be that your father inherited at that time."

Ravi shrugged, "I suppose he would have had to."

"If your grandfather had stolen jewels in strong boxes in a bank, then your father would have suddenly inherited them and become fabulously rich."

Jayanti nodded. "It would explain how his fortunes improved at that time."

"But why employ gem-cutters?" asked Elizabeth.

Rahul had his head bent down next to Jayanti, listening to her translation. He then grunted and said. "He sneaky man. He cut the jewels so they change…"

Jayanti finished for him. "…so they change shape and can't be traced."

Sister Rosalind nodded. "This is what Rohit and two other gem-cutters from Jaipur were employed to do for three years."

Jayanti gave a gasp of realization. "I…I think I know where they must have worked, or at least have been housed."

Everyone looked at her.

"In the cellar…where I sleep." She picked up the peacock stone, turned it over, and pointed to the star of India. "This mark was carved into the stone on one of the walls."

Ravi raised an eyebrow in surprise.

Sister Rosalind, laid a hand on his shoulder. "Ravi, I'm afraid that what I have to say may be deeply wounding to you. It concerns your father…and I am sorry."

Ravi bit his lip and nodded. "I think…I think I always suspected something was not right." He lifted his chin. "We were never close. I…I used to try…years ago, but…"

The nun took his hand and held it. "Toward the end of their three years of work, two of the gem-cutters disappeared. Rohit was suspicious that they might have been murdered to keep them quiet about the nature of the work they'd been doing."

"Murdered!" exclaimed Jayanti.

"I'm afraid so."

"By my father?" asked Ravi.

"Yes."

"Goodness!" said Elizabeth, shaking her head. "But how did Rohit escape?"

"Rohit, as you know, is now dying. He knows it and I think that prompted him to share some more information with me recently." Sister Rosalind smiled sadly. "I think he was pleased to finally share the concerns of his heart. Anyway, from the day he first became suspicious about what was happening, Rohit began the practice of putting the uncut stones he was about to work on in with the already cut stones. He reasoned that if he were murdered, the stones would be sold and possibly identified because they hadn't been cut."

Elizabeth whistled. "Sort of…revenge from the grave."

Sister Rosalind nodded.

"But how did Rohit escape?"

"Evidently, someone left a door unlocked one night, and he escaped through the kitchen. The trouble was, he didn't dare go home. He knew he would be found and possibly endanger the life of his family, so he stayed in Delhi. But by this stage, his eyesight was already beginning to fail."

"And so he became a beggar," finished Jayanti. "How sad. How dreadfully sad."

No one said anything for a while.

"Who is unlucky fellow who first had jewels?" asked Rahul.

"Ah," said Sister Rosalind. She shifted her legs to make herself more comfortable. "I did some research after Rohit confided in me, but I couldn't make sense of the results until now when Rahul told us that it was Ravi's great, great grandfather who originally possessed the jewels."

"What do you mean?" asked Elizabeth.

"Well, the only big theft of jewels I was able to uncover happened in 1885."

"And?" encouraged Elizabeth.

"Let me go back a bit. The story probably begins with King Mindon, a ruler of Myanmar in the nineteenth century. He became obsessed with the rubies and sapphires mined from the legendary Mogôk Valley. It is said that when he moved his capital to Mandalay in 1859, he buried a trove of precious sapphires and rubies under the foundations of his new palace to appease the malevolent spirits."

"Wow!" exclaimed Elizabeth.

"Mindon was succeeded by Thibaw who consolidated his claim to the throne by massacring all other contenders, including their friends and families." Sister Rosalind sighed. "Thibaw also loved jewels. In fact, there are a number of photographs of him wearing gem-encrusted regalia including a sapphire ring worth, it was said, a monarch's ransom."

Elizabeth put her hand to her mouth. "My goodness!"

"Yes." She paused. "Unfortunately, Thibaw was a profligate man who put his country into debt. He destroyed the productivity of the Mogôk region by imposing excessive taxes." She shrugged. "Gem production all but stopped."

"Bad fellow," said Rahul.

Sister Rosalind nodded. "His reign ended when the British invaded Mandalay in 1885 and forced him into exile." She leaned back and glanced at each of those sitting around her. "The thing is, the royal treasury containing the jewels of King Thibaw mysteriously disappeared whilst they were in the care of the British Chief Political Officer, Colonel Sladen."

Jayanti was shocked by the revelation, and was deeply concerned for Ravi. She shot him a furtive look. He had his head bowed, but she saw him nod, as if to himself.

Groups of tourists continued to walk past them pausing now and then to take in the splendor of the marble hall. Sitting in such a place hearing stories of murder and theft seemed surreal to Jayanti.

Ravi, shifted on his haunches and said slowly, "My father's great, great grandfather served in the expeditionary force of Colonel Sladen." He chewed his lip. "I've seen a photograph of him with the Colonel in my father's desk."

Everyone remained silent.

The tourists around them chatted, exclaimed, and took more photographs.

Jayanti thought back to the time she first began to live in Gokul Panwar's house, and as she did, pieces of her own puzzle started to fall into place. She began hesitantly, "So the letter you wrote to Mr. Panwar three years ago…"

Sister Rosalind nodded. "…was dictated by Rohit. He told Mr. Panwar to look after you until you became an adult, or risk being reported to the police."

Jayanti folded her hands and lowered her head. "No wonder Mr. Panwar viewed me...with such hostility."

For a long while, no one spoke.

It occurred to Jayanti that her own future was now tenuous. She would turn eighteen in a few weeks, after which time, Gokul Panwar was under no obligation to provide a safe home for her. Having heard the dark secrets surrounding Mr. Panwar, she had no desire to return to his home. She shuddered. Could it all be true? She glanced at Ravi. The fact he'd accepted the dreadful allegations concerning this father with barely a protest, was itself a confirmation. It was as if he'd always known, but now had the details.

Rahul interrupted her thinking. He pointed to Ravi. "You still number one big trouble."

Ravi raised a questioning eyebrow.

"How so?" asked Jayanti.

"Mr. Walker is not the boss of bad fellows. He work for someone big—a big man from Mumbai. Walker tell me he not stop until he have the jewels." Rahul pointed to Ravi. "You still in shit."

Elizabeth leaned back on her arms. "Ravi, wouldn't it be safest for you to return to your father's house? It has good security and you'd be under the care of Mr. Singh. He gives the impression of someone who takes his responsibilities very seriously."

Ravi closed his eyes and rubbed his forehead. "I have no desire to be under my father's protection—or in any place where he can make decisions about my life. Nor do I relish the idea of being a prisoner in my father's home."

Sister Rosalind nodded and said nothing.

"But where will you go? What do you want to do?" Elizabeth persisted.

Ravi glanced at Jayanti. "What do I want to do?" He kept his eyes on her. "I didn't know until a week ago, but I'm now very sure. The thing I want to do, is train to be a doctor."

Jayanti blinked in surprise.

Rahul nodded appreciatively. "Doctor is very good. Make plenty money."

Sister Rosalind let her gaze rest on Ravi. "Why?" she asked.

"Doctors have the power to change people's lives. It is…" he seemed to search for the right words. He tried again. "It is…the power to effect change for good." He shrugged. "There is nothing more significant."

"And lots of money," said Rahul.

Jayanti punched his arm.

"What?" he protested.

"The trouble is, I'm not sure my HSC marks will be good enough to get me into medical college. I don't get the results for another five weeks."

"Will the results be sent to your home?" asked Sister Rosalind.

Ravi nodded. "But I'll also be able to get them online."

"And will your father underwrite you financially—given that you don't want to live with him?"

"Yes. He knows that I want to train at the Christian Medical College in Vellore. It's a very good college…and has the best…attitude."

"…to the poor?" finished Sister Rosalind.

"Yes."

She nodded.

Jayanti felt a chill run through her. She tried to focus her attention on a group of myna birds fluttering in the bushes edging the lawn outside. Her world was again imploding. The one thing that was different this time, however, was that it was taking her heart with it. To be without Ravi after all these years seemed unthinkable. Whilst she never allowed herself to forget she was a mere servant, it was impossible for either of them to deny that a very special friendship now existed between them.

What on earth would she do with her life now? Fear stabbed at her heart with a fresh intensity. She reached across and took hold of Elizabeth's hand. It had become almost an unconscious action she'd allowed to develop over the last three years. More than ever, Jayanti needed the special peace that Elizabeth exuded.

Elizabeth seemed to understand and flashed her an encouraging smile.

Jayanti's thoughts returned to her home village on the edge of the canals in the backwaters behind Cochin. The village hid from the enervating heat among the trees through which the waterways cut. Although she only had childhood memories of her village, she ached now for the simplicity of its life and for the dense network of relationships that meant that you became everyone's responsibility.

Her brother was still there. He was two years older and had stayed in the village with an uncle after their parents drowned in a boating accident. The uncle and aunt had been too poor to care for Jayanti as well, so she'd been sent to her great-aunt in Delhi.

She'd written to her brother every fortnight over the last three years, sending him postcard letters. It was the cheapest way of writing in India. He wrote back very much more infrequently—even allowing for the habit of India post to lose letters now and then. He'd now got himself a mobile phone and had begged Jayanti to also get one so they could communicate more easily. So far, she hadn't had the funds to do so.

Ravi…wanting to be a doctor. She was not altogether surprised. He was a serious man, schooled in pondering things deeply by long hours of his own company. It was not uncommon for him to share his reflections on an incident weeks after it had occurred. He also drove himself hard. It was as if he were trying to expurgate some hidden demons from his soul. Jayanti suspected that it had something to do with the disconnection he felt from his father, and the absence of a loving mother. She'd certainly had a hard time keeping up with him academically. Their tutor, Ainsley Hodges, had trained initially as a physicist, and it was plain that he loved the subject almost as much as he loved a drink. He'd sourced the latest Internet technology to enable him to teach them both physics and chemistry, augmenting it with evening classes run in the laboratories of St Columba's School. He'd set them both a punishing study schedule.

But now what? Ravi needed a place to hide, at least until he could apply to do the entrance examination for the Christian Medical College in Vellore.

"When do you have to apply to the Christian Medical College?" she asked.

"I have to apply online in February. Then I have to do a written test in May." He shrugged. "If I pass that, I have to go for an interview in June. The first classes start two weeks later."

"Wow, that's all pretty quick."

He nodded. "Thousands apply, and they only accept about one hundred new students a year. So, I've got to be realistic about my chances."

Jayanti reached out to him. "You are an excellent student, Ravi."

He pulled a wry face. "I've had to be to keep up with you."

"Rubbish."

Keep up with you. It came to her in a flash. The germ of an idea— an outrageous idea.

Sister Rosalind looked at her. "What are you thinking of?" she asked.

How does she do that? thought Jayanti. *It's as if she knows.*

She cleared her throat. "Um, I...I thought that maybe I could take Ravi to Kerala, to the backwaters of Cochin, and hide him in my village until...things become clearer." She lowered her head. "My brother's there. He lives with my uncle and aunt."

Rahul scoffed. "It will take days to get there by train. And why go there? Kerala is full of coconuts, communists, and Catholics."

Jayanti looked at him imperiously. "Have you ever been there?"

"No."

"It is my home."

"Pah!" said Rahul. "Delhi is your mother now."

"I would be concerned about the propriety of such an arrangement – with just the two of you going to Cochin," said Sister Rosalind.

Jayanti translated for Rahul. He scoffed, and waved a finger at Ravi. "You be good to Jayanti or I cut your balls."

Ravi ignored him.

"Could it work?" he asked.

"I...I think so," answered Jayanti. She smiled at Ravi. "You have kept me safe in your home for years. Perhaps it is time for me to keep you safe in mine."

Ravi shook his head, as if to clear his thinking.

Sister Rosalind turned her gaze to Elizabeth. "My dear Elizabeth, you have talked with me about doing a pilgrimage to the places where St Thomas first brought the Christian faith to India." She smiled. "You are overdue for some leave. "Would you like to go to Kerala and do that pilgrimage?"

Elizabeth smiled her understanding. "I'd love to."

Sister Rosalind patted Elizabeth on the hand. "Your leave is granted, effective today." She rose to her feet. "Now, we need to do some shopping. Elizabeth will pick up her bag from the convent, and she and I will do some shopping for Jayanti." She glanced at Ravi. "Can I get anything for you, Ravi? I think it best that you stay here until an agreed time when we can meet in front of the fort."

Jayanti replied. "You won't need much. I suggest you buy most of what you'll need in Cochin. You can buy a lightweight mundu very easily there. It's good in hot weather."

"Mundu?" he queried.

"A lungi, a sarong, usually white."

He nodded.

Sister Rosalind turned to Rahul. "When is the next train to Kerala, Rahul?"

Rahul told her.

She looked at her watch. "Right. That gives us three hours." Sister Rosalind laid a hand on Ravi's arm. "Are you sure you can fund this trip, Ravi."

Ravi gave a tired smile. "That, at least, I can guarantee."

"Your father…" said, Sister Rosalind, then paused.

"I'll ring him and tell him that I am going away with Jayanti for a few months and won't be able to be contacted. He will call me a fool but I doubt he'll object very much."

Sister Rosalind nodded.

Rahul began to scowl.

"What's the matter?" asked Jayanti.

He shook his head. "I don't like this going away. Bad business."

She glanced at him, hoping it was enough to convey the things she dare not voice.

Rahul thrust a mobile phone at her. "Take this," he said. Call me if there's trouble. I will come."

Jayanti took it and turned it over in her hands. "It looks very good," she said.

"It is. I only just got it, so look after it. I want it back."

She looked into his eyes and read his expression. It was there, clearly on his face. *I want you back.*

Chapter 14

"I want to sleep in your room."

Jayanti raised a questioning eyebrow.

Ravi colored slightly. "No. What I mean is: I think I should sleep in the same hotel room as you and Sister Elizabeth—for safety reasons."

"Ravi, you've booked two rooms in this hotel. One will be wasted. Surely we should all be quite safe now we are here in Cochin."

"No, I can't be sure. I think it best if we stay together."

Jayanti inclined her head in acquiescence. She had been tempted to wobble her head as so many around her seemed to do. The incidence of head wobbling was greater in the south of India—a habit that Jayanti had almost forgotten from her childhood. Being back in the steamy heat of her home state of Kerala had brought a resurgence of childhood instincts. It was September, so the tail end of the southwest monsoons were still bringing heavy rain. One of Kerala's unusual features was that it had two distinct monsoon seasons. She was grateful for them. They filled the rivers and the backwaters in which they were planning to hide.

The journey was grueling. Ravi was scandalized by the filthy toilets on the train, and the three of them had very little sleep. There were four passengers in their compartment. The fourth was a Sikh businessman who remained aloof throughout the entire journey, except at night when he snored. He'd entertained them unwittingly with his fastidious ritual aimed largely at keeping his mustache and beard in order, as he readied himself for bed.

A taxi deposited them at a hotel late in the afternoon. Ravi had insisted they stay there for two days to recover before being picked up by Jayanti's brother.

She and Ravi quarreled over who would sleep where, as there were only two single beds in the room. Sister Elizabeth would have one; the question was: who would have the other?

Ravi insisted on sleeping on the floor. Jayanti wouldn't hear of it and pointed out that she was used to sleeping on the floor and that she was the servant. She prevailed, only to discover Ravi's arms lifting her onto the bed after she'd gone to sleep. Such was her weary state, she hadn't the strength to protest.

The next day, they went shopping in the bazaars and bought Ravi some clothes, in particular, two mundus. "What do you think?" he asked turning around in front of Elizabeth and Jayanti."

Jayanti nodded her approval. She didn't say that he'd look even better if he exchanged the western shirt for a loose cotton jacket. The traditional jacket was usually worn open so that the chest was visible.

On the second night at the hotel, all three of them slept soundly. The emotional demands of the travel, and the drama of the attempted kidnapping had taken its toll. All three of them were exhausted.

When Jayanti woke, she looked at the time and saw that it was very late. She dressed quickly and went downstairs to the restaurant to check that breakfast was still being served. She'd set her heart on eating the local breakfast specialty, a masala dosa, or perhaps some idli.

As she walked past the foyer, the attendant behind the desk called out, "Good morning miss. Have your two friends found you yet?"

Jayanti's thoughts were elsewhere, and she wasn't paying much attention. "Yes, we're all fine thanks."

It was only after she returned to the stairs from the dining room that she thought about what the receptionist had said. *Two friends?* Odd. She'd left Elizabeth fast asleep upstairs. She wasn't looking for anyone, which left only Ravi. A prickle of apprehension began to disturb her. *Surely, no one could possibly…*

Two men bounded up the stairs behind her.

She spun round, but it was too late. One of them ground the end of a silenced pistol into her side. "If you scream, we'll kill you and your boyfriend." The man pushed the silencer into her kidney, "Now, let's go visit him." He snorted in mirth. "We want to borrow him for a while."

No. No. It couldn't be happening. Terror, anguish, and questions tumbled over each other as she was pushed up the stairs to the first floor. She glanced at her captors and recognized them as the two who had tried to kidnap Ravi earlier. *How could they have tracked them all the way to Kerala so quickly?* Despair washed over her.

Jayanti came to a stop outside her room and was about to shout a warning when she was cuffed savagely around the head and dragged to the room next door.

"Don't trick us, bitch. We know his room number."

Jayanti was bewildered.

"One of the men knocked on the door."

"Wait," came a muffled reply.

A moment later, the door was unlocked.

The two men pushed Jayanti through and kicked the door shut behind them. It slammed with a bang.

There standing in front of her was Rahul. He was dressed as she'd never seen him before, in European clothes. He presented an extraordinary sight.

Without thinking, she exclaimed, "Rahul, what are you doing here?"

He flashed her a warning glance. "Who are these men?" he asked.

"What did you call him?" demanded the man with the pistol.

Jayanti said nothing.

"Who are you?" said the man pointing his pistol at Rahul's head.

"Who do you bloody well think? I'm Ravi Panwar. Who the hell are you?"

"Shut up." The man paused. "Give me your wallet."

Rahul resignedly put his hand in his pocket and produced a wallet. Jayanti recognized it instantly as Ravi's.

The man flicked it open and read the name on one of the credit cards.

At that moment, the door of the room pushed open. In their haste, the kidnappers had not locked it.

Jayanti felt her legs go weak. Ravi stood there dressed only in his mundu.

The pistol swiveled and aimed at Ravi's head.

Jayanti screamed in alarm, "No!"

Ravi stepped inside and closed the door. "I'm Ravi Panwar."

"Don't bullshit us. Who are you?" demanded the man with the gun.

"I told you: Ravi Panwar."

"Then…" the pistol turned back to Rahul. "Who are you?"

"As I said, I'm Ravi Panwar."

The man with the pistol swung the gun back to Ravi.

It was a mistake. Rahul jack-knifed and slashed upward with his knife, burying it into the armpit of the man holding the gun.

Phssst. A muffled shot rang out. A bullet hole appeared in the wall as the gun fell to the floor.

Rahul spun on his feet and slashed the other man's chest, laying open his pectoral muscles.

At the same time, Ravi dived for the pistol. He grabbed it and rolled onto his back so he could point it at the kidnappers.

Neither of them was inclined to offer any resistance. They whimpered and gasped as they sought to staunch the flow of blood from their wounds.

Rahul nodded approvingly to Ravi, then held out a hand to Jayanti.

Mechanically, as if in a dream, she took it and allowed him to lead her away from the wounded men.

Rahul then walked to the door of the room and opened it. "Right, you two assholes; get lost."

It took a moment for the men to realize that they were being released. Clutching their wounds, they staggered through the door. Rahul shut it behind them and turned around.

"That went well," he said.

Jayanti fainted.

Elizabeth thought that filling a bullet hole in the wall with toothpaste was probably not something she would be called to do again in her lifetime. She made as good a job of it as she could, grateful to be out of Jayanti's way.

She was in full flight, interrogating Rahul and Ravi in turn.

Rahul had both his hands up signaling surrender as Jayanti slapped him on the arm for failing to take her question seriously. "It was Arjun who told me," he said quickly. He's good with technology. He said that the phone I took from Mr. Walker was a very good one, and that it probably had a phone-tracking app installed. But I'd given it to you before I found out."

"But how did you come to be here, nearly three-thousand kilometers from Delhi?"

"I caught the next train."

"But…that's a very expensive ticket."

Rahul shrugged. "Who needs a ticket?"

Jayanti rolled her eyes and swung at Ravi with her hands on her hips. "How long have you known?" she demanded.

"Rahul rang me when he knew."

"When?"

"When we arrived here."

"Was that why you booked two rooms? One for Rahul when he arrived?"

Ravi nodded. "This room was booked in my name. Ours was booked under your name."

Jayanti glared at Ravi. "Why didn't you tell me? All this could have gone horribly wrong."

"It didn't," said Rahul getting to his feet.

Jayanti pushed him backward so that he fell back into the chair. "Why did you let those two men go? Why didn't we call the police… even the hotel staff?"

Rahul sighed. "It would cause too many complications." He shook his head. "Trust me, you don't need it. And those guys aren't going to cause you any more trouble. They're flat out trying to find a doctor."

She seemed to reflect on his comment for a moment before saying, "Well, I suppose it's lucky they weren't killed. Then the police would certainly be upon us."

"Luck had nothing to do with it," growled Rahul.

Elizabeth deemed it safe to get down from the chair, and screwed the top back on the tube of toothpaste. She looked around the room. The boys had done a good job cleaning up the blood and all looked to be in order—superficially at least.

"May I suggest," said Elizabeth in her now passable Hindi, "that we leave here as soon as we can and have breakfast at a stall somewhere?"

"What are we going to do with my phone?" asked Jayanti.

Ravi drummed his fingers on the arm of the chair. "I think you'll find it has gone missing."

"Where?"

Rahul broke in. "I've got it. I'll put it on a train that is going up the coast to Goa." He smiled. "That should give them something to think about."

Half an hour later, they were sitting in a market stall eating breakfast. Their luggage, such as it was, was with them.

Jayanti ate both a dosa and a plate full of idli.

Elizabeth looked at her covertly. She no longer looked like the little girl she'd first met. There was a strength and maturity in the way she carried her head. Someone might have thought her carriage imperious until they saw her eyes. Elizabeth sighed. Jayanti's eyes were dangerous; they had the capacity to melt anyone's heart. She glanced at Ravi and Rahul. Both men had fallen under their spell.

Elizabeth shook her head at the complexities of life and began to feel a longing to return to her convent in Delhi. She missed the quiet, the order, and the permission to be with God. Elizabeth was now a novitiate. She'd taken her first vows and was more certain of her vocation than she'd ever been. That's not to say she was finding things easy. The challenges of living with different personalities from various parts of the world were very real. Yet the spirit of Christ's love pervaded everything, bringing its own unique form of healing.

She'd been concerned at one time that her interest in Jayanti was fueled by a desire to live her life vicariously through her, through her vibrancy and zest for learning. Elizabeth now knew it was not so. Jayanti had needed her love and care—at least initially. Now it had grown into a mutual friendship.

Rahul belched and patted his stomach. "We should go. I've a train to catch."

Elizabeth nodded and decided that she too would return to Delhi with Rahul. She'd pass up the opportunity to do pilgrimage to the sites St Thomas was said to have visited two thousand years ago. In truth, although she'd loved the story of Thomas and the brave way he'd faced death just outside of Chennai, she hadn't found what she'd seen of the local Catholic Church very appealing. The local churches were highly ornamented things. Many had a glass box on a post outside them containing a statue of Jesus showing his bleeding heart. Elizabeth shook her head. Quite where the boundary between Catholicism and idol worship was in India, was hard to judge. She felt safer staying closer to the Christ that was spoken of in Scripture—the Christ of compassion.

Two autos carried the four of them to the shore of the backwaters, the inland sea into which canals flowed from the dense jungle. Dirty, oily water clouded by the filth of the city, lapped near their feet. Logs were tethered near the beach alongside long boats with curved, elegant bows. To the left, a crowd of locals gathered, waiting for a ferry to take them somewhere.

It was a world of water—and of people who understood it.

Elizabeth watched a man paddle a boat into the shore. He was carrying a single passenger who was standing up in the boat. It should have been a precarious thing to do in such a long, narrow vessel, but he appeared perfectly at ease.

A smudge of green marked the beginning of the jungle on the other side of the water. The palm trees were particularly visible. They were everywhere. But what particularly attracted Elizabeth's attention were the rickety-looking fishing traps that sat offshore. A massive lever supported a huge dip net that was held open by four long poles. The whole structure sat on top of a platform of coconut tree posts driven into the sea floor. A tiny rounded hut sat at one end, presumably to provide shelter for the fisherman.

Elizabeth shook her head. It was an extraordinary world—so totally foreign. Seeing it made her feel more confident that it was a world in which Jayanti and Ravi could hide successfully while giving them time to plan.

She rested a hand on Jayanti's shoulder as they gazed out across the water. Only a moment earlier, Jayanti had been speaking to her brother on Ravi's mobile. Elizabeth couldn't guess what she was thinking. She'd left her home in the backwaters as a child of twelve and was returning as a woman.

Not that she was behaving like one. She pointed eagerly at a narrow boat a hundred meters off shore. Its solitary occupant raised a paddle briefly in the air to signal his identity and then continued to paddle toward the shore with deft economic strokes.

Jayanti began to point excitedly. "It's him. It's him. It's my brother Aalok. See." She paused. "My goodness," she said, as she shielded her eyes from the sun with her a hand, "he looks so grown up."

Elizabeth noted that she had her emotions under control by the time the boat glided against the pontoon. Jayanti's reunion with her brother was a diffident, circumspect thing. Her brother got out onto the pontoon, put his hands together and bowed a formal *wai*. The three of them returned the gesture.

Namesté, said Jayanti, and then she began to speak in another language that Elizabeth assumed must be Malayalam. After a brief conversation, Jayanti introduced Aalok to each of them.

Aalok appeared to by over-awed by them all, including his sister, and did little other than stand wide eyed, waggling his head.

Elizabeth couldn't blame him. Jayanti was looking splendid in her aqua sari. It would take time for him to come to terms with seeing his sister as a well-to-do adult. Elizabeth suspected that when they did, nothing would stop them talking.

She saw Aalok glance nervously at Ravi and Rahul. There was nothing there to make him feel very much at home, either. Ravi still managed to look every inch an aristocrat, even in his mundu. As for Rahul: he simply looked intimidating.

Rahul didn't help things by speaking to Aalok in Hindi. "So you're Jayanti's brother, eh?"

Aalok nodded.

"So it's your job to find Jayanti a good husband. Have you begun your search? You need the very best fellow."

Aalok looked too startled to reply.

Jayanti rescued him by chatting to him in Malayalam. Every now and then, Aalok interrupted with a question. Once or twice he darted a look at Ravi. Elizabeth could only assume she was explaining their situation. By the end of the conversation, a slightly bossy, querulous demeanor of an older brother had begun to creep into the exchange.

Elizabeth smiled to herself. They would have their first quarrel soon, and it would do much to restore a relationship that had been so tragically ruptured six years earlier.

Ravi cut in to the conversation with his own questions. "Aalok. Is it possible for Jayanti and myself to stay with you in your village for a few weeks? I can pay for my board and perhaps help by doing some work. Is that possible? Do you have a wife who will be inconvenienced? Is there a place where we can sleep?"

The very directness of his question seemed to shock Aalok. He replied in Malayalam.

Jayanti translated. "He says, of course. There could never be any doubt about my coming back to the village. It issue is, where you will stay." She gestured to Aalok. "He says you and I can stay at his house—our parents' old house where he lives." She smiled. "…Although Aalok often stays away with the love of his life, Pambadi Rajan, in the next village. It's only a kilometer away."

Rahul grinned. "He has a beautiful woman there, eh?"

Jayanti shook her head. "No. Pambadi Rajan is an elephant."

Chapter 15

Jayanti sat on her seat in the long, narrow boat facing Ravi. He leaned forward and whispered in English, "An elephant?"

Jayanti was trailing her fingers in the water taking in the sights of her childhood. A humid haze hung over the water as Aalok propelled them steadily toward the distant tree line. She pulled her thoughts together. "Um, yes. Aalok is a paappaan, an elephant handler."

"How on earth did he become an elephant handler?" he inquired.

"It was my father's profession—our business." She shrugged. "That's why Aalok had to stay here when my father died and I had to go away."

A puzzled expression showed on Ravi's face.

Jayanti realized she would have to explain. "When Aalok was an apprentice, he was assigned to Pambadi Rajan when Rajan was a young elephant. This establishes a bond that lasts a lifetime. Aalok is now the main paappaan for Rajan, but two boys from the neighboring village help to feed Rajan and keep him clean. They're training to be elephant handlers."

"Is there an elephant school in the village?"

"There is a kraal where their training is finished, but the elephants usually come partly trained from a larger elephant school. Pambadi Rajan was different, though. He has been entirely trained by Aalok in the village." Jayanti turned around and spoke to Aalok in Malayalam.

Aalok grinned and yabbered back enthusiastically.

Jayanti turned back to Ravi. "Aalok says that Pambadi Rajan is the tallest elephant in the region."

"What does he use him for?"

"He does all the heavy work in areas that tractors can't reach; hauling logs or carrying palm branches for thatching. The best pay, however, comes from attending the many religious festivals around the city. He's quite popular because of his size. The downside is that they need a specially strengthened trailer to carry him in."

"Wow!"

It occurred to Jayanti that her family's life in the village must seem distinctly odd to anyone living in a city. She turned back and spoke to her brother again.

Aalok shook his head and answered sadly.

Jayanti laughed. "Aalok says that Pambadi Rajan is grumpy at the moment because there are female elephants nearby that are in season."

"Good grief," said Ravi. "How on earth do you control a grumpy elephant?"

Jayanti knew that it was a rhetorical question but, nonetheless, she passed the question along to Aalok.

Aalok smiled at Ravi for the first time and replied in Hindi. "A paappaan has three possible ways of controlling his elephant." He rested from his paddling and flexed his arm. "He uses cruelty;" then he tapped his head, "he uses cunning;" he tapped his chest, "or he uses love."

"Which do you use?" asked Ravi.

"Love. It is strongest."

Jayanti was well pleased with the conversation. The men were developing a rapport.

The boat glided toward the bank of trees. As it did, Aalok

stowed the paddle under his seat and pulled out a long pole that lay along the bottom of the boat. A moment later, an expanse of water opened up between the dense foliage. Aalok stood up at the back of the boat and began punting them along a shaded canal. Trees all but covered the waterway.

Jayanti had forgotten the sense of serenity that existed in the backwaters, and she allowed herself to soak it in. She saw a flash of vibrant blue as a kingfisher darted past them. On the shore, a heron stood silent and still—searching; embodying the very essence of the backwaters.

She could hear a distant *woop, woop, woop* sound.

"What's that?" asked Ravi, clutching the gunwales as he glanced around.

"It's a type of pheasant," she answered, surprising herself that she still remembered.

Modest fishermen's houses were occasionally seen on the shore. An old man stood in the shallows outside one of them washing a gossamer thin fishing net. Jayanti knew that he would use it later to catch tilapia, throwing it expertly from his narrow boat whilst standing up.

Aalok nodded to him as they glided past. No words seemed necessary.

"Is this a river or a canal?" asked Ravi.

"Technically, it is a canal, but we often refer to it as a river."

Moments later, a large canoe heavily laden with sacks and bundles of produce passed silently by in the opposite direction, punted along by a young man standing at the stern.

The peace of the backwaters was palpable.

Jayanti wanted to cry. This was where her thoughts had strayed to on those lonely nights when she had been terrified by Delhi's noisy harshness.

She was home.

They moored at a wooden landing and walked fifty meters back among the trees where Jayanti's village stood on higher ground. By this time, Aalok's reserve had fallen away, and he hailed people in the village as he saw them. "Hi Taksheel, my sister Jayanti, has returned home. Now I'll have to tidy the house, eh."

Calls and waves followed them as they found their way to her parent's old home.

The house was exactly as she'd left it six years ago—but also different. Aalok had maintained it in good condition, but the heart of it was gone. Her parents were not there. There was no cooking fire and there were no smells. It had become a utilitarian bachelor's dormitory and little else. And, yes, the inside was untidy.

Aalok waggled his head and apologized for its state. "I eat next door with Uncle Sachin and Aunty Tulasi when I'm here." He waved his hand around. "But at least I have space for you both. You can sleep with me in my room, Ravi."

A crowd of villagers were at the door when they came out.

Jayanti hugged anyone she could reach and exclaimed over many of them. It didn't take long for the villagers to get over their reserve and begin peppering her with questions and fingering her sari. "Ravi," she called, "Come meet Sachin and Tulasi Asaan, my uncle and aunt."

She could see that Ravi was feeling overwhelmed. He was polite and good-natured, but there was a hint of desperation in his expression. It was understandable. Ravi had been thrust from a privileged but very solitary life into the noisy, dense relationships of a village where privacy was unknown.

It would be good for him.

Aalok looked at the scrum outside his door and said, "I'm off to give Pambadi Rajan a wash."

Ravi seized his opportunity. "Can I come with you...so I can meet Rajan?"

"Sure."

Moments later, he was sitting on the crossbar of an ancient pushbike as it squeaked its way down the path with Aalok peddling. Jayanti smiled. It was a far cry from the BMW sports car.

She realized that she too, would very much like to see Pambadi Rajan, so she yelled after them. "Wait. I'm coming too."

The bike wobbled to a stop, and the men waited for her to catch up. Aalok tried to fit two of them on the bike but was spectacularly unsuccessful—due largely to Jayanti's sari. In the end they leaned the bike against the tree and walked.

"Why is your elephant called Pambadi Rajan?" asked Ravi.

"Aalok ran his hands through the leaves of a tree beside the path. "Pambadi is a small town south of here. It was where he was born. And 'Rajan' means 'king'. He grinned. "Wait till you see him."

They cut off the main path to the kraal that was outside the next village on the canal. Jayanti could see the tall roofed enclosure, walled with the stout wooden bars that caged an elephant when it was being schooled.

There in the clearing beside it, was Pambadi Rajan.

Ravi stopped in his tracks, and his mouth dropped open.

"Come," urged Aalok. "He is quite safe."

The mighty elephant was sashaying back and forth swaying his head left and right, impatient to be free of the chain that held his front foot to a tree. His trunk curled around Aalok's shoulder.

Aalok patted it briefly before he bent down to unshackle the giant.

Ravi put a fist to his forehead in an expression of alarm.

"Relax. Aalok won't be trampled," assured Jayanti.

The great trunk came down on Aalok's shoulder again, frustrating his attempt to unshackle the chain. Aalok reached up to the huge belly above him and pinched it.

Ravi laughed. "Don't tell me the elephant can actually feel that pinch?"

"Oh, the elephant's skin is surprisingly sensitive." She smiled. "But no, the pinch doesn't trouble him. It is just to remind him of the *thotti* because he's being naughty."

"Thotti?"

"It's a short pole with a hook at its end, used to control elephants. Although he'll carry it, Aalok's boast is that he never needs it. He usually just uses a short cane to give a tap now and again. Aalok actually gives most of his instructions with his feet. He tucks them behind Rajan's ears when he sits astride him."

"Amazing."

Aalok called out. "Rajan is letting me know he is cross at having the chains. I usually just have a thin rope. But he's frisky at the moment because the elephant over the back is on heat."

"Can't he break the rope?" asked Ravi.

"Of course. Easily. But he has been so conditioned in the kraal, he doesn't—at least, not usually." Aalok slapped the giant's massive leg. "He'll only need the chain for another week."

Jayanti discovered that she was holding Ravi's arm, willing him to understand her world.

When the chain dropped away, the elephant lifted its right leg. Aalok stepped onto the raised foot, then onto the knee and slipped his leg around the neck of the elephant. "Follow me down to the river," he yelled.

Jayanti walked with Ravi behind the lumbering giant as it plodded down to the water. She squeezed Ravi's arm. "Rajan knows he's going for a wash when Aalok doesn't put the chains on him."

"Chains?"

"They're put on when he works. I think they're actually required by law. It stops them running." She pulled a face. "Aalok hates having to use them."

The elephant waded into the shallows, knelt down in the water and rolled onto its side with every appearance of contentment.

Aalok lifted a leg up to avoid it being crushed and slid off the elephant into the water. "Ravi, come," he shouted.

Jayanti folded her arms and watched from the bank as the two men splashed water over the elephant's flanks and rubbed him down with their hands.

She sighed. It was good to be back.

Over the next few days, the rhythm of the village embraced Jayanti with the gentleness of a mother. She allowed herself to relax into it. She and Ravi ate next door with Uncle Sachin and Aunty Asaan. Her aunt was bossy, opinionated, and everything an aunt should be. Uncle Sachin was quite often out on his fishing trap, so her aunty Asaan was grateful for their company. Their son worked in Cochin and came home only a few weekends each year.

Jayanti was, of course, co-opted into helping her aunt with the protracted task of cooking. Her aunt always over-catered and seemed to relish having more people to cook for. Fish formed the staple diet, plus anything else that was in season—*karela*, a knobbly skinned bitter gourd; *parwal* pods, with their pale flesh; and *tinda*, a small spherical squash. The bounty of a tropical climate was particularly evident in the village diet. Coconuts, jackfruit, pineapple, papaya, and bananas of every sort were available.

Life was less relaxed for Ravi. His hands became badly blistered in the first week, but he didn't complain. The only thing he did insist on was the purchase of two mosquito nets, insect repellent, and a first aid kit when they went back to Cochin on their first shopping trip.

Ravi's blisters had come about because he'd been helping the village's master boat-builder construct Uncle Sachin's new boat. It was being built on trestles that allowed the boat-builders to work all around the hull. Ravi's job was to bore holes on the edge of the linseed and jackfruit planks with an auger, so they could be stitched together with synthetic cord. He'd expressed amazement at the notion of actually sewing a boat together. The seams were made waterproof by stuffing strips of coconut fiber as caulking under the stitching. When hot pitch was poured over the joints from the outside, the boats became completely waterproof.

"Evidently the boats can last about twenty years if they're dried out and painted with linseed oil every year," Ravi said.

"Hmm," she said, pretending she didn't know.

He worked with a team of six men, all of whom worked at the leisurely pace of men who knew their business well. Ravi was particularly impressed with the skill of the master boat-builder who edged the planks. He did it by eye with a mallet and chisel.

"What amazes me, is that everyone is so content," he said, wincing as Jayanti dabbed alcohol onto his blisters.

As Jayanti packed away the first aid kit she decided to share a concern she'd heard about her uncle. "Ravi, I've been speaking with Aunty Asaan; she says he's getting too old to be spending the night on his fishing trap all alone."

Ravi said nothing and waited for her to elaborate.

"She wondered whether you would go with him. He goes out there twice a week, as you know."

Ravi nodded slowly. "It would mean having to learn a whole new set of skills—how to paddle and punt a boat…"

"…and how to find your way back into our canal at night after delivering the fish to the market." She smiled. "We'll make a waterman of you yet."

Chapter 16

Rahul turned the pistol over in his hand. He liked it. It was a G41 Glock adapted to take a suppressor. He screwed the silencer into place. Its dull metal added an extraordinary sense of menace.

Good. That's what he'd use it for. The skill would be to let the right people see enough of it at the right moment to take Rahul's interests seriously.

The trouble was, it was bulky. He'd not thought to search the wounded men in Cochin for the holster before he'd appropriated the gun. Still, that was a minor inconvenience.

Rahul had been practicing with the gun in the cellar of an illegal printer for two weeks and was now quite proficient at using it. Arjun had researched the weapon on a computer for him and taught him how to use and maintain it.

Luckily, the .45 ammunition had been easily sourced through his own contacts. He'd gone through hundreds of rounds. *Practice. It was all about practice.*

"Rahul," Durgamma called from kitchen. "Arjun is here for you."

He wrapped the gun up in a cloth and tucked it under his bed. "Tell him to come up."

A moment later Arjun ducked through the doorway of his bedroom and flopped down in a chair. Rahul lay on the bed with his hands behind his head.

Without a word, Arjun threw a wad of money on the bed.

"What's that from?" Rahul asked.

"It's not from any of our businesses. It's ticket money for you to buy a first class rail pass to Chandigarh." Arjun handed across a slip of paper. "It seems as if you have a fan. Someone wants to meet up with you to discuss a business proposition." He pointed to the wad of money. "That's a token of good faith. There's a phone number on the bottom."

Rahul read the note. It didn't tell him very much other than to allude to Rahul's growing interest in passports. The note talked of tripling his business. There was nothing in it that was incriminating but its message was clear. He flicked the paper. "Sounds interesting. Do you think we should follow it up?"

Arjun shrugged. "You're the boss. But I don't think there's any harm." He grinned, "Chandigarh has the richest per capita income in India. It's full of dodgy businessmen and politicians. Should be okay. Do you know what the first words are of a baby born there?"

Rahul was pretty sure he didn't want to know.

"Visa, visa, visa." Arjun laughed as he leaned back to pull out a packet of cigarettes.

⸻

Rahul didn't like the five-hour train trip to Chandigarh. He was disturbed by what he saw, and by what he was thinking.

It began as the train headed through the northern sectors of Delhi. Rahul was used to poverty, but he was unprepared to see the miles and miles of one of Delhi's major rubbish dumps that ran alongside the rail track. The rubbish was heaped as high as a three-story building. Smoke, or was it steam?, drifted over the tattered mounds where pigs, dogs, women, and children scavenged for hope.

Hovels made of sheets of plastic, scraps of wood, and pieces of beaten tin stood beside the railway line. He watched a naked child spit out water and rub his eyes, as he was washed by a woman—presumably his mother. She was pouring water from a metal pot, the sort carried by almost every Indian woman. He could see her bending over the boy, her back made strong by years of hard physical work.

He hated poverty. He feared it. Security, the sort that is guaranteed by wealth, was what he craved. And yet, even though he was now moderately well off, he hadn't found the happiness he hoped for. Worse, he wasn't enjoying the sort of person he was becoming.

Rahul kicked at the seat in front of him. It was weird. The crazy nuns actually chose poverty; they vowed to embrace it. He shook his head. And they never seemed to be without anything they needed and, dammit, they were the most contented and fulfilled people he knew.

He thought of Jayanti. He often did. The nuns had cast their spell over her too. She also had their inner...what was it? Serenity, he decided. He smiled ruefully, not that she was without spirit and resolve. He'd bumped up against that often enough.

She was intoxicating, and he seemed to be a better person when she was around.

Jayanti hadn't been around for a while, and he definitely didn't feel like a better person. Right now, he didn't know what he felt. He kicked again at the seat. He didn't know who he was.

As the train headed north, the massive curtain of the Himalayas started to appear in the distance. The mountains were majestic. There was no subtlety about them. They erupted out of the northern plains without any introductory foothills.

Outside the window, he could see women taking lumps of cow dung and mixing it with hay. Others were patting them flat and laying the dung patties, *upla*, out to dry. He shook his head. *They were placing a value on cow dung!*

He shivered and vowed that he would never be brought that low. He watched the women arranging the cow dung patties, herringbone fashion, in stacks that they protected with dung walls and straw roofs. He shook his head. They even decorated the walls with patterns!

His thoughts turned again to Jayanti. She was so far away—with Ravi. He gritted his teeth and nursed a dark mood all the way to Chandigarh.

Two grim looking men in jackets met him at the station. They were holding a board with his name written on it. Rahul didn't trust people with jackets. You could hide too many things behind them.

They escorted Rahul to an expensive car and drove him out of the city into the country.

Nothing was said.

Fifteen minutes later, they drove off the highway, down a dirt track to a mean little village. Everything looked poor.

The car came to a halt outside a Hindu temple. As it did, the man sitting beside the driver turned around to Rahul. He held a pistol. "Get out and put your hands against the car."

Rahul did so. He'd expected it.

He was frisked, and his knife was confiscated.

The man with the gun nodded toward the temple.

Rahul walked toward it.

The temple had a porch with a thatched roof. This led into a more substantial room with plastered walls. The image of the god Shiva, stood in the middle of it. The god was dressed, as usual, in a crimson dress, edged with gold, and was bedecked with garlands and necklaces. His three-pronged iron trident stood in front of him. Shiva, the destroyer. Rahul shivered. Behind the god were two small altars in front of a back room made of brick and plaster. Its walls were covered with framed pictures of Hindu deities. In the middle of this room was a large gold statue of a snake—a cobra, with its neck flared ready to strike.

Two men were lying on mats under the porch. They stared at him with hostile eyes.

Rahul caught the whiff of cigar smoke.

A small man in a gray suit, with immaculate silver hair, stepped out from the entrance into the room with the cobra. He had the smooth skin and features that spoke of both Indian and Arab ancestry.

The man drew on his cigar and then pointed to the men lying on the mats. He said in a soft voice, "They are paralyzed with fear because they believe someone has cursed them with the evil eye." He laughed. "They're waiting for the local witch doctor to come and release them." He gestured with his hand. "He can't come until tomorrow because he also works as the local tinker. Don't you love it —the confusion between religion and superstition?"

Rahul said nothing.

"Fear: it is a great motivator, isn't it?" He looked at Rahul. "You'd know something about that, wouldn't you?"

Rahul nodded slowly.

The man sighed. "I love this place. My grandmother came from this village. She was quite a beauty, by all accounts. She was sold as a sex slave to my grandfather and taken to Iran."

Silence.

Rahul cleared his throat. "Is she still alive and well?" It was good to show respect.

"Lord no. She was used up and exhausted by the time she was in her thirties—died at thirty-five."

Rahul was momentarily distracted by the sight of a small girl creeping into the temple. When he faced her, she clasped the end of the wall and looked at him with wild, deranged eyes. She was dirty, unnaturally so, from head to toe. Mud covered her skin, and her hair had been molded into beaded clumps of cow dung that rattled when she walked. Rahul judged her to be about four years of age.

The man nodded toward her. "She's been dedicated to the gods."

Bile began to rise in Rahul's throat. The man had chosen their meeting place well. It was intimidating and reeked of fear and evil.

He took a deep breath and decided to get down to business. "You have a proposition for me?"

"Yes: and it has nothing to do with passports." The man smiled a smile that failed to touch his eyes. "I want to employ you to kidnap Ravi Panwar for me."

Rahul tried not to react with shock.

The man continued. "You have frustrated my last two attempts to capture him, so I thought, why not employ you to do what my men could not." He smiled again. "Mr. Walker sends his regards, by the way. His nose is healing well. He'd like to meet you again."

Rahul shrugged. "It's a dangerous world. But what makes you think I can find Ravi Panwar? I don't know where he is."

"Oh, I think that a resourceful man like you wouldn't have too much trouble finding him. You are closer to his contacts than I am."

"And why would I be interested in getting him for you?"

The man drew on his cigar and watched the smoke curl up toward the ceiling. "If it enables me to get what I want from his father, you can expect to make one million American dollars."

"His father must have something very valuable."

"Oh he has. But I am more interested in what I will be able to do with what he has—what it will enable me to buy."

"And what is that?"

The man waved his cigar in a circle. "There is a pleasing amount of violence in the Middle East at the moment."

Rahul nodded. "You're an arms dealer."

"Perhaps. I have many interests."

"Any in the jewel trade?"

The man's eyes hardened. Then he shrugged. "I have offices in Amsterdam."

Silence.

"This is something I'll have to think about." Rahul watched warily as the man put his hand inside his jacket. He withdrew a wad of money and threw it to Rahul.

"That's to help your thinking. You have a week."

"What do I call you?"

The man laughed. "Well let's see." He looked around him. "Why not call me Mr. Nāgá."

Nāgá; the cobra.

"And I can reach you on this number you gave me?"

"You will be able to reach someone who is able to reach me."

Rahul nodded.

The irony of the situation was not lost on Rahul. He was being given an opportunity to rid himself of his rival for Jayanti's affections and set himself up financially for life. In so many ways, it was perfect.

But it was also unsettling.

Chapter 17

"A storm's coming." Jayanti looked at the dark clouds beginning to boil on the horizon to the southeast.

"Better get home quick then," said Ravi as he pushed the canoe off the pontoon. He scrambled into the boat and picked up the paddle.

Home. He'd said it so naturally. She allowed the pleasure of hearing it wash over her. Ravi had called their village house, home. It was silly to attach too much significance to it of course, but she couldn't help but be thrilled at hearing it.

Seeing him emerge like a butterfly from his socially isolated ways and engage in the life of the village delighted her. In the few weeks he'd been living in the village, he'd gained the reputation of being the one to go to for medical help. The fact that he had a well-stocked first-aid kit probably helped. But people also seemed to genuinely appreciate his care. She smiled. He would make a fine doctor.

Ravi paddled the boat away from the mud and detritus of the shore. How good it would be to be able to say that she had a doctor as a friend. Fancy knowing a doctor! They were esteemed like gods in India.

She sighed. First, however, he had to be accepted and get through his training.

The thought of that caused her to reflect on her own future. Once Ravi decided to call in the police to sort out the current threat to him and his father, she would have to decide what to do herself. She shook her head to rid it of such mournful thoughts and busied herself picking up some of the vegetables she'd bought at Cochin's markets that had fallen out of the bag.

Ravi was paddling well. He was a natural athlete and had learned the basics easily. He'd been paddling out to the fishing trap with her uncle for the last two weeks.

A puff of wind ruffled her hair, and the temperature dropped a few degrees. She looked up at the glowering clouds. The late afternoon sun highlighted their leading edge, accentuating the menace that hung in the sky to the east. Jayanti pulled her shawl around her.

Ravi was naked to the waist. The muscles on his chest looked good. Four weeks of hard physical work showed well on him.

"I think we're going to get wet," he said. "We should have left earlier."

No we shouldn't. I love every minute I spend alone with you. "Yes," she said.

Jayanti had turned eighteen two weeks ago but had told no one. She pondered it. Technically, she was an adult.

Did she feel like one?

She looked at Ravi and felt again the familiar stirring of blood.

Yes, she decided; very much.

Then she wondered what she would do with her life. She sighed. Perhaps she was not quite ready to be an adult yet.

Waves were now kicking up across the backwaters, and the wind was gusting with a fresh intensity.

They pushed on further until a shuddering blast of wind hit them, bringing with it a heavy shower of rain. Almost as it began, it ceased.

Ravi looked around him, his face grim. "I'm not sure I can paddle through this," he said. "The wind is against us, the light's almost gone, and it's going to pelt with rain soon."

"Do you want to paddle back to Cochin?"

"Your uncle's fishing trap is only a few hundred meters away. We can sit out the storm there."

Jayanti nodded.

Ten minutes later they had tied up to the rickety fishing trap. It was swaying in the wind, tugging and knocking against the canoe tethered against it.

Intense tropical rain had been falling for the last five minutes and Jayanti was totally saturated. She clambered up the few horizontal bamboo poles that laughingly passed as a ladder and hauled herself onto the platform beside the little round hut.

Ravi passed the two shopping bags up from the canoe. Fortunately, the bags were plastic.

They crawled into the hut and hauled the shopping bags in behind them.

The sky was now very dark. It was impossible to tell how much of the darkness was from the setting sun or the storm. A rumble of thunder could be heard as the wind rose in strength yet again so that it started to howl.

Ravi looked out of the back of the hut. "I think we're going to be here for a while."

Jayanti felt a frisson of alarm. "What? All night?"

Ravi nodded.

"But...but if we spend the night here, it could be..."

"Compromising?" he finished.

She nodded.

"Well," he said, reaching for the hurricane lamp. "I don't think we've got much choice."

"But people will think that I am...no longer..."

"A virgin." He grinned.

"Seriously. It's important," she said angrily, slapping his shoulder.

Ravi, lit the lamp and hung it up on a hook from the roof. "Well, in my book, you've already lost your virginity."

"What!" she exclaimed, barely believing what he'd said.

"Hmm," he said, swinging around on his haunches.

"I'm a virgin," she said, affronted.

"No. I'm afraid I took that away."

"Don't be stupid. When?"

"In my bedroom in Delhi, six weeks ago."

"But we didn't…"

"Yes we did. It was the best sex I've ever had."

"But we didn't actually…"

He smiled. "Nonetheless, it was very good." He reached out and stroked her hair, squeezing the water out of it. "I will always remember it as my first time."

She closed her eyes and luxuriated in the feeling of his hands on her hair.

But then she remembered who she was…or wasn't, to be more accurate. A familiar mocking voice within her began to make itself heard. She twisted away from him.

"Don't," she said. "Don't you dare raise false hopes and fill a girl's head with silly notions…just so you can have your…way."

He furrowed his brow and shook his head. "No, no. That's not what's happening," he protested.

She held her arms up in front of her, clenching her fists. "Yes it is."

"No!" he shouted, leaning forward.

"It is." She pushed him away with her hand. "You're nothing but a…a James Steerforth."

"What!" He said bewildered; "as in David Copperfield?"

Jayanti nodded. She screwed her face up desperately trying to contain the tears that were welling up within her.

Don't cry. Don't cry. But it was a losing battle. She held a hand to her chest as she began to whimper.

Then the dam broke, and she began to weep. Deep, shuddering sobs wracked her body.

Ravi looked at her wide-eyed. Then he reached out and took her by the shoulders.

"No, no," she shouted, beating his chest with her fists, fighting him off. "No. It's impossible."

"Why?"

She cried out the anguish of her soul. "Aargh!" and hit him again on his chest. "We cannot marry—that's why. You will not, you must not, be allowed to. It can't work."

He kept hold of her and continued to ease her toward him.

Finally, she could bear it no longer and collapsed against him sobbing…defeated.

He lay back so that she rested on top of him, and began caressing the back of her head.

She could feel the warmth of him through her wet blouse.

Her body responded.

No, no, she must not. She pushed herself away from him.

He let go of her instantly, lifting up his hands to show acquiescence.

She looked at him, bewildered.

He wasn't pressuring her at all.

It was the last straw. "Ohhhh," she cried in anguish," and collapsed back onto his chest and wept. It was impossible.

Outside, the rain poured down with savage intensity and gusts of wind caused the fishing platform to rock and shudder. Thunder growled and lightning cracked around them.

Inside, in the yellow glow of the hurricane lamp, her damp sari pressed against him and steamed gently.

They did not have sex.

Her feelings about that were ambiguous.

The certainty of his love for her, however, was not. Whether anything could ever work out between them long term, given that she came from a very low caste, was too much of a problem for her to ponder at the present. She resolved to live only in the present, to luxuriate in Ravi's love and to fall asleep nurtured by the knowledge of it.

In the morning, Jayanti woke to find Ravi leaning up on one shoulder looking at her. She pushed her hair away from her face and returned his stare. Then, very slowly, she reached out, took him by the back of the neck, drew him close, and kissed him.

Every nerve ending within her fizzed with pleasure. It was intoxicating, heady, and bewildering.

The soft, yielding kiss soon gave way to a fiercer hunger.

Many minutes later, Jayanti, pulled herself way, laughing. "Thank you," she said as she fought to catch her breath.

He looked at her questioningly.

"For sex," she added.

"But we didn't…"

"But it was the best I've ever had."

He laughed and kissed her again.

They breakfasted on one of the papayas they'd brought with them. As they ate, Ravi delved into a shopping bag and produced a black plastic folder. He unzipped it and laid it out in front of him. "I've got some news for you."

Jayanti wiped some papaya juice from her chin. "What's that?"

"I went online in the Internet café when you were in the market."

"And?"

"I've got my HSC results."

She froze and searched his face for clues. "And?" she said eventually, holding her breath.

He grinned. "Eighty-seven percent."

She launched herself at him. "That's wonderful." She hugged him. "You'll be able to apply to the Christian Medical College in Vellore. Oh, that's wonderful, wonderful, wonderful."

He laughed and extricated himself from her embrace and held her by both hands. "And there's more."

"What?"

"You got eighty-eight percent."

Chapter 18

Jayanti swept the floor with a broom made from palm leaf fibers, flicking the dust out through the front door. She stood on the step and looked up into the night sky. The moon was full and ghostly shadows fell across the village roofs.

She sighed. Ravi had already left for a night's fishing with Uncle Sachin, and she hated not having him near her.

Their sleeping arrangements were complicated. When her brother Aalok was with them, they all slept in his house, with Ravi sleeping in Aalok's room. If Aalok was away, Jayanti slept next door in her auntie's house in the room set aside for their son. It was an arrangement that worked well and preserved decorum.

Jayanti and Ravi had told no one that they'd spent the night together on the fishing trap, electing to say instead that they'd slept under a shelter near the market for the night.

Uncle Sachin had been alarmed. "That's very dangerous," he'd said.

Jayanti had felt guilty.

Aunty Tulasi called out from next door. "Jayanti."

Jayanti leaned the brush against the wall, and walked across to her Auntie's house. When she arrived, she found her aunty under the front veranda, stirring a pot on the cooking fire. A delicious smell made Jayanti realize she was very hungry.

"Your brother's very late," her auntie said querulously. He's probably still with that wretched elephant of his. Will you go and get him, otherwise his dinner will be spoiled?"

"Yes, Auntie."

The truth was, she didn't feel at all comfortable walking to the next village at night. It was not something Indian girls did alone. But the kraal was only eight hundred meters away, and the moon was full.

She set off down the path.

The trees were dark and quiet. The frogs, however, were not. They were in full voice. Resonant 'boinks' and croaks filled the night air.

After a few minutes, she veered off from the main path to head toward the kraal. It wasn't long before its skeletal silhouette could be seen.

She could see no sign of Aalok or of any firelight. That didn't particularly alarm her. What alarmed her was seeing the massive bulk of Pambadi Rajan in the center of the compound. He was loose and standing by the well.

Whilst the river water was drinkable, it was slightly brackish and many villages elected to build a well to get water that was of better quality. None of the wells were very deep as the water table was high. This particular well had a wooden gantry above it from which buckets could be lowered into the water.

Jayanti hurried across to it.

Pambadi Rajan was tossing his head from side to side. There was nothing unusual about that; he did it habitually. What he did not do routinely was to flap his ears in the manner he was currently doing. It signaled agitation and distress.

"Whoa, Rajan," she said slowing down her walk. "Gently, gently."

Pambadi Rajan swung away from the well and took a few steps toward her.

Jayanti stood still. "What's the matter, Rajan?"

The elephant lifted its trunk and draped it on her shoulders for a second before turning and heading back to the well. She could see a broken rope on one of her front legs. Rajan was not meant to be free.

It was then that she heard Aalok's voice calling weakly. The sound was faint and echoed slightly.

With a shock, she realized it was coming from the well.

She rushed over to the stone parapet. It was impossible to see anything in the inky blackness. But she could hear.

"Jayanti, is that you?" Aalok's voice could be clearly heard. She could even hear him panting, as if he was catching his breath.

"Aalok. Are you all right?"

"No. I'm hurt."

"How bad?"

"Bashed up…and my right arm is dislocated."

"Wait. I'll go and get help."

"No!" Aalok yelled. "They'll catch you, too. Stay here."

Jayanti bent back over the parapet. "Who?" she said, gripping the stonework in alarm.

"Never mind. Just get me out of here."

Jayanti looked around her. "How?" she cried desperately.

Rajan was pushing in beside her causing her to stumble sideways.

She gave him a slap and repeated her question. "How?"

"Get the rope that's hanging on the gate of the kraal."

"What?"

"Get the rope. It's hanging on the gate of the kraal."

"Oh."

She ran across the compound, unhitched it from the railings, and returned with it panting. It was heavy. "Now what?" she yelled.

"Throw an end over the gantry and drop it down to me."

She did as she was told.

As she did, she yelled. "Aalok, you do know that I'm not strong enough to pull you out of the well. Please let me go and get help."

"No!" he yelled in alarm. "Just do as I say."

"Okay, okay."

She listened to the sounds of groans, curses, and scuffles coming from below her.

"Right," He yelled. "Rajan will pull me out."

"But I don't know how to control him," screamed Jayanti on the edge of hysteria.

"Don't worry. I'll tell him what to do from down here. But I need you to manage him from up there as well."

The elephant buffeted her again as she stood beside the well. She gave a yelp of surprise.

"Quiet him down. You need to quiet him down. Just stroke the side of his trunk as I speak to him."

Jayanti reached up and rubbed her hand against the leathery skin. Rajan refused to be pacified and continued to sway from side to side. It was hard for her to keep contact with him. Aalok began to call out to Rajan using strange words she didn't understand. She remembered fleetingly that her brother had told her about such words when she was little, saying they were magical words handed down by the gods.

Whatever they were, they seemed to work. The giant stopped swaying.

"Jayanti, tap Rajan's trunk and offer him the rope."

She did so.

At a command from Aalok, Rajan's writhing trunk took hold of the rope.

"He's got it," she yelled.

"Now Jayanti, this is important. Stand in front of his chest, just to one side, by his right leg. When I give the command. Slap it and give him a push. Keep doing it. Badger him. Don't stop 'till I tell you. Be firm."

Aalok called out more words Jayanti didn't understand.

Rajan's massive bulk soared above her. She swallowed and gave his wrinkled chest a slap and a push. Jayanti felt as if she might as well be slapping the side of the Himalayas.

Its effect on Rajan was instantaneous. He edged back and took up the slack. As the rope hardened, Aalok gave a scream of pain.

Rajan stopped immediately.

A few seconds later, Aalok called out. She could hear the desperation in his voice. "Don't stop. Keep pushing him."

The giant continued to back away, and seconds later, Aalok's head appeared above the parapet. He continued to rise until he was suspended from the gantry, like a man hanging from the gallows.

"Stop," yelled Aalok.

Rajan stood still.

Jayanti ran to the well and pulled Aalok's legs toward the side.

Aalok barked another command, and Rajan stepped forward.

Jayanti toppled over as Aalok's body fell on her.

Unbidden, Rajan lumbered forward and blocked out the moonlight. The end of his massive trunk tapped over Aalok's body, as if doing an inventory.

Aalok winced as he rolled himself upright.

Jayanti fumbled at the knotted rope, clumsy in her desperation to free him.

Aalok patted the leathery trunk as it waved in front of him and winced when it dropped on his shoulder. "Aah. I think that arm is dislocated. Can you check it's not broken."

Jayanti was not at all sure of her competence to diagnose anything, but she felt along the bones of his shoulder and arm. "They all seem to be in place."

"Lift my arm out to the side."

"Are you sure?"

"Just do it."

"Now grab the arm as if you were holding a battering ram, and give it a sharp push."

"Really? Do you know what you're doing?"

"Push," he commanded as he braced himself against the side of the well.

She did—and she heard a click.

Aalok screamed and fell backward.

Rajan lumbered forward and again began feeling over him with his trunk.

Aalok grabbed the trunk with his left arm and used it to pull himself upright. He sat there panting. "Gee, I'm glad to see you."

Jayanti wasn't sure if he was speaking to her or the elephant. "How long have you been down there?"

"Not sure. About three hours, I guess."

It was now Jayanti's turn to inspect her brother. He was a mess. His clothes were torn and there were bloody welts across his face, torso and legs.

"How did this happen?" she cried, tentatively fingering the bloodied edges of a gash across his cheek.

"I got bashed up."

"What!" she cried in alarm. "By whom?"

"Two men who wanted to know where Ravi was."

Instant alarm stabbed at her heart. "They wanted Ravi?"

Aalok nodded. He reached out, took her by the wrist and looked at her, almost pleading, "I...I'm afraid...I told them." He dropped his head.

"Oh..." she cradled his head to her shoulder.

After a moment she said, "I'll go and get the first aid kit."

He grabbed her urgently. "No, don't do that. The men are in a car—some sort of jeep. They'll be waiting near the landing for Ravi to get back from the fish markets in the early morning. That's when they'll take him. He glanced up at her. "You didn't see them when you came here, I suppose?"

Jayanti shook her head.

Neither of them said anything for a while.

All around them, the frogs kept up their incessant chorus.

"What do we do now?" asked Jayanti.

Aalok rolled over onto his hands and got to his feet gingerly. He swayed slightly and steadied himself by leaning against the side of the well. After catching his breath. He said, "I'll finish it; that's what." He looked up at her. "You stay here."

"No!" she protested. "Don't do anything stupid."

Aalok called to Rajan, then turned around to her. "It's not stupid."

Rajan swayed over to Aalok and lifted his right foot.

Aalok climbed up onto it and swung himself astride Rajan's neck. "Stay here," he said to Jayanti.

145

She watched as the giant lumbered away with her brother down the track.

She did not stay. She followed.

Once the track had joined the main path, Jayanti could barely hear Rajan. It was extraordinary. There was no sound of breaking foliage, just a gentle clumping as he plodded along. It was barely audible over the sound of the frogs and cicadas.

Rajan appeared to move slowly, but it was deceptive. Jayanti needed to walk at a fair pace to keep up.

The black fingers of the trees above her looked menacing. It was as if they were trying to block out the moonlight—to keep the deeds they were doing secret.

She noticed a tire track in the dust of the path and wondered why she hadn't noticed it earlier when she'd come to look for Aalok. Jayanti shook her head. It seemed like a decade ago—when life was simple and they lived in peace.

They were not far from her village now. Up ahead, Rajan came to a halt. She could see his ears flapping in the slanting moonlight.

She edged forward and looked toward the river for any sign of a vehicle.

Rajan tossed his head sideways. She guessed that he had probably heard her creeping up behind him.

She stood still and watched.

Over to the right, by the river, a match flared as someone lit a cigarette. There, thirty yards upstream of the wooden landing, a vehicle was tucked in among the trees on the canal bank.

Jayanti knew with a dreadful certainty what was about to happen. She wanted to scream, to stop it, to warn, and protect.

But the vehicle was only fifteen yards off the track.

Rajan turned.

Jayanti could see Aalok nudge Rajan's cheeks with his feet. The elephant pushed through the foliage.

The men in the jeep would have had their night vision destroyed by the match. They would not see the danger bearing down on them.

Jayanti ran forward and dashed among the trees to try and reach the jeep. She gave no thought as to what she would do when she reached them; she only had a firm conviction of what would happen if she did not.

Aargh. She tripped over a tree root and sprawled headlong into the undergrowth. As she scrambled to her feet, she watched with dreadful fascination as the giant leaned its forehead against the side of the vehicle. Rajan's rear quarters dropped down and then his back legs heaved forward.

The jeep tipped up on two wheels, teetered for a moment, and tumbled over into the canal.

Rajan tossed his trunk, and stepped back from the riverbank.

Aalok steadied the elephant and stared at the water.

Jayanti came up behind them both.

The big elephant flapped his ears and turned its head.

"It's me, Rajan. Steady."

The giant swung back.

Jayanti pushed to the front and instinctively held onto Rajan's trunk, patting it as she searched the water for life. The vehicle was upside down. Only the four wheels and a part of the under-chassis were visible.

Rajan stamped on the ground, but it was his last act of aggression. Jayanti could feel the adrenaline seep away in the big giant as the frogs began to resume their chorus.

"I don't see anyone," she said.

"No."

Silence.

"What will you do now?"

"Go back, get a chain, and pull them out."

"Really!"

"They obviously came to grief driving carelessly on an unfamiliar track at night. It would be my duty to get Rajan and help them."

"And the elephant tracks would be explained," she finished.

Aalok didn't answer. He swung Rajan around and pushed through the undergrowth to the track.

———

Ravi cut off another strip of adhesive bandage and stuck it over the stitching on Aalok's back. "You did a good job sewing that up," he said quietly.

Jayanti had done the stitching after swabbing the wound with alcohol. Ravi pointed out to her that she was more proficient with a needle than him, and so she should do the sewing.

She protested, but eventually allowed herself to be persuaded.

After an initial bout of squeamishness, she'd found the task absorbing.

Aalok forced them both to attend him as he manifestly refused to go to a doctor. "I don't want any record of me visiting a doctor," he'd insisted.

"Well, you'd better keep out of sight. You're not exactly a pretty picture," said Jayanti.

Aalok wasn't. He had two lines of butterfly Steri-Strips across his face pinning the edges of two gashes together. Jayanti had refused to stitch them reasoning that the Steri-Strips would do a better job at not leaving scars from badly healed wounds on his face. There would be some scarring, but Jayanti hoped it would be minimal. "You're not married yet," she chided. "So you can't look too ugly."

Ravi handed Aalok a tube of antiseptic cream and a roll of adhesive bandage. "Keep the wounds clean. Change the top bandage every two days and dab the antiseptic gently over the stitching. It's only sewing cotton that's been soaked in alcohol, so it needs to be kept sterilized."

"How long do the stitches have to remain in place?"

"Two weeks," said Jayanti.

Ravi looked at her and raised an eyebrow.

She shrugged. "I paid attention when I was with the Missionaries of Charity."

He nodded and turned back to Aalok. "When are the police coming?"

Aalok shrugged. "Not sure. I doubt they'll be here for another hour or so."

"And the two men…"

Aalok raised his hands. "Didn't have a close look—and I don't want to."

"Shouldn't we…get them out?" asked Jayanti, biting her lip.

Aalok glanced at her. "Rajan has turned the vehicle onto its wheels, but I don't want to do anything more. Best leave it to the police."

Jayanti shook her head. It was surreal. Attempted kidnapping, murder; and all in her own village. She shuddered and looked up at Ravi who was standing by the door. He was staring out into the village as it began waking up to the morning sun.

Ravi turned back and saw her looking at him. He reached out a hand and touched hers as she lifted it toward him. "Jayanti," he said. "Somebody obviously knows we're here." He squatted down. "I think we have to leave as soon as we can and get lost to everyone in the world until we can think this through."

Jayanti nodded. "But where? We don't know anyone outside of Delhi and Cochin."

"That might be a good thing. It'll mean we can't be traced." He put a hand on her shoulder. "But what I am sure of is that we need to leave—now if possible." He turned around to Aalok. "Is there a boat or a vehicle going anywhere this morning?"

Aalok stretched his back tentatively and winced. "Um…" he paused. "Well, yes, actually. One of the paappaans who helps me with Rajan is setting off this morning to get his own elephant. He's been waiting for ages and is very excited about it."

"Where's he going?"

"To Munnar: to one of the tea plantations. A wildlife warden has found a young wounded elephant who's old enough to leave its mother."

Jayanti furrowed her brow. "Munnar! Where's Munnar?"

"It's a town up in the mountains—four hours drive from here.

It's where the tea plantations are." Aalok stood up and smiled "It's a good place, very mild climate—and there are lots of wild elephants there."

"But what shall we do when we get there?" protested Jayanti.

Ravi rubbed his forehead. "I've absolutely no idea."

Chapter 19

Jayanti scolded herself for being childish. She was timing the number of seconds between beeps of the horn. The maximum was twenty-two seconds. Their driver was impatient to get to his elephant.

As the jeep climbed up into the high country along a twisting road, she became too interested in the view outside to continue her game. They'd been driving for almost four hours, and the views outside were spectacular. Massive slabs of granite soared into the sky from the green mosaic of the tea plantations covering the hills. Lines of trees had been planted among the tea bushes, presumably to help break up the wind.

Deliciously, the temperature outside was cool—a consequence of being at an elevation of over four thousand feet.

Jayanti was sitting in the back seat watching a waterfall cascading down the rocks beside the road when the crash happened.

There was a skid and a sickening crunch. She spun around in time to see a motorbike bounce off the front of the car ahead of them, flinging its driver so that he skidded across the road on his face.

Jayanti screamed as their jeep swerved and braked violently to avoid the car in front.

The motorbike was not the usual lightweight bike, but a heavy, diesel powered Enfield, an old-fashioned looking bike considered a status symbol by India's young men. It was big enough to cause so much damage to the car in front, that the car's driver was not able to accelerate off, and escape the crash site.

Almost immediately, people from the nearby village started gathering at the scene. Jayanti had seen too many accidents in India to be under any illusions as to what would happen next. If the car looked to be driven by someone who was well off, they would be dragged from the car, beaten by the crowd and hauled to the police where they would be made to pay—regardless of who was at fault.

The motorbike rider was soon surrounded by the curious, the calculating and the concerned. They were waiting for someone to lead them into a general consensus as to who was to blame: whom they should direct their anger toward.

Ravi was fingering his head. It was evident that he'd hit it on the dashboard. Jayanti could see blood on his hands. But before she could voice her concern, he'd opened the door and was pushing through the crowd standing over the body of the motorcyclist.

Jayanti followed.

When Ravi turned the young man over, Jayanti gasped in shock. His lower jaw and mouth were a bloody mess. A gurgling noise told her that the man was drowning in his own blood.

She knelt down beside Ravi as he tried to clear the man's airways. He shook his head in frustration. "Jayanti, get me a knife."

Jayanti yelled the request for a knife at the crowd in Malayalam.

In short order, a kitchen knife was thrust into her hand. She handed it to Ravi.

The crowd pushed in closer to watch. Ravi yelled at them in Hindi to keep clear. They stepped back slightly, although Jayanti suspected that many of them didn't understand his words.

"Jayanti, grab the ballpoint from my pocket, take out the ink tube and give me the barrel as a hollow tube."

She reached around him, pulled the pen from his pocket and dissembled it.

As she handed it to Ravi, she gasped in horror. Ravi was pushing the knife into the man's throat.

Jayanti glanced at Ravi. He'd not taken leave of his senses. Ravi had a look of fierce determination and was being careful with his movements. "What are you…?"

"Give me the pen," barked Ravi.

She did so, dumbly.

Ravi inserted the pen into the hole he'd made and pushed it into the man's windpipe.

Almost immediately, there was a whistling sound as the man began breathing through the tube of the pen.

"I've got to stay with him to make sure it's not pushed in too far and not being pulled out," Ravi said. "And we need to get him to hospital—quickly."

Together, they hauled the wounded man into the back of the jeep.

"Where's the hospital?" Jayanti shouted at the crowd.

A man started to explain. He was not, however, good at making himself clear. In the end, Ravi pushed the man into the front seat of the jeep with Jayanti. Then he got into the back seat with the wounded man and shouted, "Go!"

They weaved their way past the crowd of people now hauling the unfortunate driver out of the crashed car, and continued up the winding road to Munnar.

"You saved his life," Dr. Nambeesan said as he finished putting a bandage over Ravi's eyebrow. The cut underneath it had required five stitches. "Where did you learn to do a tracheotomy?"

Jayanti thought she knew the answer. Ravi had bought a book on emergency first aid in Cochin and read it almost every night since. Sometimes, he'd asked Jayanti to allow him to practice the various techniques of tying bandages on her. She smiled. It hadn't been long before they were tying each other up, sometimes with rather more hilarity than educational merit. She looked at him as he sat on a chair in the surgery. It did him good to laugh. He didn't do it often.

"I've got a book on first aid. I'm familiarizing myself with it to help me get ready to apply to CMC in Vellore."

The doctor nodded. "CMC, eh. It's a good college. What did you get in your HSC results?"

"Eighty seven percent."

"You have proof of that?"

"Yes." Ravi pointed to his rucksack. "In there."

Jayanti, anxious to show Ravi off, unzipped the front of it, extracted the black folder and handed it to the doctor. She'd expected the doctor to wave it away, but he took the folder and leafed through its pages. A few seconds later, he looked up at her and asked, "You are Jayanti Panikkar, I presume? Your results are here too."

The question caught her off guard. "Y...yes," she stammered.

Doctor Nambeesan inclined his head. "Hmm."

Nothing was said for a few minutes.

Ravi broke the silence. "How is the man we brought in doing?"

"Well enough now. His face is still a mess. We're prepping him for an operation to reset his jaw at the moment." The doctor looked at his watch. "I'm doing it, so I haven't long before I need to get in there."

"Do we know who he is?" asked Jayanti.

The doctor nodded. "He's a deputy manager at one of the Kanan Devan Hills tea factories. He lives in one of the tea gardens at Chinnakanal, a small settlement about twenty kilometres east of here."

Ravi stood up to put on his jacket. "So this hospital treats patients from all the tea plantations?"

The doctor nodded. "Yes. Although Kanan Devan Hills Plantations have taken over most of Tata Tea in this area, Tata Tea has retained the hospital. We still care for most of the local tea plantation workers." The doctor felt in his pockets and pulled out a packet of cigarettes. "I have time for one cigarette before I go in to surgery."

Jayanti and Ravi accompanied the doctor along the terracotta tiles of the corridor to the hospital entrance. The building was a white-walled, single-storied building fringed with a veranda. The doctor leaned against one of the square pillars and lit a cigarette.

"Where are you going now?" he asked.

"No idea," said Ravi. "We don't know whether to stay or just pass through." He shrugged. "Ideally, we'd like to find a place to stay for a few months and maybe get a casual job."

The doctor glanced at Jayanti, looking her up and down, letting his gaze linger on her breasts. "Do you speak Malayalam and Tamil?" he asked her.

Jayanti nodded.

"I need a personal assistant for a few months to help us reorganize the hospital's records." He blew cigarette smoke in her direction. "I estimate that it's about a year's work."

Jayanti's skin prickled. "I'm afraid that Ravi and I are a package deal. I couldn't do anything that did not also include him."

"I could write you a good reference for CMC—if you worked well for me," he said as he examined the tip of his burning cigarette.

Jayanti was put momentarily off balance. "I'm not applying to CMC," she stammered.

"Really!"

Hard on the heels of her shock came stirrings of anger. She looked at the doctor. "And anyway, as I said, we want to stay together."

The doctor stared at her through the smoke.

Jayanti was as able to recognize the overtures of lechery as any girl. Drawing a deep breath, she decided to go on the offensive. "If, however, we were both employed, you'd manage to re-order your records in half the time."

"Hmm, perhaps," said the doctor with a shrug.

"But I'd also insist on one more thing."

The doctor raised his eyebrow. Jayanti gripped her hands in

front of her. "I'd like a good reference for Ravi, written for him…
before we start work."

The doctor guffawed. "Before! Isn't that a little unusual?"

Jayanti lifted her chin. "You know you will have a highly intelligent man—one who has just saved the life of a motorcyclist—and I
know he has an excellent work ethic. Also, having a reference
beforehand will ensure no…er, undue pressure is put on anyone."

"On you."

"Yes."

Doctor Nambeesan smiled. "You don't trust me very much, do
you?"

"I suspect that you are a very fine doctor and that women find
you attractive. This can lead to expectations. So you are right; I
don't trust you."

Ravi's mouth dropped open.

Nothing was said for a while.

After an eternity, the doctor nodded his head. "Very wise." He
flicked his cigarette butt away. "Tell you what, why don't you write
the reference for Mr. Panwar, and I'll sign it. After all, you know him
better than I do."

"Alright," she said immediately.

"Hang on," protested Ravi. "Shouldn't I have a bit of a say in
this?"

The doctor turned to him. "Not really. It would seem your
woman is fighting for you." He headed toward the door. "Come
with me to admin," he said over his shoulder.

A nurse knocked on the door of the doctor's office as Jayanti sat
down to the computer at his desk.

"Doctor," said the nurse, "We're running twenty minutes behind
schedule, so there's no need to rush."

"Thank you."

The nurse turned to Ravi. "Are you the man who saved the
motorcyclist who came in?" she asked.

"He is," replied the doctor for him.

"Then, can I ask you to come to the front desk? The man's wife is here, and she wants to thank you."

"Oh!" said Ravi rubbing his hair, "I suppose so." He followed the nurse out of the office.

Doctor Nambeesan lounged in an armchair and watched Jayanti. "Well, Jayanti, I wonder what you will write about your Mr. Panwar."

"I shall write the truth," she said, straightening her back.

"A truthful reference," he laughed. "Now that would be a first."

She began to type.

To whom it may concern:

"How long will we be working here?" she asked.

"Say three months and see how you go. If all goes well, there'll be an option for another three months."

She nodded.

I have known Ravi Panwar and worked closely with him for three months. In that time, he was employed by me to help in the essential task of re-ordering the hospital's records.

"Will Ravi be able to go with you on your rounds and perhaps observe some surgery."

"Would you like him to?"

"Yes."

"Then, I suppose so."

He did this partly so that he could experience life in a hospital.

Because he impressed me with his integrity, initiative, and intelligence, I allowed him to attend doctor's rounds and observe some surgical procedures. Where possible, he was allowed to help, under supervision, with simple medical tasks.

He performed these duties well.

On one occasion, his quick thinking saved the life of an accident victim.

He performed a tracheotomy with improvised tools, displaying remarkable self-control under pressure.

I can report that Mr. Panwar's attention to detail and work ethic are excellent and that he will prove to be a valuable asset to any team lucky enough to have his services.

As such, I have no hesitation in commending him to you.

"Done," she announced.

The doctor got up and read the text over her shoulder. He nodded. "That's very good. Perhaps I should ask you to write one for me."

"It wouldn't be the same."

"Write it anyway," he teased, resting a hand on her shoulder.

She began to type.

I have known Dr. Nambeesan for one hour. In that time he has not impressed me with his character. He assumes that his status as a doctor gives him the right to make sexual advances to women. As such, he is a predator.

Dr. Nambeesan has displayed no understanding of the correct way to handle power; nor does he appreciate that it is a sacred entrustment.

I suspect that inside, he feels empty and unfulfilled despite his commendable academic achievements in becoming a doctor.

This is, of course, regrettable as underneath, I suspect there is a good man —a wise man, perhaps even a noble man, waiting to be born.

But as it is, Dr. Nambeesan does not yet know who he is, or why he is. He does not know his calling to live life well. Tragically, he has allowed his baser instincts to kill off what is truly fulfilling. He has chosen to live life in the shallow end of the pond.

"Stop. Stop," laughed the doctor. "I surrender." He twisted the office chair around and waved Jayanti away. "Off. Off. Let me sit down. I think it only fair that I now write your reference."

The doctor took her place in front of the computer and drummed his fingers. Then he too began to type.

Jayanti read over his shoulder.

To whom it may concern:

Very rarely do I have the chance of being so confident and honest in writing a reference, even though I have known Jayanti Panikkar for only three months. In that time she has worked…

Jayanti slapped the desk. "If you say 'under me', I shall walk out of here."

The doctor waved her away.

…as my adviser and work colleague, particularly in the task of re-ordering the hospital's record system.

Miss Panikkar has three qualities that particularly stand out. The first is her fierce loyalty to those she holds dear. She is definitely a person you would want with you in a tight corner.

Secondly, she is intelligent and intuitive.

Thirdly, she is principled—a trait that is all too rare in today's world.

I can, of course, also commend her work ethic.

Jayanti will…

The doctor paused and tapped his lips with a finger.

…refresh and revitalize any workplace lucky enough to attract her services.

I can therefore highly commend her. I, for one, would welcome the chance to work with her again if the opportunity arose.

Jayanti swallowed, and wasn't sure what to say. Eventually, she found her voice. "Does this mean we've declared a truce?"

Dr. Nambeesan nodded.

A knock on the door announced Ravi's return. He came in looking slightly bewildered.

"Is everything okay?" asked Jayanti with concern.

"Hmm. I think so. Um, would you like to come to the front desk and meet Millie? She's the wife of JP, the fellow we brought in." He rubbed the back of his neck. "She's insisting that we stay with her whilst we are in Munnar—in gratitude for saving her husband.

"Oh." Jayanti turned to Dr. Nambeesan. "Is there public transport from where, er Millie lives, into town?"

"From Chinnakanal—easy: there are buses—and you'll probably find a plantation jeep coming into town, almost every morning."

She turned back to Ravi. He shrugged as if to say, I don't know. What do you think?

Jayanti closed her eyes and consulted her instincts. At first, there was nothing. She waited—and finally she caught it, a delicate whiff of peace, a sense of being given a gift.

Jayanti opened her eyes. "Fine," she said.

Chapter 20

Jayanti looked at Millie's tear-stained face and tight, drawn expression. She was trying to keep her composure, but it was a struggle. Jayanti reached out and took her hand. The simple action was enough to break down all reserve. Millie began to weep. She momentarily fluttered her hands in front of her seeking comfort, but unsure of propriety. Jayanti stepped forward and enfolded her in her arms.

Millie held onto the front of Jayanti's sari, her fists in front of her, and howled.

Jayanti tucked her under her chin and caressed her shoulder. "Millie," she said. "It's been horrible, totally horrible for you. I'm so sorry." She used the language of a close friend, not someone who had only been introduced two minutes earlier.

Millie seemed to be beyond caring. Her tiny, pert body, dressed in casual western clothes, was pressed against her.

Minutes later, the crying subsided. "Oh, I'm being stupid," she said as she disengaged and reached for a handkerchief.

Ravi quickly offered his own.

She took it and blew on it without much delicacy. Millie scrunched the handkerchief up in her fist. "That bloody, bloody motorbike. He loved the wretched thing." She dabbed her eyes and glanced at Ravi. "And you found J.P..." Her breath caught, but she continued, "...and saved him."

"Yes."

Millie sniffed. "Well, I'm grateful." Another sniff. "You must come and stay with me. I'll be on my own..." and she started to weep again.

Dr. Nambeesan interrupted. "I'm going into surgery now. Look, it's pointless you staying here. Why don't you go home? I'll let you know when he's out of surgery. It'll be quite a while."

Millie nodded, accepted Jayanti's hand and walked outside with her to the parking lot.

Ravi followed, carrying the two rucksacks. When Millie indicated a blue saloon, Ravi held out his hands for the keys.

She handed them over, dumbly.

Soon Ravi nosed the car through the busy town, passing lines of gray Mahindra jeeps that seemed to be the favored form of local taxi. Millie sat beside him, giving directions.

"Take the Madurai road."

Towering granite peaks pushed up from steep hillsides covered in tea bushes. It was spectacular scenery. Jayanti could see women picking the tips of the shoots of the bushes and tossing them into a woven basket they carried on their backs. From what she could observe the basket was supported by a strap worn as a headband. The baskets were big, and she wondered how heavy they were. The workers looked happy enough, and Jayanti caught herself envying their slow pace of life and structured order. She sighed. Her own life was very different.

Ravi drove down the twisting road for fifteen minutes.

"This is our tea garden," said Millie pointing to tea bushes sweeping up the sides of the hills. "Turn left onto Suryanelli road."

A small village was tucked down the gorge to the right. Long white buildings with rusted tin roofs nestled between huge, rounded rocks. Some boulders were as tall as multi-story buildings.

"This is Chinnakanal. Some of our workers live in those houses.

Each building is divided up so they can house six to eight families."
It was evident that Millie needed to talk.

"That's our house up the hillside among the tea bushes to the left."

The house was a well-built colonial bungalow. It seemed to sit gently amid the plantations like an aged local, waiting to tell stories of the past.

Two servants came to meet them. Millie told them the news, and soon Ravi and Jayanti were being ushered to their rooms.

"You're not sleeping together?" Millie asked.

"Sadly, no," said Ravi. "Jayanti is instilling in me notions of propriety and principle."

Millie put a hand on her hip. "How odd. Oh well. Never mind. Dinner is at 7:30. Drinks on the veranda in half an hour. Please excuse me: I need to make some phone calls."

Seeing Millie in her own home helped Jayanti understand her more. Even through her shock and grief, it was evident that Millie had a natural self-confidence. She dealt easily with people. She was small in stature and very pretty. Her petite frame was squeezed into jeans. A belted blouse highlighted her thin waist and generous bosom.

It was bewildering for Jayanti to have a servant hover around her offering to help. Being a servant was her role. She felt awkward and undeserving—a fraud.

After she'd unpacked, she made her way to the veranda. A jug of iced lemon tea sat on a cane table with some glasses.

As she sat down, she couldn't help overhear Millie through the plantation shutters behind her. She was talking into her phone.

"JP is having surgery to stabilize the damage and have a proper tracheotomy inserted. The doctor says he'll probably have to be driven down to Cochin for more reconstructive surgery and ortho-dontic work...No idea. We'll have to plan for six months, I think... No, I can look after him here. This place is ideal for rehabilitation... Yes I can...No, I don't need any help. And anyway, I'm not on my own. I've got friends staying...No: absolutely not! I can oversee the accounts and do the rosters. No!"

There was a sigh of exasperation.

"No, no, no! Who knows more about managing J.P's responsibilities than me? Aargh!…Well, let me do it for a month, and then you can review my performance…Right…good…okay…I'll ring you when I know something."

Millie came out onto the veranda, threw her phone on the table, and flopped into a chair.

Jayanti felt she should make it clear she'd overheard. "Did you win?"

Millie wrinkled her nose. "I know as much about running the tea garden as anyone." She sighed. "But because I'm a woman…"

Jayanti nodded. "But you managed to persuade your boss?"

"Yes. But only because he's my father." She slopped some iced tea into a glass. "My family's been in tea for generations. I was brought up with it."

Jayanti said hesitantly, "Um, won't Ravi and I staying here be a complication you could do without? You'll be nursing your husband as well as administering a tea garden. That's a lot."

Millie waved a hand dismissively. "You're nice. Ravi is a hero, and I will go mad without company. So let's agree to do each other a favor." She sipped her tea. "Ravi's told me that he's hoping to apply to the Christian Medical College in Vellore."

"Yes, he is."

"What about you?"

Jayanti experienced a stab of anxiety. "Um, I've no idea. Nothing's organized yet."

Millie looked at her quizzically. "I hope you don't mind me asking, but what exactly is your relationship with Ravi—just so I know where I stand."

"Oh, of course." *What on earth was it?* They had kissed passionately as lovers and allowed the sexual desires they had for each other to be seen. Marriage, of course, was out of the question—but life without him was unthinkable. She sighed. "We, er, studied together…and we're very fond of each other. But nothing…permanent will be allowed."

"And nothing temporary is morally acceptable. You poor darling: you're trapped."

Jayanti bit her lip and nodded.

"Well," said Millie brightening. "I'll just have to see if I can't help you break your resolve. How long can you stay?"

"I have no idea."

"I...I would probably appreciate having you around for a few months."

Jayanti smiled. "That's a long time...and very generous." She paused. "Why don't we aim for one month...and then do a review?"

Millie smiled. "One month, just like with Dad. These are going to be interesting days." She got up from her seat. "I've got some more work to do. Just make yourself at home."

Ravi passed her as he stepped through the archway onto the veranda. Millie stopped him. "You're staying a month, by the way; probably more." She raised herself on tiptoes, gave him a kiss on the cheek, and carried on into the house.

"Wow!" said Ravi as he took his seat beside Jayanti.

She smiled.

They sat in silence, enjoying the peace of the vista before them.

"It's been quite a day," he said, eventually.

"Yes."

"What on earth persuaded you to go for Dr. Nambeesan?" I was about to give him an ear-full when you blind-sided me completely. You were magnificent and outrageous. Don't you know that doctors are supposed to be revered like gods?"

"He crossed the line between god and demon—and I don't like demons."

"You seemed to have patched things up with him by the time we left."

"I gave him my boundaries. He'll flirt of course, but I'm not worried about any more serious sexual advances."

Ravi put his hand over hers. "I don't want you to have to put up with anything or anyone you are not comfortable with. So promise me you'll let me know the instant you feel uneasy."

She nodded.

"Do you think the doctor is married?" she asked.

"It would be unusual if he wasn't, but I didn't see a ring."

The sun continued to edge toward the horizon bathing the maze of tea bushes with a golden light.

"Oh, I forgot to give this to you." She handed Ravi an envelope. "It's a reference telling people how brilliantly you will work in the next three months."

Ravi smiled, but didn't open it. He tapped it up and down on his hand. "Jayanti, you do know that we must talk about...us, at some stage, don't you."

A frisson of fear washed through her. "Yes, but please, let's just enjoy this moment for now."

Elizabeth pressed the phone close to her ear as she listened to Jayanti.

"Ravi and I are both well, Elizabeth auntie, so do not worry."

"Where are you?"

There was a pause before Jayanti replied, "I must not tell you, auntie, it would betray a promise to Ravi. I'm not sure I am even meant to phone, but I knew you would be worrying."

"That's quite all right, dear." Elizabeth pinched the top of her nose and tried to understand the significance of what she'd just been told. There'd been another attempt to kidnap Ravi, this time from Jayanti's home village in the backwaters. Fortunately, those attempting the kidnapping had been tipped into the water—by an elephant, of all things! The police were now attending to the matter. Jayanti had been vague about the details.

The fact that someone was able to find the whereabouts of Ravi and Jayanti, despite the extraordinary lengths they'd gone to in order to ensure they remained hidden, was deeply disturbing. *How on earth...?*

Jayanti interrupted her thoughts. "I must go, auntie, and return Ravi's phone. But, please don't worry. We are safe and well. We've both got temporary jobs and are being cared for by a local family."

"I'm relieved to hear it, Jayanti; very relieved indeed. But before you go, I have some sad news for you."

"Oh?"

"I'm afraid that your old friend, Rohit died yesterday."

There was silence on the other end of the phone, followed by a sob. Elizabeth continued. "I'm so sorry, Jayanti. I know he was very special to you." She paused. "You should know that we spoke a number of times just before he died, and the subject we spoke about most was you. He valued your friendship dearly and treasured it."

Sniff. "Thanks for saying that, auntie." *Sniff.* "When is the funeral?"

"Tomorrow."

"Will you place a flower for me?"

"I will."

"Goodbye auntie. Give my love to Sister Rosalind. And please share our news with her."

"I will. God bless you, Jayanti."

Elizabeth needed peace and a place to think what her next move might be. She made her way to the chapel, sat down, and waited in God's presence for her thoughts to fall in place.

One of the things she didn't understand was the relationship, or lack of it, that existed between Ravi and his father. Whilst Ravi had rung his father to assure him he was well, she couldn't imagine many Indian fathers of eighteen-year-old sons being particularly sanguine about their boy going into hiding without knowing all the details. Theirs seemed to be an unusually distant relationship.

Indian fathers typically lived through their children—and for good reason. If a child gained good employment, a family thrived. If it did not, it could threaten a family's survival. India had no Western-style social security. Life here was a grim, competitive business. It was little wonder that Indian parents exercised a high level of control over their children. They had honor codes, and high expectations for their children's education and marriage. Pages and pages advertising the merits of daughters or sons as marriage partners existed in the matrimonial section of Indian newspapers.

Elizabeth had once asked Sister Rosalind how marriages could possibly work in India. She remembered her reply.

"Aah, my dear Elizabeth: in the west, you marry the person you love; here in India, we choose to love the person we marry."

Elizabeth had tried to pursue the subject but Sister Rosalind had declined to talk further about it.

From what she had observed, honor and status mattered to Gokul Panwar. He certainly surrounded himself with displays of wealth. So why was he so *laissez faire* with his son?

She sighed, straightened her back, and folded her hands in her lap.

The last of the evening light fell across the face of the cross above the altar. Elizabeth allowed the image to play on her heart and waited for that soft call, the tender idea that came from silence.

Half an hour later, the dinner bell rang.

Elizabeth caught up with Sister Rosalind afterward during the recreation time. They sat down in chairs on the veranda.

"Sister Rosalind," she said, "I have an idea."

Next afternoon, Elizabeth sat next to Sister Rosalind and hung on to the side rail as the auto stuttered and spluttered its way along Raisina Road. It turned and drove past the end of Rajpath, the 'King's way', the processional road that headed east to the India Gate. The gate, built in honor of the soldiers of the First World War, was India's equivalent to the *Arc de Triomphe*. At the moment, however, it was looking less than impressive in the hazy afternoon light.

Sister Rosalind seemed to share her thinking because she said, "The best time to see the India Gate is at night when it is floodlit. Have you seen it then?"

Elizabeth shook her head and returned her thoughts to the issue at hand.

"What on earth am I going to say?" she said.

Sister Rosalind patted her knee. "Simply say what you shared with me." She smiled. "And don't worry. God will not call you to say anything that he hasn't given you the ability to say."

Elizabeth didn't have much time to worry any more as the auto was soon pulling up in front of Gokul Panwar's house.

She stepped out of the auto but Sister Rosalind stayed where she was. "I think I will be of more use if I stay here and pray," she said. "It's enough for Mr. Panwar to know there is another sister at his gate waiting for you."

Elizabeth swallowed. "I...I'd much rather..."

Sister Rosalind smiled and waved a hand. "Go on, Elizabeth. I shall wait for you here."

Elizabeth swallowed her protest, walked over to the gate and pressed the button on intercom.

"Who is it, please?" came the deep voice of Aakar Singh.

"It is Sister Elizabeth from the Missionaries of Charity," she replied in Hindi.

There was a pause, before Aakar replied in English, "Miss Jayanti is not here."

Elizabeth leaned toward the intercom. "I know. I was hoping to speak to Mr. Panwar and give him some news about his son."

It was partly the truth, so she managed to wrestle a pang of guilt to a standstill.

"Please wait, memsab."

Minutes later, she was being escorted to the house by the giant Sikh. He was his usual stern and forbidding self, but as he held the door open for her, he said, "Tell to me please, is Master Ravi safe?"

Elizabeth glanced at him and could see authentic concern in his eyes.

"Yes, Aakar, both Ravi and Jayanti have told me they are safe, although they have not told me where they are."

The giant nodded.

Gokul Panwar did not get up from behind his desk when Elizabeth was led into his office. He made a show of tidying up some papers, tapping them together and putting them in a drawer.

The door behind her closed as Aakar left.

Elizabeth realized that Gokul was already seeking to stamp his control on the interview. She decided to wrest it back. "Is that the drawer with the photo of your great, great grandfather and Colonel Sladen?" she asked.

He froze momentarily before closing the drawer. "And what do you want?" he said, only just on the civilized side of rudeness.

"I've come to report a death."

Gokul jerked his head around. "Ravi?"

Elizabeth held up a hand. "Oh no. Rest easy. Ravi and Jayanti have rung me to report they are both well, but not where they are."

Gokul nodded. "So, the Kerala woman is still with him, then."

"Yes."

"Fool."

Elizabeth cleared her throat. "The death is that of a Jaipur gem cutter who worked for you fifteen years ago; the one who escaped before he too…er, was scheduled to go missing."

Gokul hunched his shoulders fractionally and glared at Elizabeth from under his eyebrows. "I don't know what you're talking about." He spat out the words, exaggerating the consonants.

"Oh, we've got his story, and some information on the other two gem cutters." Elizabeth smiled. "One of them even carved the gem-cutters mark on the wall of your cellar. I imagine the police will be very interested in the report that's been put together." She shrugged. "There are a number of copies of it."

Elizabeth could hear the ticking of the carriage clock on the mantelpiece.

Gokul leaned back in his chair crossed his legs and began tapping the end of a pen on the desk. *Tap tap.*

Elizabeth recognized it for what it was—a charade.

"As I said: What is it that you want?" he growled.

"It rather depends on how many jewels you have left."

Silence.

"They could be put to such good use…perhaps in propitiation for the evil that has been done," she continued.

"You play a dangerous game for a nun."

Elizabeth smiled. "Oh, I'm not in danger. I've a colleague in an auto at your gate waiting for me; and others know I'm here. No," she said, "It is not me who is in danger, it is Ravi."

Tap, tap. "How so?"

Elizabeth rubbed her forehead with a finger, allowing him to see her frustration. "You cannot be indifferent to the fact that people have tried to kidnap your son to force you to hand over what's left of the jewels to them."

"And…?"

"They will try again, or kidnap you until they get what they want."

"I have excellent security."

"But Ravi does not. He hopes to train at the Christian Medical College in Vellore. Elizabeth lent forward and placed a hand flat on the desk. "He cannot remain hidden or be protected there."

"He shouldn't go there, then. The boy is already independently wealthy from the shares and investments that have been bought for him."

"I think you'll find that Ravi wants to do something worthwhile with his life."

Gokul flicked a finger in irritation. "Tell him to come home. Aakar Singh will keep him safe enough."

"And live in fear because of his father's actions!"

Gokul swung back to the desk and gripped its edge with two hands. "Right, woman, he snarled. "Let's take off the gloves—on the understanding that I will deny saying anything to you." He threw himself back in the chair. "What have you got? What have you really got: the ravings of a dying man—with no independent verification? Pah! All you have is conjecture. If you inspect any strongroom of any bank in India, you'll find no jewels of mine. Your case is absurd."

Elizabeth began to panic. She was losing control.

She prayed.

The carriage clock ticked.

"The jewels are overseas." She'd meant to say it as a possibility, but it ended up sounding like a fact.

Elizabeth stood up and folded her hands in front of her. "I

should also point out that I'm presenting you with a chance to do the right thing."

"Let's get one thing straight: I own the jewels. They can't be returned. Who would get them? The British government who pillaged them? A king of a kingdom that no longer exists—who extorted them from local miners? Who should get them?" He waved his hand. "Legal ownership would be impossible to determine."

"I think you're right. But you've not been listening. I've not suggested that you find their original owners."

Gokul slapped the desk. "What, then?"

"That you give them to charity, with a generous amount going toward the families of the gem cutters you employed for three years."

"Hah! You mean that I should give my millions to the Missionaries of Charity." He leaned back and sneered. "It is pleasing to me to know that you are just as greedy and corrupt as anyone else."

"I've never suggested that. No, I'm sure you will find charities wanting to build hospitals and other facilities for the poor to which we have no affiliation. One of them might even offer you a sinecure and look after you for life, in gratitude for your donation." She shrugged. "Once those wishing to extort the jewels from you discover they have been given to charity, you and Ravi will no longer be in danger."

"Hah! You have no idea of the lifestyle I currently enjoy. A sinecure from a bunch of do-gooders simply will not do." He leaned forward and stabbed at an intercom button. "Aakar".

"Yes, sahib," came a tinny voice through the speaker.

"Come and conduct our visitor off the property."

"Yes, sahib, I shall come. One moment please, I am at the gate."

Elizabeth glanced out the window and saw Aakar Singh standing next to the auto talking with Sister Rosalind.

Gokul pointed to the door. "Wait in the entrance hall for Mr. Singh." He swiveled in his chair, presenting his back to her. "I don't want to see you again."

Chapter 21

"What the hell are you playing at?"

Rahul spun on his heel as he paced up and down the alleyway with the phone pressed to his ear.

There was silence on the other end of the phone.

"I've spent six days on bloody trains; three days making inquiries in Cochin's stinking fish markets—and when I discover where Ravi Panwar is, he's fled the village to God-knows-where because of the stupidity of your two goons."

Mr. Nāgá's silky voice purred in his ear. "May I remind you that two of my men have died."

"Why the hell didn't you tell me you'd also be attempting to get Ravi Panwar? Am I going to make a habit of running into your incompetence and lack of trust?"

There was a pause. "Be very careful what you say, Rahul."

"No, I'm not inclined to be careful with someone who has wasted a good deal of my time and money." Rahul massaged his forehead. "You've made a simple job a lot harder, and blown any deadline out of the water. Why didn't you warn me you had another team working on the same project?"

"It shouldn't surprise you. Every bull has two horns to fight with."

Rahul slapped a piece of corrugated iron covering a window that once looked out into the alleyway. "A cobra only needs to strike once if he does it right?"

Silence.

Rahul continued. "Am I employed to get Panwar or not?"

"Can you do it?"

"No, I can't promise—not now. But I have a better chance than anyone else because I'm in contact with people he knows."

"Do you have any idea where he might be?"

"None. All I know is that he hopes to be accepted to the medical college in Vellore. If, and I stress, 'if,' he gets accepted for a final exam and interview, he will have to be in Vellore in May. That's almost six months."

"I've waited a long time to launch this project; another six months is of no real significance."

"Vellore is at the other end of India. I'm going to need considerably more to cover my expenses."

"That can be arranged. How much do you need?"

When negotiations were completed Rahul felt the need to dissipate his anger. He strode out of the alleyway and along the main street to one of his favorite restaurants. The people there had become quite used to his patronage over the last year. It was the price of protection. Compared to what the restaurant used to be paying another gang, Rahul's rate—food whenever he needed it, was very generous indeed.

He always ate when he was agitated, and he was agitated now. In fact, he had felt agitated for the last month, so much so, that he was beginning to put on weight.

He stepped past a bullock that was having new shoes hammered onto its hooves. The cobbler had tied the animal's legs together and pushed it over onto its side in the dirt. The bullock's terrified eyes were rolled upward so that only the whites of its eyes could be seen.

Rahul never wanted to be constrained by anyone, and yet, there were constraints around his heart he didn't fully understand that were exerting altogether too much influence. The truth was, he admitted, he didn't like himself very much.

He caught sight of his reflection in a shop window and slowed down to inspect it. His excess weight was not showing very much, which pleased him. He could see that his skin color was lighter than that of most Indians in Delhi. That was good, too. Like many Indians, he was obsessed with skin color and believed light color indicated good breeding.

He snorted. Rahul had no idea about his breeding.

He touched his face. His high cheekbones probably indicated a Mughlai influence somewhere in his history. Rahul concluded, much as he'd done before, that he was a mixture of many cultures.

He ducked into the doorway of the restaurant and made his way to the table nearest the kitchen. It would provide an emergency exit if he needed it.

Rahul inspected the menu. He would eat a lot tonight. His heart, if not his stomach, required it.

He smiled ruefully at the menu. Like himself, the food had a Mughlai Persian influence. It included kebabs, korma, biryani, and naan bread.

Rahul ordered paratha, a multi-layered flatbread smeared with ghee and toasted on a griddle. It was stuffed with vegetables and served with a spicy pickle and curd. Next, he ordered mattar paneer, curd cheese in a pea sauce spiced with garam masala.

He knew he'd eaten too much, so he decided to compound the problem by ordering a mango kulfi. It was his favorite dessert—made by gradually reducing flavored milk, and freezing it slowly until it was smooth and free of ice crystals.

As he waited for it to come, he looked at a poster of the popular Hindu god, *Ganesh* on the wall beside him. He was depicted with his usual elephant head.

Rahul fingered the edge of the poster.

Hey Ganesh, you're meant to be pretty clever and able make people good. I could use your help right now because I don't much like myself at the moment.

An empty silence followed.

Rahul flicked the poster dismissively.

The kulfi arrived.

He didn't feel any better once he'd finished it.

He wished he'd ordered the pistachio, or maybe the saffron flavor instead.

Chapter 22

Jayanti and Ravi were usually able to get a lift into Munnar in one of the tea-factory's jeeps each morning. Millie had seen to it.

The hospital, on the edge of town, was in stark contrast to the bustling chaos of the town center. It exuded an aura of peace and order. Jayanti found herself looking for the red roofed hospital as it came into view. That was not to say that she found the first few weeks easy. They weren't. It took a while for her and Ravi to find their place in the hospital community, as both they and the hospital staff took time to work out their status. The work was mundane and they were paid very modestly, yet both Jayanti and Ravi attended the doctor on duty on his medical rounds. This made them oddities. It didn't help that Jayanti was almost the only staff person wearing a sari. The doctors wore lab coats and the nurses had white uniforms over which they wore blue jackets when it was cold.

The hospital had one hundred and fifty beds and was fairly busy. Jayanti learned that it particularly catered for the health needs of tea plantation workers and their families—about one hundred thousand people. As it was the only hospital in the area, locals also used it, particularly the intensive care unit and its pediatric facilities.

Jayanti enjoyed doing the rounds with the doctor. Initially, she went with Ravi on the rounds to escape the tedium of her work—and it was certainly tedious. It was little wonder that the monumental job of transferring records and data to the new computer system had been delayed for so long. It was a massive and intimidating task.

Jayanti sighed and began typing.

An hour later, she glanced at the clock. "It's time to go to the nurses station for ward rounds," she said to Ravi.

Ravi did an elaborate final tap on the keyboard then swiveled around in his chair. "You're keen," he said, standing up.

"Really?" She looked at Ravi and smiled inwardly. He'd hooked his thumb into the pocket of his trousers. It was a mannerism of the senior surgeon at the hospital. Ravi was both consciously and unconsciously absorbing the culture around him.

They went off to the nurse's station and waited for the doctor and the senior matron to arrive and begin the rounds. A few minutes later, they arrived and the group of them began to stroll from ward to ward; bed to bed.

Jayanti discovered she was learning a lot by tagging along. It was her habit to stand back from the knot of medical staff as they did the rounds. Sometimes, she would linger at the bedside of a patient to speak with them when she felt there was a need. She learned to read how patients were feeling by their body language, and sometimes questioned them about it. As a result, it was not uncommon for patients to talk to her with a degree of honesty they found difficult to adopt with the medical staff.

It wasn't long before the doctors noticed and began asking Jayanti how a patient was feeling when they were uncertain. The doctor on duty had just done so. "How is Mrs. Kaimal, really?" he'd asked her.

Jayanti swallowed. "Mrs. Kaimal has only said she's feeling better because she wants to get home to her youngest child. Her husband is at work and she's not sure the children are being adequately cared for by the neighbors."

"Thank you, Jayanti," said the doctor. "We'll send a welfare officer out to check on them."

They went on to stand beside the bed of a retired tea plantation manager. He'd been badly gored by a wounded bison—on a golf course, of all things, but he was now recovering well. The retired manager knew Millie and JP well. He winced as he pulled himself up on his pillows so he could speak with Jayanti. "Ah Millie; she's a firecracker, that one. She's got raw Kerala tea flowing through her veins. Give her my regards."

"I will."

"Has she taken you to J.P's factory yet."

"No."

"Ask her. It's interesting to see how the tea is rolled, fermented, and graded." He smiled. "You might even get a cup of their premium tea. It's pretty good."

"She's been very generous to us."

"That's Millie, positive and generous…although I've always felt there is some sadness in the background somewhere. She hides it well, but I've seen it."

Jayanti said nothing. She'd seen it too.

There was certainly a lot to occupy Millie's mind at the moment. JP had been driven down to Cochin for specialized facial and orthodontic surgery. He needed to be there for a month, so she made the gruelling journey down from the hills to see him each weekend, leaving Jayanti and Ravi to look after themselves.

Jayanti loved this time of being together. It gave her the illusion of being married. Her favorite time was in the evenings when she would sit with Ravi on the veranda, watching the sunset.

JP was eventually brought home. However, he still far from well. JP could only consume liquids, and was not yet able to leave the bedroom—except for short periods in order to exercise.

The tedious work at the hospital continued. After each working day, Jayanti and Ravi would catch the bus back to Chinnakanal and join Millie on the veranda. Quite often, Millie would talk about the tea industry.

"It's going to 'hell in a handcart' at the moment," she said.

"Why?" asked Ravi.

"We're finding it hard to compete with other world tea producers."

"But this whole region is given over to tea. It's been growing tea for ages," said Jayanti. "What's the problem?"

Millie shrugged. "We're expensive. The labor force has a history of being quite political, and so is well paid." She smiled. "You may have seen a bit of communist graffiti around the place."

Jayanti nodded.

"On top of that, we fall between two stools. We make good tea, but we can't quite match the quality of Darjeeling. These days the western market either wants 'rubbish' tea in tea bags, or they want top quality tea." She shrugged. "We hate making rubbish, and we can't quite make the world's best."

"Does this area have a future, then?" asked Ravi.

Millie smiled. "Oh yes. We're pretty resilient, but I think things will become fairly difficult. The one great thing going for us is that our mild climate means we can harvest all year."

"It's certainly beautiful," said Jayanti. "What are those trees growing among the tea bushes?"

"They're Australian eucalypts mostly, and silver oaks. The eucalypts are good for firewood. Not a lot of what you see is indigenous to this area, I'm afraid. Most of it has been imported as a result of our English colonial history."

"Are there still any tigers in the area?" asked Ravi.

"No, they had their habitat stripped away from them, and they've been hunted to extinction. We still have a lot of wild elephants, though. One killed a Welfare Officer last month when his motorbike stalled on the road."

"Good grief," said Ravi.

They watched a mother with a small child on her back walk from the bus stop up the hill through the tea bushes beside them.

Jayanti looked at Millie and saw a cloud of darkness momentarily eclipse her buoyant nature.

"Is there a village up the hill?" Jayanti asked.

Millie didn't reply. She seemed to be deep in thought.

Jayanti tried again.

"Sorry," said Millie. "What did you say?"

"Oh, I just wondered if there was a village up the hill somewhere?"

"Yes, just a small one. Technically, it is an illegal encroachment on our property, but we turn a blind eye to it." She sniffed. "Have you walked up the hill yet?"

"No," said Ravi. "What's up there?"

"Devikulam Lake, It's very beautiful. There's even a couple of old row boats up there if you feel like getting out on the water—and you can fish for trout if you want to. J.P's got a rod somewhere."

"That sounds fantastic. Anything else we should look out for?" asked Ravi.

Millie smiled. "Well, you can always look out for *neelakurinji*."

"What on earth is that?"

"It's a purplish-blue colored flower that grows in bunches on a bush. When the bushes flower, they do so simultaneously and in great profusion." She smiled. "I've only seen them once in my life. It only flowers once every twelve years."

"Once every twelve years!" exclaimed Ravi.

"Yes."

He shook his head. "That's a long wait."

Ravi and Jayanti walked up the steep path behind the house toward the top of the hill behind them. Jayanti noticed that Ravi was looking more than usually thoughtful.

She said nothing, confident that he would share what was troubling him when he was ready. He tended to do a lot of thinking before he spoke, and it wasn't always easy to wait. She was not finding it easy now as she had a suspicion of what was on his mind.

As if by common consent, they had both elected not to speak of the future after their dangerously physical time together on the fishing trap. It was as if it was too hard.

Indeed, thought Jayanti, it was. They couldn't marry: she knew that, and had made it clear to Ravi that she was not holding any expectations. And yet their time together was making it harder and harder for her, at least, to be physically restrained.

They turned left, away from a tiny village hanging precariously to the side of the hill, and continued up the hill through vegetation that was almost alpine. Suddenly, they came to a beautiful lake edged with grass.

A sagging boat shed stood by the shore with two wooden rowing boats inside. The scene looked peaceful and idyllic.

A puff of wind disturbed her thinking.

The two of them sat down on a weathered bench near the water's edge.

Ravi cleared his throat.

"Jayanti, what do you see happening between us? What do you hope might happen—given you said it can't be marriage?"

Oh no. Here it is, the conversation I've been dreading. "Can't we just see what happens?"

He looked at her with his dark eyes. She could see the longing of his love in them. Suddenly, she wanted to be wet again, and to be pressed against his body. The one thing she did not want to talk about was anything that might spoil what she was able to enjoy now. "Must we talk about it?"

He nodded. "Yes, we need to. We need to craft the future, if we don't want to be casualties of it."

Jayanti sighed.

He drew a deep breath. "The thing I want to ask is this: Are we a couple who want to be committed to each other for life?" He lifted his head. "Is that what you want?"

Yes, yes, yes...and I have wanted to be so for years. "I...I don't know." She sniffed. "I don't want to be your girl just because I happen to be traveling with you."

Ravi bit his lips. "You mean you don't want a James Steerforth."

"No," she said irritably. "It's just that you need to think what will happen when you get back to Delhi. Your father will require you to marry the woman he negotiates for."

Ravi said nothing for a long while. Eventually he said, "Things are not only complicated for me, they are complicated for you."

"In what way?"

"Well, someone of your quality should find a husband pretty soon."

"What!" exclaimed Jayanti. "How can you..." she was lost for words. She finally spat out, "Don't you understand, it's totally shattering for me to hear you say that after we...after so many years of...and on the fishing trap." She buried her face in her hands and cried in a muffled voice, "Did it all mean so little to you. Am I...am I just the romantic diversion, the girl who's conveniently at hand?"

The wind moaned in sympathy among the treetops and ruffled the waters.

Ravi remained where he was, watching her. He didn't put an arm around her as she'd expected.

It was too much. She began to weep.

Ravi began to reach out to her, but he pulled his hand back to his side. He wore a strange expression, one of savage determination.

It did nothing to mollify her grief. She turned away from him and sobbed the private hell that was hers.

The wind rose in strength, insisting on being heard.

Jayanti shivered.

Ravi stood up, removed his jacket and placed it around her shoulders. But that was all. He got up and walked to the shore of the lake.

Jayanti could smell his musky scent on the jacket. She pulled it around her shoulders and gripped the lapels together on her chest.

Eventually, her sobbing eased.

Ravi did not turn around. He picked up a stone and hurled it into the lake. "You told me you couldn't marry me, Jayanti."

"Of course not," she retorted angrily. "No one in your family would allow it, and you know it."

Ravi threw another stone. It flew an impressive distance.

"So you wouldn't let yourself even entertain the possibility?"

"No," she lied.

He turned to face her. "Yet you know that I love you."

She dropped her head. "Yes." She paused. "At least, I let myself believe it sometimes."

"Sometimes?"

"Ravi," she said with exasperation. "I'm almost the only one you have had a chance to love. It's...it's a big world out there, and you're about to enter it. Who knows who you will meet."

Ravi nodded. "So, if you cannot marry me, someone has to find you a husband."

She wanted to say, *Yes, but not you. That would be rubbing salt into a wound that has savaged my heart for months.* She elected to say nothing.

Ravi continued. "The question is, who's going to find him for you? You have no parents; your brother has his head full of elephants and is not moving in circles where he's likely to find a good husband. Your uncle and auntie are good people, but they only know people in their village locality. It's hard to imagine them doing you justice either."

"That is my problem, not yours." She said stiffly. "There may be a very nice boy in the next-door village who they will find for me.

Ravi shook his head. "No, Jayanti. I'm afraid you've been ruined."

"I have not!" she replied, tossing back her head and glaring at him.

"Oh yes you have. You've been ruined by education. You've tasted the forbidden fruit of knowledge. You've seen too much and experienced too much to ever be satisfied with cooking meals for someone in a village."

Jayanti lowered her head. She could think of nothing to say. It was true, and she knew it.

"So, we need a better plan."

I don't want a plan, I want you to love me. I don't want solutions, I want understanding. "A better plan?"

"Yes." He strode to the bench, sat down and took her hand. "Why not allow me to find a husband for you?"

"What!" She stared at him, snatched her hand away and punched his arm—a good deal harder than she'd intended.

He didn't flinch. "Why not? I'm the person who has been closest to you these last three years. I…um, care for you a lot. I know you very well, and I'm well connected."

Jayanti couldn't believe what she was hearing. "I think it best if I don't get married," she said. "After all, I have no dowry."

"True," he nodded. "You would bring almost nothing to a marriage…"

She looked up at him sharply.

He continued, "…other than a beautiful character; a brilliant, well educated mind; courage…and…well, never mind."

Jayanti experienced a flush of warmth through her, but she banished it almost as quickly as it came. "Others may think differently," she said. "They may simply see those qualities as arrogance, strong-will, and poverty."

"Then we won't invite them to marry you. We'll find someone who values you."

Jayanti frowned. "I…I'm not convinced that I understand everything that is going on in that head of yours, Ravi—or what you are hatching." She gave him a searching look. "That's the trouble with people like you; people who are quiet and think too much. It's hard to know what you're really thinking."

Ravi held up his hands. "No. I'm serious. Honestly. I really do want the best for you." He leaned back on the bench seat. "So I need your help. Tell me: what would you look for in a husband?"

The question shocked her. "I haven't given it much thought," she said, evasively.

He put his head to one side. "Come on. Every Indian woman has a wish list for a husband—and has had almost from birth. Seriously: what do you want in a husband?"

Jayanti said nothing.

Ravi persisted. "Well, let's begin. Would you like him to be rich or poor?"

"It would be helpful to be free of abject poverty." She glanced at him. "I hope you don't think me selfish, it's just that I'm frightened I might not be strong enough for my principles to remain intact if I was faced with dire circumstances."

"Morality is the privilege of the middle class. The poor can't afford it, and the rich don't care about it." He nodded. "It's perfectly understandable. Where do you want him to come from?"

"I don't mind. As long as he understands me and my culture."

"How academic should he be?"

"I wouldn't like to be…"

"Frustrated?"

She nodded.

"Pretty clever, then. What belief system should he have?"

That brought her up with a start. It was the first time she'd been put on the spot. She lowered her head.

He raised an interrogating eyebrow.

"Oh," she said in irritation. "Atheism requires you to believe everything came from nothing…or from infinity…and there's no scientific precedent to suggest such a thing."

"What about religions?"

She waved a hand dismissively. "Hinduism is based on fear and self-effort. Buddhism is inherently negative—seeking ways to escape reality. And Islam, in its pure form, advocates violence, needs to dominate, and is careless with truth."

"And Christianity?"

Jayanti dropped her head. "Yes," she said eventually. "I have faith in Christ, but I'm afraid I have rather less faith in the institutional church."

Ravi waited for her to say more.

She breathed in deeply and continued. "It seems to me that Christ-like principles have brought more justice, equality, and education than anything else that's about." She shrugged. "They instill a culture of sacrificial love."

"So, how important is it that your husband is a Christian?"

"Fairly. It's the foundation on which everything else is built. But a foundation should not be agreed on just for pragmatic reasons, it needs to be agreed on because it's true."

Ravi nodded. "Would you like your husband to allow you to work at your own profession?"

"Yes."

"Okay," he said. "I think I've got enough to go on."

"What are you going to do?"

"I'll put an advert in the paper, inviting people to write to me at the hospital in Munnar."

"Really?"

"Would you allow me to?"

No. I don't want you to do it. I know exactly what I want. "Yes."

"Thank you."

Chapter 23

"How's JP doing?" asked Jayanti as she and Millie walked arm in arm past the tea bushes. They had decided to go for a walk whilst Ravi went for a jog up to the lake.

"He says he's going to trim his beard tonight, and that we all have to tell him how handsome he is."

"Sounds positive."

"It is. It's his first try at believing in himself."

Jayanti nodded. JP had been fairly subdued in his months of rehabilitation at home. Once all the stitches were removed from his face, he'd decided to grow a beard. Given the extent of the scarring on his face, Jayanti was not surprised. However, the scarred facial tissue did not grow a beard well, and so it struggled to grow evenly. It needed more length to hide the gaps so JP had never trimmed it —until now.

"I hope it hasn't been too much for him to have us sharing his home."

Millie shook her head. "No it hasn't." She sighed. "This accident has really knocked his confidence. He used to be...," her voice caught, "he used to be the life and soul of the party. Everyone loved him, but now...the scarring, and the shock of nearly dying—he's lost his confidence." Millie turned Jayanti around to face her. "You and Ravi have ensured that life still happens in this house, and that's actually been very important for us both."

"That's lovely of you to say." Jayanti smiled. "You know you never actually reviewed us staying here after the first month."

"Oh I did, I very much did." Millie grinned, "I just never told you." She drew a deep breath. "If you weren't here, I suspect that I would be a morbid, depressive alcoholic."

"You! Rubbish."

"Oh, yes. All this could have easily tipped me over the edge." She gazed into the distance. "I actually walk closer to the edge than most people think."

Jayanti didn't know what to say.

They continued on down the track until they stood looking over the tea planters' village of Chinnakanal with its houses tucked in beside the massive granite boulders.

Some huts made of mud bricks and corrugated iron stood a few hundred yards away from the village on the roadside. They'd been built hard up against a road cutting. Jayanti watched as a truck passed dangerously close to them. "Are those buildings more of those illegal encroachments?"

Millie nodded.

"Wow! That's a precarious life."

"Yes," said Millie. "Life is precarious, and can be a bitch."

One hint that all was not well in Millie's life could be forgiven as an accident. A second hint could not be ignored.

"Millie," she said softly. "Would it help to talk about whatever it is that's eating away at your heart?"

Millie stiffened.

"I don't want to pry, and I'm not a local who's going to betray secrets to people in the community. But I'm happy to listen if it will help…" she trailed off.

Millie was silent for a long while. Jayanti was concerned that she'd offended her. However, Millie wiped her nose on a handkerchief and said, "I, er…gave JP a bit of a cuddle last night—first time in ages."

Jayanti managed not to show her surprise, and nodded.

Millie gave a bitter laugh. "I used to cuddle him a lot before the accident. Wore him out, actually."

High over to the east, Jayanti could see clouds growing above the peaks.

There was another sniff and a wipe of the nose. "The thing is, I can't have a baby."

Silence.

Jayanti waited for more.

Millie scrunched the handkerchief up in a fist. "We've been trying for nine years, and I've been on the IVF program for two years." She lifted a tear-streaked face to Jayanti. "Nothing." She started to weep. "Always nothing—month after month."

Jayanti put her arms around her and drew her to herself. "I'm so sorry."

"I've been trying so hard, so hard…"

More sobbing.

"Yes. It must be difficult to bear. Do the doctors hold out any hope?"

"Oh, they always try and put the best spin on it, but the fact is, the IVF process is still pretty chancy." Millie sniffed. "Evidently J.P's sperm count is very low."

Jayanti gave her a squeeze and rubbed her back. "I wish there was something I could do for you Millie; I really do."

Millie gave a shuddering sigh and turned around. "Let's go back and rejoin the men on the veranda."

As they walked up the hill, the clouds began to thicken, bringing an early twilight to the evening.

They were halfway back to the homestead when Millie said, "Jayanti, I've asked you this before, but I want to check…" She fell silent.

"Check what?"

"What is your relationship with Ravi? Do you have sex with him?"

"No. Of course not."

Millie gave her a searching look.

"Really," Jayanti insisted.

"Hmm. And do you have plans to marry him?"

Anguish stabbed at Jayanti's heart. "No, not at all." She tried to put on a brave smile. "His family would never allow it. I was a servant, a laundry maid in his father's household."

Millie frowned and looked Jayanti up and down. "Wow! You're some laundry maid."

"I was lucky enough to be educated with him. He needed a classmate."

"A classmate."

"Yes."

Silence shouted between them.

"Why do you ask?" said Jayanti.

Millie stopped walking and turned to face her. She took Jayanti's hand and looked at her from under her dark eyelashes. "Please don't think me presumptuous or think badly of me, but might I borrow Ravi...you know...at night whilst he's here, to...to be a sperm donor...to..."

"To impregnate you," finished Jayanti.

Millie nodded. "I...I, need hope...a chance..." She looked at her pleadingly.

More silence.

Jayanti turned away and rubbed her forehead; she had to do something to stop herself from screaming. Life was so cruel, so unbearably cruel. *No, no, no, no, no.* "What does JP think of it?" she said, desperately trying to give herself time to think.

"Oh, he has no idea; and he must not know. He's...he's a proud man." Millie shook Jayanti's arm in emphasis. "Both Ravi and JP are similar in build; both are intelligent and both are fabulously handsome."

"You've not asked anyone else?" said Jayanti, floundering.

"No."

"Um, Ravi is fairly highly principled, he may not..."

"But would you mind if I asked him...as a friend...as an act of compassion...an act of generosity?"

Jayanti rubbed her temple.

"I haven't offended you, have I?" said Millie.

"I...I don't know what to think." Jayanti tried to smile. "It's all a bit of a surprise, that's all."

The air around them became colder.

"Do you mind if I think about it for a day or so?"

"Of course not," said Millie.

Jayanti froze for a moment before she pushed down the door-handle. Slowly, oh so slowly, she levered it down as far as it would go.

Should she continue?

No.

She closed her eyes and then pushed the door.

It opened with barely a squeak.

Relief.

Jayanti slipped inside the room and eased the door shut behind her.

The curtains were open. She was not surprised. Ravi had often spoken of his love of being woken by the morning light.

Moonlight streamed into the bedroom and fell across the bed where he lay. He was lying on his back with his head turned away. His hair had grown over-long and was in need of a cut. It lay in waves, falling to his shoulders, gleaming blue-black.

She crept forward and looked down on his face. The long straight nose, the dark eyelashes, the strength of his jaw—the face she loved.

A tiny zephyr of wind blew in through the window causing the shift she was wearing to flutter. It was the only piece of clothing she was wearing. She put one hand on her chest and reached over with a forefinger to stroke his cheek.

Except, she didn't. Instead, she moved her finger just above his skin tracing the contours of his face in the air—imagining.

But she'd not come to imagine, she'd come to make love to him. She wanted to do it gloriously, with abandon and with complete self-giving. There were words she wanted him to hear, endearments and declarations of love. She wanted him to know the truth of what she felt and what she truly yearned for.

Jayanti felt the swell of her breasts under her hand.

The thought of someone else, particularly someone as shapely as Millie, making love to Ravi was unthinkable. She was the one who should be making love to him.

Jayanti had lain awake for half the night, tossing and turning until she could bear it no longer. Finally, she'd got up, combed her hair and tucked a flower from the vase behind her ear.

Now she was here. She only needed to touch him.

A shadow from the sash window scarred the moonlight. It fell like a cross over the blankets as they rose and fell with his breathing.

She lifted her head in anguish. She'd just professed that she was a Christian—and that it was really important to her. Was this what…? She sighed. *It was all so difficult.*

Ravi's mobile phone was beside his bed. She picked it up. Slowly, she took the flower from her hair, bent down, and laid it down in the phone's place.

Quietly, she exited the room.

Back in her own room, she rang a familiar number. She desperately needed to hear from someone with more strength and wisdom than she possessed.

"Sister Rosalind speaking." There was no hint of surprise or complaint that it was ten minutes past three in the morning.

Jayanti gave a brief sob and then poured out her story. "Sister Rosalind; I went into Ravi's room because I want to have sex with him—and have wanted to for so long. I love him so much and he loves me but we can't marry—but when I told a dear friend that we don't sleep together and that I can't marry him, she asked if she could sleep with him so she can have a baby because she and her husband, whom she loves, can't."

There was a pause, then Sister Rosalind said, "Perhaps you should tell me a little bit more."

Jayanti did.

When she'd finished giving the details, including what happened on the fishing trap when she and Ravi had declared their love for each other, Sister Rosalind asked, "And where are you at the moment?"

"I'm back in my own bedroom but unless you tell me otherwise, I'll go back into Ravi's room."

"My darling Jayanti, I won't tell you to do anything."

There was a pause.

"But shouldn't you. I told Ravi I'd become a Christian."

"That's wonderful, dear. I'm delighted."

"But Christians don't…"

Sister Rosalind sighed. "I'm afraid that I'm not really in the 'telling' business. Ours is more the loving business."

"But…"

"…and because I'm in the loving business, I point to God's best plan for people—when appropriate."

"But could it conceivably be God's plan for Ravi and I to…"

"…get married?"

"That wasn't quite what I was about to say, but yes, now you've said it, 'get married'?"

"It's worth asking God about it."

"Oh, I wouldn't dare."

"Why not?" Sister Rosalind sighed. "What father wouldn't want their daughter to share the secrets of her heart with him?"

"But it's so personal…and selfish."

"Jayanti, God knows the secrets of your heart already, he's just waiting for you to invite him into your situation and to guide you through it."

"But surely praying won't make my having sex with Ravi more likely."

"Maybe not. God is not a good luck charm you wear around your neck to ensure you get what you wish for."

"Then why…?"

"Because he whispers what's best for you into your heart, and gives you the ability to pursue it in a way that honors him."

Another silence.

Jayanti sniffed. "I very nearly didn't honor him tonight."

"Don't beat up on yourself. You're doing okay."

Silence. "It's just that I love Ravi so much."

"Jayanti, as I said, being a Christian doesn't mean things will go magically well for you. In fact, things could very well get tougher. It's not easy being a Christian. It's just that being a Christian gives you the right to intimacy with God, a right to represent him, and the assurance that you will be part of an eternal adventure with him."

"So you're not going to tell me what to do?"

"No. All I'll say is that Jesus had a very high view of marriage, and that the commitment of marriage is the best context for sex."

Jayanti twisted the edge of her sheet in her fist. "Oh, Auntie…" She wept.

"Weep your tears child, and picture your Heavenly Father holding you."

"Why, why, why?" she said angrily, "Why is marriage so hard?"

"Is it?"

"The whole thing is horrible," she said. "Did you know that my mother told me that she was required to strip in front of her prospective mother-in-law so that her body could be inspected for the position of any moles to see whether or not it was propitious that she should marry my father?"

"I think I can promise that no mother is going to ever ask that of you, Jayanti."

"Hmph!"

"Changing the subject. What have you and Ravi decided to do? You can't remain in hiding forever. As you know, Sister Elizabeth was unsuccessful in persuading Ravi's father to give what's left of his jewels to charity. So Ravi is still in danger."

Jayanti dabbed her eyes with the bed-sheet. "If there is no breakthrough soon, we'll go to the police before Ravi takes up his position at CMC or comes back to Delhi."

"Has he put in his application?"

"Yes, he applied back in February. He should hear any moment now whether he's been accepted to do the preliminary written test."

"When's that?"

"In May."

"Will he have to go to Vellore for that?"

"Yes."

Silence.

"How are you feeling now, Jayanti?"

"Exhausted." She laughed despite herself. "So I think I'll manage to go to sleep."

"Sweet dreams. Oh, and one more thing: Rahul was asking about you both. What do you want me to say to him?"

"Tell him we're both fine."

"Just that?"

"Yes."

Chapter 24

"Whoops," said Jayanti as she made to enter Dr. Nambeesan's office." Ravi nearly bumped into her as he was leaving it.

"Sorry," he said.

She raised a questioning eyebrow.

"Just reporting that we've nearly finished transferring the records to the new computer system." Ravi smiled. "I'll leave him to you."

She knocked on the open door.

"Come," said the doctor.

Jayanti drew a deep breath and walked in. "Dr. Nambeesan, may I speak with you?"

The doctor swung around on his chair and looked Jayanti up and down. "Of course," he said with a slow smile.

Jayanti shut the door behind her and stood in front of the doctor's desk. She licked her lips. "Doctor, may I ask some personal questions before I put a proposition to you?"

The doctor raised his eyebrows. "Sounds intriguing; go ahead."

"Are you married?"

"I am, as it happens, and I have two sons. Why?"

"But this doesn't stop you from, er…engaging in affairs of the heart elsewhere?"

"Miss Jayanti, you are full of surprises this morning. Why do you ask?"

"You don't have to answer my questions," she said hurriedly. It's just that…"

"…you might make me a proposition." He smiled. "Well, let's put it this way. I have a certain appetite that Mrs. Nambeesan, with all the laudable work she does as a mother, can't fully satisfy."

"Does she know?"

"Oh yes. She'll always be my wife, and we do have a sex life, but not much of one. She knows that my arrangement means that I'll never be tempted to marry anyone else."

Jayanti blinked, but kept a straight face. She drew a deep breath. "I have someone who may want to engage your sexual services."

The doctor put down the pen he was holding. "Not you, then."

"No."

"A pity." He paused. "You'd better tell me what's on your mind."

Jayanti didn't want to betray Millie's confidence. "I…er, have met a very pretty local woman who has been unable to conceive. She suspects that her husband's sperm count may be low."

"There are all sorts of reasons why a woman can't conceive," said the doctor slowly.

"Anyway, she is too poor to afford IVF treatment," *forgive this small white lie*, "…so she was wondering whether I could ask you to, er, inseminate her, perhaps on several occasions, to see if she can get pregnant."

All was silent for a moment before the doctor laughed. It wasn't a very convincing laugh. "This woman wants to recruit my services to get her pregnant?"

"Yes. Rest assured, she's very beautiful. I wouldn't have asked you otherwise."

"As if I was some sort of stud bull."

"Yes."

The doctor was silent for a long while. "Very beautiful, you say?"

"Yes. But you'd have to be very discreet. Her husband mustn't know."

"The doctor waved his hand dismissively. "I'm used to being discreet." He rubbed the back of his neck. "Well, this is extraordinary. I must say, I'm taken aback."

"Why?"

The doctor looked nonplussed. "Well, strange as it may seem, I'm feeling a bit coy about this."

"But you've had plenty of affairs. What's the difficulty?"

Dr. Nambeesan lowered his head and fiddled with the pen in front of him. Eventually, he looked up. "I think I've worked it out."

"What?"

"When I pursue a woman, I'm the hunter. I'm looking to take a sexual experience from them." He shook his head. "This is the first time someone has hunted me, even if it's only for my genes."

Jayanti couldn't restrain herself. "How does it make you feel?"

He again rubbed the back of his neck. "It makes me feel…that I might be a little more careful and restrained in future."

"So, is that a yes or a no?"

The doctor looked up at her. "Rather strangely, I can't answer that now. I'll have to think about it." He shook his head and said, half to himself, "I can't believe I'm not jumping at the chance to have sex with a beautiful woman."

Jayanti smiled. "I think you are changing, Dr. Nambeesan. But on this occasion, your…um, service would be a kindness."

"A kindness." He laughed and waved her away. "Get out of here."

That evening, only Ravi and Jayanti were sipping iced tea on the veranda. Both Millie and JP had stayed on late at the tea factory to oversee the installation of a new roller.

Ravi picked up a folder beside him and put it on his knees. "I've got five applications which I think sound promising," he said.

Jayanti was looking at the view and not paying much attention. "Promising for what?"

"A husband."

Jayanti jerked herself upright. "What!"

"Seriously." He tapped the folder. "These are all very good candidates. "I've already had a phone interview with their parents and have the details here. They're impressive." He looked up at her. "Honestly, Jayanti. I've got rid of all the rubbish applicants, and these are the good ones."

She could feel the color drain from her face. "Oh."

"Do you want to know how your advert read?"

Jayanti nodded dumbly. The truth was, she wanted to talk about something else—anything else.

Ravi cleared his throat. "Extraordinarily beautiful woman from Cochin, from a good family (parents deceased). Scored eighty eight percent in her HSC. Seeks intelligent Christian husband. Ring... blah, blah, blah." He lifted his head. "Good enough?"

Jayanti inspected her glass of iced tea. "It's okay, I suppose."

He shuffled the papers in front of him. "Okay, tell me what you think." He picked up the top sheet. "This guy is thirty eight years old, but he's..."

"Too old," said Jayanti waving her hand.

"Oh, right." He picked out the second page. "This fellow is twenty-two, works in a family business in Delhi, and is from the *Vaishyas* merchant caste. He scored an HSC result of sixty-five."

"Spare me," said Jayanti.

"Hmm. We have Massoud. He got an HSC result of eighty. He works in IT in Bangalore and loves gaming." Ravi looked up. "Are you okay with gaming?"

"Computer gaming?"

Ravi nodded.

"I suppose so."

"Well, this guy has very wealthy parents but they are nominal Muslim. The thing is, Massoud is willing to convert to Christianity in order to marry you."

Jayanti shook her head. "I don't want anyone to convert to Christianity just so they can marry me. That's absurd."

"Really? I thought that was a pretty good offer."

Jayanti gave a sigh of exasperation. "If there is any truth in a faith, it has to be a whole lot more that what is convenient or what 'works for you.'"

"Oh," Ravi sighed. "Okay. Well, that brings us to Sandeep." He bent the piece of paper in his fingers and then straightened it again. "His HSC results are in the high seventies, which is pretty good."

Jayanti nodded.

"He's attended a Christian school in Pune. His parents tell me that they are delighted at the prospect of him finding a wife. They come from the *Vaishyas* caste and have a large house. His parents made it clear that they would need to continue living with him if you got married." He looked at her. "Is that okay?"

She said nothing.

Ravi continued to read. "The downside is that he's only a hundred and sixty three centimeters tall."

Jayanti eased herself up from the cane chair and stood in front of Ravi with a hand on her hip. "For goodness sake, Ravi, look at me. I'm a hundred and seventy eight centimeters tall. Don't make it hard for me."

Ravi ran his eyes up and down her, and smiled. "Then we only have one more."

Jayanti sighed and sat down. "And what are his details?"

Ravi extracted the final piece of paper and glanced at it. "He's pretty good, except for his name."

"What's that?"

"Nemo."

"Nemo?"

"Yes."

She shrugged. "I suppose I could live with it. What else?"

"Wealthy background and quite sporty."

"Education?"

"Over seventy five in his HSC."

"Hmm. How old?"

"Under twenty-five." Sorry, I sent them a tick box, so some questions aren't answered exactly. But his father says he's very good looking. He's going to send me a picture."

"That's good. What else? Where's he from?"

Ravi looked at the sheet. "From Tamil Nadu."

"A southerner."

"Hmm."

"What do we know of his faith and character?"

"Bit woolly: he says that his faith is a work-in-progress but that he's committed to going wherever the truth takes him." He looked up. "Will that do?"

"If it's sincere, then yes," she said.

"Anyway, he's asked to meet you."

"He has!" squawked Jayanti. "When, where?"

"In Vellore."

"Vellore! Why Vellore?"

"Because that's where we're going in a fortnight's time."

"Why?"

Ravi smiled. "Because you've been accepted to do the preliminary written test to train as a doctor at CMC."

She choked. "Me? That's ridiculous. I haven't even applied."

Ravi looked at the ceiling. "Well, actually, you did. I applied for you." He steepled his fingers under his chin. "It was easy. I've got all your details—even a copy of the testimonial written for you by Dr. Nambeesan."

"What! Don't be ridiculous. I can't afford to apply…"

Ravi waved dismissively. "All paid for." He held out his hand. "Congratulations."

Jayanti ignored his hand, frowned, and tried to understand.

As something of what she heard began to impinge on her, a dreadful thought occurred. "But, but what about you? Did you get accepted? I couldn't possibly…"

Ravi thrust his hand at her again—insisting. "You may congratulate me also." He grinned. "I've been invited to do the test as well."

"You asked to see me?" said Elizabeth.

Sister Rosalind looked up from her desk and smiled. "Ah, Sister Elizabeth. Do come in." She waved her to one of the seats by an occasional table. Sister Rosalind came around from her desk and joined her in the other seat. She folded her hands together.

Elizabeth could hear the tooting and bustle of Delhi through the window. It was at odds with the peace in Sister Rosalind's office.

The senior nun cleared her throat. "Are you aware of the mission work of Ida Scudder?"

"I'm afraid not."

"She was the daughter of a missionary doctor in South India. When she grew up, she was appalled that so many Indian women died, particularly in childbirth, because their husbands refused to let them be attended by male doctors."

Elizabeth nodded. She knew that this prejudice still existed in many rural communities.

Sister Rosalind continued. "So she went back to America, trained as a doctor, and returned to build the Christian Medical College at Vellore to train women doctors. It's grown to become one of the best hospitals in Asia and is known for its work among the poor."

Elizabeth had learned not to rush a conversation with Sister Rosalind and waited for the relevance of this information to be made clear.

Christ, hanging on a cross on the wall behind the desk, looked down benignly, showing equal patience.

"Sadly, it is the nature of all Christian institutions that their ideals change as they grow in power and prestige." Sister Rosalind shrugged. "Without continual spiritual renewal, they become less Christ-like."

Christ, on the cross behind the desk, said nothing to disagree.

"Anyway, the senior chaplain at CMC has been concerned that the culture of the chaplaincy department is losing its Christ-like heart and becoming too preoccupied with education and status. He fears they are losing their love of the poor."

Elizabeth nodded.

Sister Rosalind continued. "Even though CMC is affiliated with the Protestant Church of South India, the Missionaries of Charity have had a longstanding invitation to visit them for a few months to help them recapture this love." She looked at Elizabeth. "I contacted CMC this morning to let them know that you and I will be traveling down to Vellore to work with them." She smiled. "Evidently, we'll be staying at the training college a few miles out of town and will travel into the hospital each morning."

Elizabeth nodded. "I'll look forward to it. When do we go?"

"Next week."

Silence.

"Sister Rosalind, isn't Vellore the college that Ravi wants to apply to go to for his medical training?"

Sister Rosalind smiled. "It is."

Rahul watched as the cow poked its head into the open door of the café. It always amused him to see the social dilemma caused by incidents such as this. The cows that roamed the street were a nuisance to almost everyone—and were often dangerous, particularly when they got among the traffic. But they were sacred—hence the dilemma.

The pale-skinned cow had obviously smelled something it liked. It moved its head from side to side, inspecting the patrons from under long, sleepy eyelashes, before it began to push its way into the café.

Rahul handed a newspaper across to Arjun. "Go bang it on the nose with this," he said as he mopped up the last bit of biryani from his bowl.

Moments later, Arjun came back and threw the rolled up newspaper onto the table. "I hope that when I get reincarnated as a cockroach for beating a sacred cow, you might put in a good word for me with the gods."

Rahul pushed his bowl away. "I don't think the gods listen to me very much."

Arjun sat back down and slouched untidily in the chair. He looked at Rahul. "I'm a bit worried about you, mate."

Rahul fixed him with a look that betrayed no emotion.

Arjun continued. "Getting richer is meant to make people happier. But you've become grumpier. He lent forward and prodded Rahul on the arm. "You were happier conning tourists at the station when your ass was hanging out of your pants. What's the matter?"

Rahul thought fleetingly of those early years, of the times spent in the late afternoons with Jayanti. He snatched his arm away, irritated at the world and at himself.

Arjun gave an exaggerated sigh. "Okay, forget it." He reached over to take a handful of *mukhvaas,* a mouth-freshener made of sugared dill, fennel, and coriander seeds. "Now tell me more about this little plan you're hatching."

Rahul grunted. "This one doesn't involve a big team."

"You don't need Kumar's muscle?"

"Yeah, I'll take him. It'll be a bit physical."

"Do you need my brains?"

"Entertainment, more like. No, I don't. Kumar and I can handle it."

"So, what's the job?"

"I've got to snatch a bloke and sit on him until someone flies in to take charge of him."

Arjun pursed his lips. "Sounds simple enough. Who do you have to grab?"

"I'm keeping that to myself at the moment."

Arjun nodded and held up his finger to order another glass of chai.

After the tea was poured. Arjun asked, "Has the job got you worried?"

"No. But it might take a while to work out where my target is. We could be gone for a few weeks, maybe a month."

"Where are you going?"

"To Tamil Nadu."

"Bloody hell, that's a long way away." He shook his head. "Who would want to go there?" He brightened. "I know a joke about Tamil Nadu."

Rahul rolled his eyes.

Arjun was not to be deterred. He rubbed his hands together.

"There was a man from Tamil Nadu who had lost his job and was stony broke. He prays to his favorite god, *Ganesh*, saying. 'Oh *Ganesh*, I will serve you faithfully if you let me win the Lotto. I desperately need the money.'

"However, when the Lotto results come out, he learns that he's won nothing.

"'What's the matter, *Ganesh*? Don't you realize that my wife has produced yet another baby and I'm penniless? Please organize it so that I win the Lotto. Come on. I know you can do it.'

"But next week he's won nothing.

"The man yells at *Ganesh*. 'What is wrong with you *Ganesh*? I've served you faithfully for years. Why haven't you let me win Lotto?'

"And then, a blinding light comes from heaven and *Ganesh's* voice booms out like thunder. 'If you want to win the Lotto, you must first buy a ticket.'"

Arjun laughed at his own joke, sighed, and said, "Seriously; why on earth would anyone want to go to Tamil Nadu?"

Rahul knew he should not be going, but was equally sure he would.

Chapter 25

Indian Railways had written, rather optimistically 'Happy Journey' on the top of the ticket. Jayanti turned it over in her hands and decided that she was not enjoying the journey very much. She and Ravi were sharing their compartment with a couple who had reunited with each other after the husband had returned from Dubai. They'd married the previous year just two months before the husband went off to the Middle East.

Jayanti felt sorry for them. The couple spent a lot of time whispering to each other, shyly getting to know each other all over again —and unable to express much intimacy because she and Ravi were present. Jayanti wanted to apologize. Then she grew to wondering if she, as a young bride, could bear to be separated from Ravi for reasons of work?

She pulled herself together when she realized what she was thinking and forbade herself to muse on the fantasy any more.

The train tugged them through a day and a night into the hot interior of India.

Ravi dozed through much of the journey, or gave the appearance of it. Jayanti suspected that he had retreated to the inner part of his mind, the place he went to when he needed to think.

Certainly, both of them had much to think about. What would happen to them in Vellore? How could Ravi get free of the danger that stalked him? And—heartbreak of heartbreaks—how soon would it be before she and Ravi were separated? She reached for her handkerchief. It was absurd to think that she had any chance of winning a place at CMC. But if she and Ravi did, by some miracle, pass the entrance exam, it would mean that they would be together for another five years. That's what she wanted more than anything else. It was such a faint chance, but she was desperate. She resolved to study all she could on Ravi's computer to prepare for the exam.

Jayanti had grilled Ravi about why he'd applied on her behalf to CMC. She'd hoped to hear him say it was because he could stay with her, but he didn't. His maddeningly logical reply had been:

"Jayanti, I know you really well, but even if I didn't, blind Freddie could tell that you love the medical profession."

"Blind Freddie? Rubbish. What are you talking about?"

"Who knew how long your brother should keep his stitches in place? Who sewed him up, for that matter? Who loved going on the doctor's rounds? Who did the doctors consult when they wanted to know what a patient was really feeling?" He smiled. "You're a natural."

She'd interrogated him with a searching glare—but that was the trouble with Ravi, he could operate from deep places that were hard to fathom.

The train eventually pulled into Katpadi Junction just north of Vellore. Jayanti watched the teeming crowds of people on the platform—the passengers, the coolies, and the beggars who lived on the station. As she watched the faded Victorian architecture—so typical of Indian rail stations—slide to a stop outside, she caught sight of the two people she least expected to see. Their white saris made them fairly conspicuous.

She squealed with delight, "Elizabeth and Sister Rosalind are here. Ravi, look." She shook Ravi's arm."

He smiled. "Go and meet them. I'll get your rucksack."

She leaped to the door of the compartment, paused and looked back at Ravi. "You knew they would be here, didn't you?"

Ravi waved her away. "Go and meet them," he said again.

An hour later, she was sitting with Elizabeth, Sister Rosalind, and Ravi in cane chairs on the veranda of 'Big Bungalow'. This was the guesthouse set aside for distinguished visitors to the medical college. It was where Elizabeth and Sister Rosalind were staying. Jayanti was pleased to be sheltered from the enervating heat of Vellore by the veranda. She reflected ruefully that six months in Munnar's mild climate had made her soft.

It was lovely being with the nuns again. She and Elizabeth had hugged each other and danced up and down. Sister Rosalind placed her hands on her shoulders, appraised her with calm eyes, and enfolded her in a tender hug. Jayanti cried.

The college jeep took them south across the Palar River, past local women spreading their newly washed saris over the reeds to dry. They looked like flower petals. Their driver then took them through the dusty, crowded center of Vellore and out to the medical college at Bagayam, seven kilometers south of the city.

Finally, the interminable journey ended.

Jayanti took a grateful sip from her lime soda, settled back in her cane chair, and looked out at the beautiful garden. *Heaven will be like this*, she decided.

It had been a revelation driving into the college grounds in the jeep. The first impression was one of peace. The college had been heavily planted with trees and built to include beautiful stone colonnades. *What a wonderful place to study*, she'd thought.

Sister Rosalind explained how she and Elizabeth were taking advantage of CMC's invitation to revitalize their mission to the poor. "It was an opportunity that was too good to miss," she said with a small smile playing on her lips.

"Does your being here have anything to do with your concern over Ravi's safety?" asked Jayanti.

"Yes dear, it has. Sister Elizabeth spoke with Mr. Panwar, but was unable to persuade him to donate the rest of his jewels to charity and remove the threat from Ravi."

Elizabeth broke in. "I'm sorry, Ravi. I tried."

Ravi nodded and said nothing.

Sister Rosalind reached out and put her hand over his. "With your permission, Ravi, we would like to try again."

"But what will make him change his mind?" said Jayanti.

Sister Rosalind turned to her, "Mr. Panwar believes there is not enough evidence to cause the police to investigate. I'm working on a plan to inject an additional factor he may not have taken into account."

"What is it?" demanded Jayanti.

"I'll tell you when I've got the details." She looked around at them all. "Meanwhile, we need to keep Ravi safe for a week or two until this business is resolved."

Jayanti nodded.

Sister Rosalind turned to her. "Why don't you go to our room and have a shower. I want to talk with Ravi for a moment." She smiled. "Then we'll take you to a place where you can hide in safety, yet still be within easy reach of us at the college."

"Where's that?" Jayanti asked, a little alarmed.

"It's a little village thirty minutes from here. I'm afraid it's very basic, but you should be safe." She sighed. "I wish you could stay here but the college has fairly exacting criteria for whom they will accommodate."

"Ravi and I will be together, though?" asked Jayanti.

"Yes, dear. You will be staying at the home of the local potter. Their daughter is one of the cooks here. Ravi will be living close by, in the home of the village carpenter."

Jayanti was surprised at the level of fear she found in the culture of rural Tamil Nadu. She came across it everywhere during her first week. The 'all-seeing eye' was daubed on the walls of houses that were being built to ward off evil. Children had green leaves tucked in their waistbands to protect them from evil spirits. What particularly saddened Jayanti was seeing beautiful children with black spots of kohl painted on their faces. She'd been told that children who were particularly good looking were disfigured in this way so as not to arouse the jealousy of malevolent spirits.

The village children, particularly the girls, gathered around the front of the house in which she was staying. They stared at her shyly with a mixture of awe and curiosity. The village had been told that she and Ravi were staying there in order to sit the entrance exam for CMC. Consequently, they were both held in high regard. It wasn't long before Jayanti was helping the village girls to learn English and basic hygiene.

Whilst Jayanti knew a smattering of Tamil, Ravi could not speak it at all, so he resorted to India's universal language—cricket.

It began with him suggesting in English that they play a game behind the village huts using a stick for a bat and a tennis ball. As things became more serious, a real cricket bat was unearthed, and the game began in earnest. Ravi conducted coaching clinics in the late afternoon, followed by a game. The rivalry was intense, and the boys loved it.

She could hear him yelling now. "Cricket is a sideways game, Tajdar. Stand sideways."

Ravi was billeted with Dakshi, the village carpenter. He first met him when Dakshi was smoothing a post with a wooden plane. The plane was fitted with handles at one end and Dakshi's twelve-year-old son was helping to pull the plane as his father pushed. When the son needed to duck away for some reason, Ravi took off his shirt and gripped the handles of the plane. Under Dakshi's direction, the two of them continued to smooth the post.

Jayanti liked seeing Ravi in an undershirt—and even more when he took it off. He looked good. Ravi had set himself an exercise routine in Munnar to keep fit. Jayanti suspected that his work with Dakshi would make the need for further exercise redundant.

She, on the other hand, was billeted with Gursharam and Deepa, a gracious and generous Hindu couple. Gursharam had fathered three daughters, one of whom was working at the Big Bungalow. He was considered very unlucky as he had the onerous responsibility of providing a dowry for each of his daughters. Fortunately, one of the mission agencies from CMC had given

Gursharam a small business loan that enabled him to buy two goats. He'd bred from the goats so successfully that he was now able to employ a worker in his pottery business. His proud boast to Jayanti on her first evening was that he had provided an attractive dowry for two of his daughters and had enough to provide for the third.

Not everyone in the village was so fortunate. She didn't have to look far to see the specter of poverty. Some in the village talked of their fear at having to offer themselves and their families as bonded laborers to the brick factory down the road. In reality, it was little more than slavery.

Jayanti screwed up her nose. She'd passed the factory many times that week. From the outside, it looked innocent enough—just a gaggle of large buildings and yards covered with clay bricks being air-dried prior to firing.

Fire. She sniffed.

Smoke hung in the air. From the smell of it, the smoke came from someone cooking turmeric. One of the men of the village would be feeding the fire under a massive cauldron filled with turmeric roots covered with hessian sacks.

People scratched for a living anyway they could. Jayanti couldn't help but feel compassion. Sometimes it took just a little thing, such as an improvement in health, for the fortunes of a family to change.

Could I bring those changes as a doctor? She bit her lip. It wouldn't be for lack of trying. Both she and Ravi spent most of the day in the medical college library researching and revising in readiness for their test. They returned to the village by bus in the middle of the afternoon, mentally exhausted.

Jayanti packed the pad of paper she used to teach the village girls into her rucksack and pushed it under her bed. The bed was a simple wooden frame with rope threaded across its top to form a base to lie on. It was a design that discouraged lice—even if it didn't encourage a good night's sleep. She shared the room with the daughter who was still at home.

Jayanti went through to the front of the house where Deepa was squatting on the dirt floor under the front shelter of the house, cooking. Her kitchen was rudimentary, but she ruled over it protectively.

She forbade Jayanti from helping with the meals, reasoning that with one daughter still at home, she had more than enough help.

Even now, the daughter was at work grinding grain in a huge granite pestle and mortar. It was a sensible design that required the operator simply to rock the pestle around and around whilst feeding grain down the crack between pestle and mortar.

Deepa had built a low brick wall around the far side of the cooking fire to protect it from the wind and the careless totterings of children. She sat on the other side fanning the tiny fire under the cook pot. "When you do exam?" she asked in English.

Jayanti squatted down beside her. "Next week."

The fire had burned down to a point where there were plenty of red coals that were useful for cooking. Jayanti stared at the tiny flames. There was something hypnotic about fire—almost soothing.

"You frightened?" asked Deepa.

"Yes."

Silence.

"You plenty smart. You be okay." Deepa smiled. "If you not doctor, you make good wife for big shot. Your good self is plenty beautiful."

Jayanti didn't trust herself to say anything. She'd tried to stop herself dwelling on the fact that she would be meeting a prospective husband next evening—Nemo. *What sort of person is called Nemo?* She'd wondered it a hundred times. The terror of the upcoming exams was more than matched by the prospect of meeting a future husband, a complete stranger—and the loss it might mean.

A small child walked over from the house next door on his stumpy little legs and, with complete trust, settled himself in her lap. Jayanti toyed with the child's hair as she pondered the uncertainties of the future.

Ravi had organized for them both to get dressed tomorrow in Sister Rosalind's room at Big Bungalow—not least because the toilet and washing facilities in the village were very basic. Jayanti had also expressed her need to have the nun's support before she set out with Ravi to meet Nemo.

She shivered.

The only enjoyable thing about the whole nightmare had been going shopping with Sister Rosalind and Elizabeth to buy a new sari. They spent a wonderful afternoon together, laughing and pointing shopkeepers to yet another sari for Jayanti to throw over herself.

It was when Sister Rosalind, Elizabeth—and most of the others in the store, for that matter—became silent as she sashayed and twirled around in a mint-green sari that she knew she had the right one.

"But how much does it cost?" she whispered to Sister Rosalind as she fingered the gold edging.

"I don't think, my dear Jayanti, that is a question you should ask." Sister Rosalind smiled. "Ravi has given me instructions not to trouble you with such details."

"He's supplied the…funds?"

"Yes."

This comment had caused Jayanti to reflect again on the enormity of what she was about to do.

Sister Rosalind had taken her by the shoulders. "What's the matter, dear?"

She'd shaken her head. "I…I, don't have any gold to wear…to show." It was not what was primarily troubling her, but nonetheless the thought had crossed her mind. An Indian woman should show gold to a prospective husband.

Sister Rosalind had smiled. "Indeed, Jayanti, you are as poor as a church mouse. You simply have the beauty of who you are." She'd smiled. "…which makes you rich indeed."

Deepa, however, was much more pragmatic. She lifted up the metal lid of the cooking pot with a stick. "How rich is this husband fellow you see tomorrow?"

"I don't really know. He's told Ravi he's quite well off."

"Well off?"

"Rich."

"That's good."

If only life was that simple.

"You are a Christian, yes?"

Jayanti nodded.

"I am sometimes a Christian…but when I want my daughter to find a husband, I tell her to spend the night with Shiva." She pushed a stick further into the fire. "Maybe you try Shiva."

Jayanti shivered. The villagers had put the red robe of the Hindu god Shiva over a termite mound at the end of the village and built a hut over it. The effigy was garlanded with yellow flowers, and had an iron trident in front of it. What was not commonly known by anyone other than the locals, was that a cobra lived in a hole at the base of the mound. The snake lived there to take advantage of the moderate climate engineered by the termites. Jayanti was horrified to learn that it was the practice for village women, desperate for a husband, to make an offering of an egg to the snake and to spend a night at the shrine. Only rarely did the snake attack and kill them.

"No, I don't think so," said Jayanti.

Deepa shrugged and sat back on her haunches. "One of the children tell me a fellow ask about Ravi. Would he be a friend?"

Jayanti frowned. "When? What man?"

Deepa shrugged. "Yesterday. He follow your bus on motorbike. He ask children."

Jayanti froze, then lifted the young child off her lap.

"Where you going?" asked Deepa as Jayanti got to her feet.

Jayanti's mind was in a whirl. The safe retreat she and Ravi had worked so hard to find suddenly seemed a lot less safe.

"I need to find Ravi," she stammered, "and let him know what you've told me."

Chapter 26

Jayanti woke after a restless night during which she'd been troubled by mosquitoes. She put on her sari and walked across to Dakshi's house in search of Ravi. Rather surprisingly, he was not dressed for another day of study at the college but was in his work clothes, drilling a hole through the end of a heavy post with Dakshi. He stood up as she approached. She could see the sweat shining on his torso.

She swallowed. "There's no way I can study today." She dropped her head. "Particularly with what's happening tonight, and…" she trailed off.

"The uncertainty?" he finished.

She nodded.

Silence.

Jayanti blurted out, "Why don't we go off together, just the two of us—all day? Let's go where no one will find us." She stepped close to him, almost touching, getting as close as propriety allowed. She needed him and wanted him to understand.

Nothing happened for moment. Then, Ravi reached out, took hold of the back of her neck, and drew her to his chest. For one heart-stopping moment, she thought he was going to kiss her.

Instead, he rested his chin in her hair in a half caress, and then pulled back. It was the action of a brother, not a lover.

"Okay. Give me an hour to finish this, then we'll go for a walk."

"What are you doing?"

"Making, um…certain provisions because of what you told me last night."

She nodded. "Come over when you're ready."

An hour later they began walking through the village toward the countryside. Jayanti looked at the white painted houses with their steep thatched roofs as if seeing them for the first time. *So much could change today.* A small girl walked past. She needed to reach high to keep the metal bin full of laundry balanced on her head. Jayanti waved to her. "Hi Maasila."

The girl smiled shyly.

To the left, a tangle of dried reeds and leaf strips lay beside a house. A woman was squatting beside them weaving a basket. To the right, calves shuffled in a stable that was little more than a thatched roof held up by poles.

She wanted to scream. *How could everything be so normal on a day like this?*

"Ravi," she ventured. "Nothing will be quite the same for us after tonight. Does that…" her voice faltered, "…bother you?"

"Seeing the woman I love being appraised by another man as a possible wife, doesn't do a lot for me."

"Then why do it?" she asked desperately.

"Because you won't marry me…and, because you are my best friend, I want the very best for you." He smiled sadly. "Even if it is only second best from my perspective."

She took his arm and shook it. "It's not that I don't love you. I do." She searched his face. "It's just that servants aren't allowed to marry above their station. Your family wouldn't allow it."

"And what do you think Nemo's family will think of you? They are well off and are also of a twice-born caste."

She pulled Ravi by the arm to avoid walking too close to a buffalo that was lying under a banyan tree. Buffalo were less predictable than bullocks, and she was a little bit afraid of them.

"If Nemo's family are anything more than *Vaishyas* caste, I feel very sure they will reject me." She brushed away a troublesome fly. "I suppose we'll see tonight how he really feels about someone of my status."

Ravi rubbed his forehead. "You do realize there is a chance that you might be accepted for training as doctor, and that being a doctor would change your status. Most men would be proud to have a wife who was a doctor."

She scoffed. "The possibility of me being a doctor is remote, and you know it."

"No. I don't know it. I'm applying to be a doctor and my HSC results were not quite as good as yours. Your problem, Jayanti, is in your head: it's lack of self-belief."

"Hmph. You're much better at math and physics than me. I'm just better at English, which is a lot less useful for a doctor."

"Oh, Jayanti, Jayanti."

"What do you mean?" she said, crossly.

Ravi shook his head.

Coming down the road ahead of them was a man on a pushbike with a pile of coconuts behind him. Ravi raised a questioning eyebrow.

"Yes please," she said.

The man selected a coconut and made it ready for drinking with a few deft strokes of his machete. Jayanti drank gratefully. It was good to have something to drink other than water.

Some of the nutty liquid spilled down her front, and she laughed despite herself as Ravi wiped her dry.

Not much else was said for the next hour.

They bought lunch from a roadside café with walls and roof made from plaited palm leaves. The man cooking inside wrapped their dry curry in a banana leaf and tied it up with string.

Ravi and Jayanti took their meal outside and sat on the plastic chairs the café owner had put out for his patrons.

"You never showed me a picture of Nemo," said Jayanti.

"That's right. He didn't send one. I wonder why."

Jayanti started to giggle. "I bet that means he's really ugly."

Ravi nodded. "The signs are not good," and he too began to laugh.

She became serious. "Promise me that you won't...be far away...if I need help with Nemo."

He nodded. "Don't worry, I'll back you up."

She laid a hand on his arm. "You always have."

"No, I haven't. It took a while for me to discover you."

She looked up at him and risked asking, "And when exactly did you...discover me?"

He answered without a moment's hesitation. "I was in awe of you when I first met you; fell in love with you when I saw you dance; and became intimidated by you when you gate-crashed my lesson with Mr. Hodges. So, I guess it took me about two weeks to discover you."

"Oh," she said weakly.

A truck growled past, leaving them coughing in a cloud of diesel smoke. On its tailgate was the usual sign, 'Please horn'. It tooted as it overtook a man on a pushbike carrying baskets of chickens. She knew he carried chickens because one of them was trying to escape through a gap by the basket's lid.

Jayanti empathized. She too was feeling trapped by circumstances.

"Let's get way from the road and see if we can find Deepa. Deepa said she'd be harvesting somewhere near here," she said.

Ravi nodded.

As they walked through the gaggle of shops and houses toward the fields, it was evident that it was market day for the local community. A man was selling bananas from the back of an auto-truck. Others were selling dried fruit. A butcher had goat meat hanging from a tripod of bamboo poles beside a chopping block. Flies were gathered all over it. The next unfortunate goat was tethered to a nearby tree.

They made their way through to the fields beyond where Jayanti could see a group of women harvesting some sort of green crop. She marveled at the strength of the women's backs and felt very sure she would not be able to bend and cut like them for half an hour, far less a full day.

"Jayanti, can I put a hypothetical scenario to you?" said Ravi, chewing on the end of piece of grass.

She nodded.

"If you were accepted for training at CMC and I was not, your status would increase massively—to the point that any family would be proud to have you join them. My status, however, would not rise at all." He spat out the piece of grass. "If that happened, would you let yourself believe my family would allow you to marry me?"

Jayanti had a flash of insight about where Ravi's comments might be leading—and was appalled. She rounded on him. "Ravi Panwar, if you dare entertain the idea of deliberately flunking your entrance exam just so our social status could be evened out, I shall walk out on you right now."

"But Jayanti…"

"'But' nothing. I know how your devious mind works." She shook her finger at him. "I've never heard of anything so outrageous. What sort of woman could live with herself knowing that she was the cause of her husband not pursuing the career he'd set his heart on? Go on," she challenged. "I dare you to deny that was your plan." Jayanti put her hands on her hips and continued to berate Ravi for a few minutes more. "Promise me that you will do no such thing," she ended.

Silence.

"Promise me," she demanded.

"Okay," said Ravi. He turned around and led the way toward the harvesters.

Deepa was one of the women working there.

"How's the harvest going?" Jayanti asked.

"It is a good year for ragi." She stood up. "You not at CMC?"

"No," said Ravi. "We have to go in tonight. Now, we are preparing."

"Ah yes." She smiled. "Maybe a husband night."

Jayanti lowered her head.

Deepa continued. "I shall be home in two hours, so tell Gursharam that dinner will not be late."

Jayanti looked around and saw that the field was almost fully reaped. "Are there two hours work left here?" she asked.

"Oh no," said Deepa. "We need time for our fight."

"Fight?"

"Yes. The owner of the field will come and make a great show of being generous in filling up our bins with ragi to take home. Then we women will argue with him and tell him he has been mean." She shrugged. "So we fight. It is expected, but it takes time."

"It sounds crazy."

Deepa bent over and continued to cut at the base of the ragi stalks with her long, curved knife. "But it won't be big fight like you two just had."

Chapter 27

"How do I look?"

Jayanti stepped into the lounge area of Big Bungalow and stood still.

Ravi twisted around in his chair, then stood up.

He said nothing.

She desperately wanted him to see her, and be surprised. Jayanti had dressed to arouse his hunger, his admiration, to present herself to him as someone too precious for him to lose. She'd taken an hour to dress—for Ravi.

Jayanti pirouetted around.

The pale green silk barely whispered.

She felt tall. Some of her hair had been plaited on top of her head, but half had been plaited with yellow flowers into a ponytail. He hair was so long that it came to her bare midriff.

Jayanti gripped the material that covered her thigh and pulled the sari out to better display it. Its gold edging glittered. Then she dropped it and waited.

Ravi put a hand out to the back of the chair, as if to steady himself.

She felt his eyes roving over her, seeing her—consuming her.

That was good.

She lifted her chin and stood up straight allowing her breasts to lift.

Jayanti watched him, knowing that she'd struck his heart.

There was a ripple of applause from behind her. Someone had obviously ducked in to tell the kitchen staff that something rather special could be seen outside. They were clapping.

Ravi came forward, took her by both hands and leaned forward so that his cheek brushed hers. "You are beautiful," he said hoarsely —"and always have been."

Sister Rosalind and Elizabeth came up beside her. "Isn't she amazing," said Elizabeth.

"Yes," he said.

Sister Rosalind took hold of both Jayanti's and Ravi's hands. "May God bless you both with his protection and wisdom."

Ravi looked at his watch. "It's time for us to go. Our taxi will be waiting at the college gate."

"Where are we going?" asked Jayanti as she settled into the back of the taxi.

"To a restaurant called *Hundreds Heritage*. It's north of the Palar River. I've asked around. Evidently it has a nice ambience and good food, although a bit overpriced."

"Nemo suggested it?"

"Yes."

She was silent for a while, before saying, "I'm nervous."

Ravi smiled. "If it's any consolation, so is Nemo."

"How do you know?"

Ravi pulled out his cell phone, scrolled through the text messages and showed her the screen. She read: 'Trust all is on schedule. I'll see you in an hour. I confess to being nervous.'

She bit her lip. *I don't really want to consider him. It's you, Ravi, I want to be with you. Can't you see that? Can't things stay the same?* She glanced at him. He was wearing a shirt she'd never seen before—a loose-fitting South Indian shirt with a deep embroidered neckline. It looked very cool and comfortable. She could see dark curls of his chest hair between his pectoral muscles. The shirt and his slim pants made him look good.

She swallowed.

The taxi drove into a gate behind a tall wall and parked in front of a bland-looking white building. To Jayanti, it looked sterile, but then she conceded, everything was looking bleak to her at the moment.

Ravi led her inside where, she had to admit, the ambience was a good deal better. A waiter conducted them to a table set for three people. Jayanti looked at the empty third place and shivered.

Ravi pulled his cell phone out and put it in his ear. He spoke into it briefly, then put it away. As he held Jayanti's chair and helped her sit down, he said, "That was Nemo. He's at the bar so I'll go and collect him when we're ready."

Jayanti laid a hand on Ravi's arm. "Does that mean he's an alcoholic? I couldn't bear it if…"

"Relax. I've talked to him about habits. He's a social drinker only and doesn't actually like alcohol that much." He looked at her. "And I think I'd have a drink if I was about to meet a woman who could become my wife."

Ravi sat down and looked at her. She fiddled with the folded white napkin in front of her. *What am I doing?* She glanced at Ravi, reached out, and took his hand, not trusting herself with words.

Ravi lifted her hand and held it briefly against his cheek. "Jayan…" his voice broke. He swallowed and tried again. "Jayanti, whatever happens in the next few minutes, know that I will always love you and want the very best for you." He looked at her. "You do know that, don't you?"

Tears began to run down her cheeks. She eased her hand away and began to wipe them. Ravi held out his handkerchief.

Jayanti took it and dabbed her eyes. "You…you've always offered your handkerchief to me when I needed it." She tried to laugh, but it wasn't convincing.

"Seriously," he insisted. "Your love is the most precious thing I have ever been given. I've never known my mother; never had love from my father…and will shortly be estranged from him, so, your love has been particularly special." He dropped his head. "Whatever loves may or may not cross my path, yours will always be special and…" he looked up at her, "frustrating because it was unfulfilled."

Jayanti felt herself coloring, and then began to cry again.

Ravi returned his handkerchief to her.

She scrunched it up and dabbed her eyes. "Your love will always be the most important thing in my life," she said between sobs.

"But will remain unfulfilled because you will not marry me."

She gripped her hands into fists and looked up at him angrily. She was about to snap at him and say the well-practiced words she'd told herself for years: *Women of my status are not allowed to marry men of your status*, when she realized the significance of what Ravi had said. He considered himself estranged from his father, a father who had never cherished him other than to provide for him financially; a father who was probably a murderer. She'd never heard anything of Ravi's extended family so who was left to object to any marriage? No one of any significance. Of course, all those in the social circle Ravi knew would be appalled, but…

She felt a shaft of hope pierce the heart she'd protected for so many years.

Surely, it couldn't be possible.

"What's going on, Jayanti?" asked Ravi.

She shook her head—as much to clear it as to wave away the distraction to her thinking.

"I really ought to go and collect Nemo. He'll be wondering," persisted Ravi.

She laid a hand on his arm to forestall him leaving.

Life without Ravi was inconceivable.

Ravi pushed his chair back and made to lift Jayanti's hand off his arm.

She gripped it hard. "I will," she said.

Ravi's eyebrows puckered. "You will what?"

She looked at him in desperation. "I will marry you," she said.

Ravi gave her a searching look. "You're saying this because you're panicking. This is fear speaking."

"No, no…" she said leaning forward to place her other hand on his arm as well. "She looked at him imploringly. "I've always loved you, always wanted to be your wife, always found it impossible to think of life without you—always…" she trailed off.

Ravi nodded slowly and leaned forward. "Always?" he asked.

"Always," she said.

He smiled.

"…as you know full well." She lowered her head.

"Yes," he nodded.

"Yes?…as in, you've always known?"

"No."

"What…"

He picked up one hand, lifted it to his lips, and kissed it. "Yes, as in: I will accept your invitation to marry you."

It took a moment for the significance of what he said to reach her. When it did, delight and relief flooded through her. She threw herself at Ravi.

He caught her and nestled her head briefly under his chin, smoothing her hair. Then, he lifted her face gently—and brought his lips down on hers.

It was delicious; oh so delicious. The delight of surrender; the delight of love; the delight of hope.

Once things had settled down, he murmured to her as he nuzzled her ear. "You do know that it is usually the man who proposes, don't you? This is most improper."

She ran her fingers through his long hair and laughed. "You've proposed to me every day for the last few years, and you know it." She pulled back from him smiling. "It was just that you only rarely said it with words."

"Hmm," he said, pulling her back to him. "You know me altogether too well."

"Yes," she said. "I do."

Jayanti suddenly realized where they were. Fortunately, their table was in an alcove and only visible to an elderly couple seated by the wall. The woman smiled at her with the confidence of a wife who understood. Jayanti smiled back.

As they resumed their seats, Ravi drummed his forefinger on the table. He sighed. "All this…presents us with a small problem."

"Oh?"

"What are we going to do with Mr. Nemo?"

Jayanti opened her mouth with the shock of realization. "Oh, of course. What shall we do?"

Ravi scraped his chair back. "I'll have a brief conversation with him."

She kept hold of his arm. As he drew away, she allowed her fingertips to slide down and hook briefly onto his fingers. "Tell him, I'm so sorry."

Ravi nodded. "I'll enjoy it."

Jayanti took the opportunity to repair what little makeup she had put on whilst Ravi was gone. When she'd finished, she looked around her. The décor and ambience of the restaurant really was much better than she remembered it. Then she hugged herself and gave a shivery giggle of glee. The relief; the delight. She giggled again. Life was wonderful.

Ravi came back to the table carrying a small parcel.

"How did he take it?" she asked.

"Oh," he said sitting down. "He was quite philosophical about it." Ravi smiled. "I think he was actually pretty relieved."

"Relieved?"

"Hmm."

Ravi handed over the parcel to her. "He asked me to give you this."

Jayanti took it and turned it over in her hands. It was wrapped in brown paper. Strange.

She opened it and withdrew an early edition of a book: it was 'David Copperfield', by Charles Dickens. She frowned, not understanding.

The front cover of the book did not sit snugly against the rest of the pages. She opened it to discover a pressed flower, a flower that she very definitely did recognize. It was the flower she had left beside Ravi's bed when she'd gone into his bedroom to make love to him.

Realization dawned. She picked up the flower and smiled. "You are Nemo," she said.

Ravi nodded. "The book is to assure you that I am no James Steerforth."

She reached for his hand. "I know that. But why Nemo?"

"I thought that calling myself David Copperfield might give the game away." He shrugged. "So I hit on the idea of Nemo. It's Latin for 'no one' or 'no name.'"

She held up the flower questioningly and said nothing, twirling it in her fingers.

"Ah, that." He smiled. "I knew you had visited me when I saw that. And that's when I knew there could be no other outcome than us being together."

"I...I came oh so close to..."

He nodded. "Which is why we need to get married as soon as we can."

"Yes," she said. "Yes, yes, yes."

He took her hand, "...which is why I've, er...already made some arrangements."

"You have?" she squeaked.

He kissed her fingers. "I had to plan ahead, with a little help from some friends."

"Really? Who?"

"Sister Rosalind, mainly."

She gave him a searching look.

"She volunteered to talk with the minister of St John's church inside Vellore Fort."

"What!"

"If it is all right with you, he's agreed to marry us next week in a small private service." He looked up at her. "Is that okay with you?"

She laughed. "You cheeky...you knew..."

He kissed her fingers again. "I couldn't countenance any other outcome, so I made plans."

A waiter stood at the entrance of their alcove and coughed politely.

Ravi leaned back and said, "We'll both have a lime soda and the panneri angoori tikka with naan bread, thanks."

"Yes sir; of course. And to follow?"

"Mango kulfi…" he paused, "for my fiancée…" He turned to Jayanti. "Gee, that sounded good."

"And for yourself, sir?"

He turned back to the waiter. "Saffron kulfi, please."

"Yes sir".

Jayanti laughed. "You didn't even ask me."

"You asked me to marry you. My bruised ego needs me to retake the lead." He picked up her hand and sandwiched it between both of his own. "There's not a single day of my life in which I've known you, Jayanti Panikkar, that you've not been the subject of my closest study." He smiled. "So, do you think for one moment I don't know you well enough to choose for you?"

She placed her free hand on top of his. "Then it should be no surprise to you, Ravi Panwar, that I choose you."

Chapter 28

Rahul only half listened to Kumar's litany of complaints.

"I hate the countryside. It doesn't work by the same rules as a city. I hate Vellore. It's dusty and hot. I hate their tandoor food; I hate drinking out of metal cups. I hate their roti bread."

Rahul glanced at Kumar's impressive girth. "You've eaten like a pig all week."

"A man's got to live."

"Well, I think you've been living pretty well."

Kumar grinned. "While you're paying, why not?"

"Well, hopefully, we'll be back in Delhi next week."

Kumar picked at the long saffron tunic he wore over his red lungi. "I feel ridiculous; particularly with this bloody mask."

"We're both devotees of Jainism and we're on pilgrimage. We wear masks to stop us inhaling insects out of respect for all living things."

"So that's what we are about, respecting all living things." Kumar laughed.

The irony wasn't lost on Rahul. He had a pistol and a knife strapped under his saffron tunic, whilst Kumar carried a short length of rubber hosepipe filled with lead pellets. It was in the begging bag he carried. The other item inside his begging bag was a large hessian sack. No one looked at anyone carrying a hessian sack.

Rahul had parked the auto-truck under the trees by the road-side. They had stolen it earlier that afternoon. He had chosen it because he was more familiar with driving autos than cars—and auto-trucks were always carrying hessian sacks in the back. They would be invisible.

"Over there," Rahul pointed. "Panwar is in that hut at the back of the village, next to the field."

Kumar nodded.

Rahul looked up into the night sky. There was very little light from the stars because of the haze. "We'll go inland, walk along the edge of the field, and cross over to his hut."

Rahul led the way down a narrow path to the edge of the field. No one asked too many questions when you walked on a path. People only became curious when you left them. After sixty meters, the path came to a T-junction. He turned right and led Kumar along the back of the village.

They didn't have to go very far. The hut where Ravi Panwar slept was the second one along. It had one doorway at the end and no window. Panwar was trapped. *Perfect.*

Six paces away, Rahul took out his knife and waited for Kumar to pull the cosh from his beggar's bag. "Ready?" he asked quietly.

Kumar nodded.

They slipped over to the hut like shadows. Rahul stood flattened against the wall in deep shadow. Carefully, he slipped the end of his knife between the door and the doorjamb and slid it up until he encountered the catch. It was a simple latch arrangement with no lock. Rahul gently lifted the latch and pushed the door.

The door groaned as it opened slightly.

Rahul froze.

He waited for what he judged to be a full ten minutes, until his legs threatened to cramp with inactivity and the tension. *Be patient; be patient. Out wait anyone's concerns. Let them get back to sleep.*

All was silent.

Rahul reached his hand back and tapped Kumar on the arm. Then he stood in front of the door and pushed.

After a moment of resistance, the door opened.

He stepped forward.

An instant later, a post swung from the roof and smashed into him.

Everything went black.

—————

As familiar as she was with the strange things that could be experienced on Indian buses, Sister Elizabeth eyed the shackled prisoner seated across from her with alarm. The two policemen standing in the aisle of the bus, made no attempt to be seated. Both carried old-fashioned rifles. Perhaps she shouldn't be surprised, she thought. The bus from the hospital in central Vellore to the medical college, seven kilometers south, passed through Kurisilapattu—where one of India's most secure prisons had been built.

Sure enough, the prisoner and his guards got off when the bus stopped outside the prison entrance. A sandbagged gun emplacement sat in front of its grim looking gate.

Elizabeth shivered. *As if there wasn't enough drama already.* She turned to Ravi sitting beside her. His head was swathed in bandages. "How are you feeling?" she asked.

"Bit better now," he said.

Elizabeth nodded. "How much do you remember?"

"Not much. I woke to discover that my booby-trap had worked well. One guy had been smashed to the floor." Ravi winced as he fingered the edge of his head bandage. "The trouble was, the guy behind him pushed through to where I was and hit me." He shrugged. "I didn't know anything until Jayanti found me and demanded I go to the hospital to get checked out."

Elizabeth was about to reply when she caught sight of a fire burning beside the edge of the road. It was too big to be a cooking fire, and too long. "What's that?" she asked.

Ravi glanced up and looked out the window. "They're getting it ready for a fire-walking festival tonight."

Elizabeth turned to have a better look. "But there's not even a temple there, just shops."

Ravi shrugged.

She shook her head. Even after living in India for three years, the country continued to defy understanding. Being half turned enabled her to steal a glance at Jayanti. She was seated behind her next to Sister Rosalind. Her face was pale.

Elizabeth turned back and said, "I don't know many people who manage a proposal of marriage and a mugging in twenty-four hours."

Ravi managed a smile. "It was still the best twenty-four hours of my life."

The bus stopped at the gates of the medical college, and the four of them disembarked. As they walked past the guardhouse into the college grounds, Sister Rosalind asked. "Ravi, have you still got your banana?"

"My breakfast: no, I ate it before we got onto the bus. Why?"

Elizabeth answered for her. "The monkeys here can be pretty aggressive, particularly when they know you're carrying bananas." She grinned. "We found that out the hard way. So far, they've stolen four bananas and three pieces of washing from us."

She'd designed her comments to help lighten the pall of uncertainty that had descended on them all—but wasn't sure it helped.

Sister Rosalind led them along a colonnade that ran beside the sunken garden toward the college chapel. The chapel's domed roof could be seen from most of the college grounds.

They descended the steps into the garden, walked past the lily pond, and came to the chapel steps.

"I think this is a good place for us to talk," she said.

It was, thought Elizabeth. The peace provided by the garden was in stark contrast with the grim events of the morning. She helped Jayanti ease the rucksack containing all she possessed off her shoulders, and then sat on the steps.

Jayanti smiled her thanks and sat herself beside Ravi. Elizabeth saw her seek out his hand—probably to seek assurance as much as to signify her love.

When they were all settled, Sister Rosalind said, "Ravi, what would be your summary of the situation?"

Ravi drew a deep breath. "Someone, or some organization, wants to kidnap me to pressure my father to give them jewels stolen from the British by my father's great, great grandfather. The fact that they have tracked me to Cochin and Vellore would suggest that they are people who are well financed and have good intelligence. They are also tenacious." He shrugged. "I can't remain in hiding indefinitely, not least because Jayanti and I will be taking our first exam tomorrow—and thereafter—well, you can't hide as a medical student."

The impossibility of Ravi's situation seemed to cast a pall over them all. "I'm so sorry, Ravi," Elizabeth said, "I did try with your father."

Ravi smiled sadly. "I think that showed great courage. More importantly, I think you were on the right track. My father has to be brought to justice."

Elizabeth nodded and wondered how a son must feel to say such a thing about his father.

Sister Rosalind looked up at Ravi. "Why is that, Ravi?"

"Because people have probably been murdered. Because a blind beggar received no justice. Because evil has had its own way too long."

"Not because you are in danger?" she probed gently.

"Not primarily—although my safety is of greater importance now because Jayanti shares my life. Her safety and well-being are vital."

"Bravo, Ravi," said Sister Rosalind.

Elizabeth smiled to herself. She understood that Sister Rosalind's question was not designed to give her an understanding of Ravi's feelings at all, but of his values. Elizabeth cleared her throat. "So, what's the way ahead?"

Ravi lifted his head. "I think we need to push harder with your initiative. Let's force my father into a meeting by sending him the documents we plan to show the police."

Elizabeth frowned. "Your father can be very belligerent and uncooperative, Ravi."

Ravi nodded. "I know. But if we work together, we might be able to persuade him to meet with us so we can make him see reason. I don't, however, think it's wise to meet him at his home. We need to meet at a neutral venue. In fact, I suggest we have the meeting here in Vellore."

"But what would entice him to come?" persisted Elizabeth.

"This time, we'll not only have information ready to give to the police but we'll also have it in a form suitable for the press. Even if the police don't have enough evidence to charge my father and recover the jewels, the press will publicize the story so that it becomes common knowledge and he won't be able to move without scrutiny. He would have no life at all."

Ravi turned to Jayanti and took her hand. "Jayanti, you're brilliant with words; will you help me draft the evidence we have so that it looks convincing?"

Jayanti nodded. "Of course."

Elizabeth was still not convinced. "Won't your father object to traveling on a train for days on end to meet with us?"

"He'll come by plane. He charters them all the time," said Ravi.

"Is there an airfield near here?"

Ravi nodded, then winced in obvious pain. He caught his breath and said, "Vellore has an airstrip at Abdulla Puram, six kilometers east of the city."

Elizabeth glanced at Ravi. "Are you all right?"

"I'm fine." He looked up. "But I think we should get this plan going as soon as possible."

"I agree," said Sister Rosalind. "I'll make some phone calls to Rev. Thomas at St John's. Jayanti and Ravi have an appointment with him this evening to plan their wedding."

"We have?" said Jayanti. She turned to Ravi. "When was this organized?"

Ravi inspected the end of his sandals.

"How long?" insisted Jayanti.

"About two weeks ago," confessed Ravi.

"What! While we were still in Munnar?" Elizabeth saw her stare aghast at Ravi.

He shrugged. "It's easier to cancel an appointment than make one."

"I'm afraid I'm partly to blame," said Sister Rosalind. "Ravi spoke to me of his intention to ask for your hand in marriage: I simply suggested a minister he might approach. I know Rev. Thomas because of his close ties with the hospital. Many of the senior medical staff worship there."

Elizabeth's mind was in a whirl trying to keep up with what was being said.

Jayanti appeared to digest the information for a few moments. Then she lifted her head and said, "You're altogether far too devious, Ravi Panwar." She punched him on the arm.

Ravi rubbed it. "I've been meaning to ask you where you learned to do that."

"Older brother," she said.

Elizabeth drew her veil across her face to hide a smile. Sometimes, they behaved more like brother and sister than lovers.

"Right," said Sister Rosalind getting up. "I'll phone Rev. Thomas to confirm all is well for tonight's meeting." She looked at Ravi and Jayanti. "You never know; he might also be able to suggest some alternative accommodation for you two." She paused. "How much can I share about your situation?"

"As much as will help," said Ravi.

Sister Rosalind nodded. "Meanwhile, I suggest that Ravi works with Jayanti and Sister Elizabeth to draft a convincing case against Mr. Panwar, detailing all the facts we have. We'll try and email it to him tonight."

Elizabeth got to her feet and wondered, fleetingly, if she could have done better at persuading Mr. Panwar in Delhi. Had she done enough?

She sighed. *Too late now*; they were committed to their next initiative. The die was cast.

Chapter 29

Jayanti watched as Ravi drew in the dirt with a stick. They were outside the college gates waiting for the 4:00pm bus into Vellore. He'd sought to hide the bandage on his head with a panama hat. She smiled. It made him look more distinguished and noticeable than ever, but she didn't tell him.

They were engaged. Engaged! It was unbelievable. The thing she'd ached for in her heart, the impossible dream, was realized. The problem was, she couldn't believe it. Her heart had been compressed by denial for so long, that it refused to take the shape of hope. What would it be like to give herself...?

Ravi interrupted her thinking. He'd circled a pair of crosses drawn in the dirt. "Jayanti, how could anyone get the information that I was in Vellore?" He pointed to the circle containing two crosses that he'd drawn in the dirt. "That's us." He then pointed to another ring outside the inner circle. It also had two crosses in it. "That's Sister Rosalind and Sister Elizabeth." He drew a circle outside of that in which he put three other crosses. "That's my father, Aakar Singh, and Rahul." He looked up at her. "Where's the information coming from?"

Jayanti blinked, and sought to reorganize her thinking from the pleasurable place it was taking her. "Um, both of us have been fairly careful, I think. We've told no one other than those you've identified."

Ravi rubbed out his and Jayanti's crosses with his sandal.

Jayanti continued. "I'd trust Sister Rosalind and Elizabeth with my life—and I think it unlikely that they've told anyone who's not on your list."

Ravi erased their crosses. "Which leaves my father, Aakar Singh, and Rahul."

Jayanti asked, "Did you speak to any of your friends in Delhi about your plans to catch the train in Vellore?"

"No, I didn't admit to anyone that I was even trying—largely because I thought my chances of being accepted for training were so slim. He pulled a face. "It seemed easier."

"Would your father have boasted to any in his social set of your aspirations?"

"It's possible, but I've never heard of him speaking to anyone about me. It's not what he…does."

Jayanti saw the flash pain in his eyes. He'd always been stoical about his lack of relationship with his father, but underneath…She took Ravi's hand and lifted it between her breasts, holding it there for a brief moment before easing it away. It was her way of signalling that she would make her love available to him, a love that would more than make up for any deficiency he'd experienced during his childhood. "Which leaves Aakar and Rahul," she said.

Ravi shook his head. "It's not Aakur, at least, not intentionally. He's always been protective of me—too much sometimes. He wouldn't knowingly do anything to…"

At that point a green bus roared toward them and came to a stop in a series of shuddering jerks. Jayanti sighed, picked up her rucksack, and climbed aboard.

They got off the bus in the center of Vellore and walked the short distance to the fort where they had planned to catch up with Sister Rosalind, Elizabeth and Rev. Thomas.

Jayanti had seen the fort often from the bus but had never visited until now. It was impressive.

As they crossed the causeway over the moat, she could see Vellore Fort had two concentric lines of walls. The crenelations on top of the outer wall were shaped liked gravestones. She shuddered. It was probably appropriate. Someone had told her a little of its history—she couldn't remember the details. It had something to do with a rebellion by Sikh soldiers because they thought that pig fat had been used to cover the bullet cartridges they had to bite open. There was a dreadful massacre; the story of an English officer escaping over the wall; of a counter-attack and summary executions —horrible things.

They followed directions to St John's church and walked past playing fields on which a squad of police was practicing some sort of drill. To the right, she could see a *gopuram*, the ornate tower at the entrance of a Hindu temple complex.

St John's church was a beautiful building. Sweeping stone balustrades edged the steps that led up to a pillared portico. The whole building was painted white. Jayanti approved. The architecture did all the speaking that was necessary. No color was necessary. It had a simple elegance.

They climbed the steps, took their shoes off, and walked through into the sanctuary area.

A woman with a cleaning cloth in her hand asked them their business and, on hearing it, conducted them to the vestry. She bowed to them and left them by the door.

The vestry door was half open, and they could hear a man's voice. He was in full flight, recounting some sort of tale. "He was a poor fellow, I can tell you. I'd asked him to preach for ten minutes on the last seven sayings of Jesus, and he, good chap that he was, said 'fine'. He did not know that I meant preaching ten minutes on each of the last seven sayings of Jesus."

Laughter.

"To make matters worse, I'd underestimated what was necessary to fill the three hour Good Friday service, so after his first message, I told him to preach for twenty minutes on each subject."

More laughter.

"So, he'd prepared for ten minutes and ended up having to preach for over two hours."

Ravi knocked on the door.

"Come in."

Ravi pushed the door and held it open for Jayanti.

Sister Rosalind and Sister Elizabeth were seated in a leather settee opposite Rev. Thomas who was sitting in a faded Chesterfield. He was small in stature, balding, and running to fat. Smile lines creased the corner of his eyes.

"Aah, you must be Ravi and Jayanti." Rev. Thomas stood up and held out his hand. "May I congratulate you on your engagement. It's good to meet you at last. Come in."

Jayanti shook his hand and sat in the straight-backed seat offered to her.

The reverend got straight down to business. "I understand, Ravi, that some bad fellows are trying to kidnap you, and that you must hide." He shook his head. "This is a bad business and the police should be informed."

Ravi nodded. "Yes, sir. We plan on giving them all the details after we find a safe place to hide. But Jayanti and I need to take the first of our medical entrance exams tomorrow. So for now, we need to make that a priority."

"Hmm, I suppose you do."

Silence.

The clock on the wall ticked the seconds away, seconds that were gone forever—never to be recovered. *Time,* Jayanti mused, *as precious as it was, offered only one gift, and that was 'opportunity.' What would it offer in the next few minutes?*

Ravi took the initiative. "I understand sir, that you might be able to marry us."

"I might, indeed. But first, let's talk about your accommodation." Rev. Thomas cleared his throat. "There is accommodation available in a building at the back of this church. We use it to house visiting clerics. However, I'm not inclined to give it to an unmarried couple without them being chaperoned—and that is impossible because it only has one bedroom." He looked up at both Ravi and

Jayanti, as if to make sure they understood this was a non-negotiable value.

Jayanti felt a chill of despair grip her heart. She reached across to find Ravi's hand.

"I understand that sir," said Ravi. "We wouldn't like to compromise ourselves or your values."

Rev. Thomas nodded and said nothing for a while. Then he turned to Jayanti. "Jayanti, what do you believe constitutes a legal marriage in the Church of South India?"

She froze.

Ravi gave her hand an encouraging squeeze. It was as well he did. She wanted to scream. She had no idea of where the mercurial Rev. Thomas was going. It was hope she wanted, not questions.

The reverend leaned back, steepled his fingers together, and waited.

She swallowed. "Well, I suppose sir, that it would require proof of identity, proof of voluntary intent, proof that it wasn't a spur-of-the-moment decision, and perhaps, proof of faith—if it were to be a Christian wedding."

"You're right. And which of those factors is missing in your instance?"

She was spared the need to answer because the vicar continued. "I have known for over two weeks of your intent, so your marriage is no sudden thing."

Jayanti tried not to blush.

"You both presumably have proof of identity with you: you'd need it in order to sit your exam."

"We have sir," said Ravi.

"So, what of your Christian faith?"

Jayanti lowered her head. "I am a Christian, sir, but I feel a reluctance to label myself with any particular denomination, at least, at this point."

Rev. Thomas turned to Ravi. "What about you?"

Ravi did not answer immediately. He rubbed his forehead and eventually said, "Authentic Christianity commends itself to me more than anything else, but I could not yet say that I am fully persuaded."

"I approve of your honesty, Ravi. Thank you. I don't often get it." The cleric sat thinking for a moment before he slapped the sides of his chair.

"I think, then, that there is a way out of your dilemma," he said.

Jayanti waited for him to explain.

Ravi didn't wait. "And what is that, sir?"

"Why don't I marry you?"

"Marry us?" said Jayanti, not understanding.

"Yes."

"What? Now?"

"Yes. It shouldn't take long."

Jayanti looked around for moral support, for someone to end this insanity. Sister Rosalind had her eyes closed and was looking very much at peace. Sister Elizabeth was holding her scarf across her face so that only her eyes could be seen. Jayanti waited for someone to object to the madness of what was proposed.

No one did.

Rev. Thomas continued. "I am happy to take care of the official paperwork." He shrugged. "I am available right now; and this…" he waved his hand around him, "is probably the most beautiful church in South India." He nodded toward the nuns. "And Sister Rosalind and Sister Elizabeth can be your witnesses. What do you think?"

This is madness. I've haven't been engaged for twenty-four hours, and now I am to be married. She lifted her head and said. "I would like that very much indeed—and I'm more grateful to you than I can say."

Rev. Thomas turned to Ravi. "Payment will be a generous donation to the organ restoration fund." He sniffed. "You'll also be expected to pay rent for the house."

Ravi smiled. "Yes, sir. Of course."

Sister Rosalind opened her eyes, reached over, and took her hand. "Jayanti, you have no parent to walk you down the aisle. Would you allow me to do that?" She smiled. "You have been a daughter to me for many years."

Jayanti knelt in front of Sister Rosalind and hugged her. Between sobs, she said. "I would love that—more than anything."

Sister Rosalind caressed her hair then bent down to kiss her on the cheek.

When the sobs had quietened, Jayanti reached out to Elizabeth. "Elizabeth, my dear friend, would you be my matron of honor? It couldn't be anyone else."

Elizabeth dropped her scarf to reveal a tear-streaked face. The young nun sniffed and smiled. "Of course."

Ravi stood up and helped lift Jayanti to her feet. He put his arms around her. "Jayanti, I know you have a beautiful sari, I saw it yesterday." His eyes had a twinkle in them. "I think it would make a wonderful wedding dress." He looked into her eyes. "But you may have to wait for me to give you your wedding ring."

Sister Rosalind lifted her chin. "Perhaps not." She undid a clasp on a leather string necklace and removed a gold ring. She held it out. "I carry this ring to remind me that I am a bride of Christ." She smiled. "I know he would love you to have it, and I certainly would."

The ring was a simple design that featured a single stone—a green emerald. Jayanti turned it over on her hand. It would match her sari perfectly. She lifted her head back and laughed: she'd ceased being surprised by anything.

Rev. Thomas rubbed his hands together. "Good. I'll take that as a yes." He walked over to the desk. "Now, let's get the paperwork done. When we've done that, Ravi and Jayanti can disappear to get themselves ready while I look for some new candles for the altar."

Chapter 30

The taxi dropped them off at Poppys Anukula Residency. It was very Western in a modernist minimalist way. Jayanti had no experience of being in such a setting. Ordinarily, she would have lingered so she could observe, exclaim, and wonder. But this was no ordinary occasion.

She was married. *Married.* In the eyes of the law and in the eyes of God, she was married.

Ravi Panwar, will you have this woman, Jayanti Panikkar, to be your wife, and cleave to her alone?

"Yes," he'd shouted.

The taxi ride to the hotel was very short. Ravi sat half sideways, wedged against the car door and the seat looking at her. Occasionally he shook his head, as if to make himself believe.

She reached out to him, wanting to feel him, to know he was there. He was wearing the same embroidered lightweight shirt he'd worn when he'd proposed to her. The dark chest hairs were just as disturbing.

She hugged herself with glee—a feeling that was instantly

followed by a small sense of apprehension. Would she be able to…please him?

Aaargh!

She hated the way that mocking, accusing part of her always sought to sabotage her enjoyment of the present. Jayanti closed her eyes. Through the mists of memory, the words of Sister Rosalind came to her. *Evil will always try to kill what is good. Please don't cooperate with it by giving it a foothold. Take authority, and banish it in Jesus's name.*

"Is everything all right?" asked Ravi.

She smiled. "It is now."

He held the car door open for her.

Jayanti had the impression of a patch of red carpet, cream tiles, a reception desk, hard modern angles, a lift, and an open hotel-room door.

Then it shut.

They were alone. Finally.

Ravi didn't give her a moment to think. He put his hand around her waist. "Jayanti, you are beautiful." He brushed Jayanti's head-scarf back. "You do know that, don't you?"

Jayanti arched her back slightly. She became intensely aware of her own sexuality. Her body was beginning its own dance, a dance as old as time: hardening, lifting, wanting to be seen.

Ravi drew her to himself. In the safety of his love, she lifted her chin and met his gaze. He brought his mouth close to hers, hovered for a moment and then pressed against her moist, partly open lips. Warmth, passion, and a raw hunger mounted within her as she put a hand behind his neck and returned his kiss, feeling him, smelling him, moving with his strength and passion—exploring.

She clutched a fist-full of his hair and tilted her head back so she could receive the trail of kisses from him down her neck.

His hand ran lightly down her side to her waist and back up to cup her breasts.

"Aaah."

Her beautiful sari, once so alluring, was now a hateful impediment. She stepped back from him.

He let her go. Their eyes never left each other.

Take it slow, Jayanti, she told herself.

She untucked the pleated end of the sari, lifted the *pallu* off her left shoulder, and handed it to Ravi.

Very slowly, he pulled it causing her to twirl around as he unwrapped her.

Finally, she was standing before him dressed only in her blouse and petticoat. She felt the need to show him more but she wanted her body to be just right—and for that, she needed a shower.

She glanced at the bed. Two white towels ingeniously folded to be like swans, faced each other nose to nose. They formed a heart-shape between them as they sat on the bed.

She leaned forward and whispered in his ear, "Let me prepare by having a shower." Jayanti nibbled the end of his ear, simply because she could. It was delicious.

Moments later, tepid water was sluicing over her body. She'd left the door to the en-suite open so she could be seen.

She looked up and saw Ravi staring at her from the doorway. He was dressed only in his shirt. She gulped. He looked magnificent.

Ravi walked to the shower cubicle, opened the glass door and stepped inside. He took her head in his hands and said hoarsely, "I seem to remember that I had the best sex ever when we were both wet."

Half an hour later, they had progressed to the bedroom.

An hour after that, Jayanti lay in his arms naked and exhausted. "I suppose it's no use telling you that both of us should be revising for our exams tomorrow?"

Ravi nodded. He rolled over and leaned on one shoulder. Then, reaching forward he kissed her neck. "This is your sternocleidomas-toid; and it's quite fantastic." He moved down lower and began to tease her with the tip of his tongue. "The sensation you are feeling now is mainly facilitated by branches of the fourth, fifth, and sixth intercostal nerves."

Jayanti giggled and reached down. "I wish to explore the func-tionality of your pudendal and cavernous nerves."

Ravi gave a small gasp. "Very good," he said. "You are an excel-lent student."

Jayanti looked at what remained of the two white swans on their bed. Both were severely mangled.

Ravi had insisted that they drink plenty of water and eat generous amounts of low GI carbohydrates at breakfast. "Our brains will need a lot of fuel today," he said. We've got over three hours of exams."

"Yes doctor," she replied.

Ravi settled the hotel account and they were starting to pack their rucksack when she said, "Ravi, have you considered that CMC may not allow two of its students to get married while they are studying. They may not even have provisions for married couples. Should we keep our marriage secret, at least until we know the results and can make some inquiries?"

Ravi took her by the shoulders. "I want everyone to know I've married the most beautiful, the most intelligent, the most..." She ended the conversation by kissing him. Jayanti leaned back in his arms and tidied a lock of Ravi's hair. She grinned. "What I'll do is wear Rohit's Peacock Stone as my *mangalsutra*, my wedding necklace. What do you think?"

"Brilliant. Every time I look at it you'll know I'm having lascivious thoughts."

She punched his arm, then began to rummage in the side pocket of the rucksack.

"Here it is," she said, turning around. "You may put it on me."

He did, but it didn't stop there—and they had to scramble to get their rucksack packed when the hotel rang through to tell them that their taxi had arrived.

Jayanti looked at the other applicants milling around waiting to do the exam. There was a curious dynamic among them. They wanted to be friendly but knew they were in competition with each other.

There were perfunctory nods and nervous smiles, but most kept to themselves.

Jayanti smiled at everyone. She wanted to tell them that she'd just got married, to show them Ravi, to hang on his arm, and laugh with delight.

Eventually, the students were led into a hall and given a rather stern lecture about the process of the day. Then they were given their exam papers.

This was it. This was the moment that Ravi had worked toward for so long. She said a silent prayer that Ravi would do justice to all his hard work. Then, drawing a deep breath, she opened the first page of her exam paper.

The first exam was the longest. It was a two-hour multiple-choice paper on biology, physics, and chemistry.

Time flew.

The exam invigilator eventually called time, and all the papers were collected. Some students had their heads on their hands; others fiddled with their pens, and none of them spoke. As they trooped outside for morning tea, some students got together in small groups. Jayanti could hear some nervous laughter.

She and Ravi found each other. "How was it?" she asked.

Ravi held her by the waist and looked around. "You know I want to kiss you, don't you?"

She shook his arm. "How was it?" she hissed.

"Not too bad. What about you?"

"Okay, I think."

In no time at all, they were back inside the exam hall.

The unsmiling invigilator again gave them their instructions. "You have before you a paper which examines your general knowledge. The exam will last seventy minutes: and your time begins now."

Jayanti turned over her exam paper and set to work.

She was about half way through when the door of the hall opened behind her. As she was seated near the back, she turned around and was able to see two policemen before the door swung shut and obscured them from sight. The man who had come in walked to the front and whispered to the invigilator. There was a brief discussion, and they inspected a piece of paper. Both of them then walked down the hall between two rows of desks and stopped where Ravi was sitting.

With horror, she saw one of the men tap Ravi on the shoulder and beckon him to follow him. *What on earth...?*

Ravi got up without demur and followed the man toward the entrance of the hall behind her. A few students looked at Ravi, feeling his shame. He'd obviously done something wrong—probably cheated.

Jayanti sat back in shock.

As Ravi passed her desk, he said quietly, "Finish well. That's your priority."

"No talking!" said the man escorting him. "Come." He held the door open for Ravi.

Jayanti could again see the two policemen standing outside.

Ravi picked up his mobile phone from the table beside the door, fiddled with it, and walked to the open door. There, he paused and spoke to the man holding the door open. Then, he whipped up the phone, took a photograph, gave the phone to the startled man holding the door, and ran.

There was an angry yell from a policeman, and the door closed.

The invigilator at the front called out. "Please attend to your exam and ignore the disturbance."

Jayanti wanted to run after Ravi, to find out what was happening. She wanted to fight for him; to plead. She pinched the top of her nose. This was disastrous. Ravi could not pass the exam if he had only done half of it. She closed her eyes in anguish. *No, no, no!*

As she tried to calm herself, his words came back to her. "Finish well. That's your priority."

She brushed away a tear and returned her attention to the exam, determined to honor Ravi's instruction by doing her very best.

Just before the exam ended, the man who had escorted Ravi from the hall came back and stood beside the invigilator at the front of the hall.

"You have two minutes to finish the exam. Please ensure that your name and number is printed clearly at the top of your exam paper."

Where was Ravi?

Jayanti finished her exam and sat back, mentally and emotionally exhausted.

She was completely unprepared to hear the invigilator's next instructions. "Pens down. Will Miss Jayanti Panikkar please come to the front. All other students may leave the hall."

Jayanti stayed where she was as students filed past her. When most of them had gone, she got up and walked up to the two men standing at the front.

"Miss Panikkar?" said one of them.

"Yes."

"Please follow me."

"Where are we going?"

"To see the college principal."

This is a nightmare. She put a hand on the invigilator's desk to steady herself.

"Are you all right?" asked the man.

"Yes."

"Then come with me, please."

Five minutes later, she was ushered into a large office.

The first person she saw was Ravi.

She rushed over to where he was seated and flung her arms around his neck. "Are you all right?" she asked.

"I see you two know each other." This dry remark came from a man in a dark suit seated on the other side of a large desk.

"Oh," said, Jayanti. "Yes sir. We are…er, good friends. Is Ravi in some sort of trouble, sir? I can vouch for him…"

The man behind the desk put his hands up. "Please be seated Miss Panikkar."

Jayanti sat down.

"My name is Dr. Chandra. I am the principal of the college." He leaned back in his chair. "Mr. Panwar has told me that he may have just escaped an attempt to kidnap him."

"Yes sir. That is very possible. There was another attempt to kidnap him just a few days ago. Sister Rosalind of the Missionaries of Charity knows about it."

Dr. Chandra held up his hand again to forestall her torrent of words. "So you can vouch for the truth of his story?"

"Oh yes, sir. Ravi and I were staying out of town in the same village when the other kidnap attempt was made."

The man who escorted Jayanti to the principal's office spoke up. "The policemen said that they had come to arrest Mr. Panwar for a serious traffic offense committed this morning."

Jayanti couldn't contain herself. "But that's not true. Ravi and I were together and we came to the college by taxi. He wasn't driving anything…"

"Please, Miss Panikkar…"

Jayanti kept quiet.

Dr. Chandra lent forward and picked up Ravi's phone from the desk. "Clever of you to take a photo of the two policemen, Mr. Panwar." He weighed the phone in his hand and then picked up the receiver of the phone on his desk. "Put me through to Chief Inspector Bhati, please."

There was a long wait.

The ceiling fan turned above them: *whump, whump, whump.*

"Aah, Chief Inspector, how are you?…Good, good…Chief, I've had some trouble at the college from two men who may be your boys…They are either your boys, or they are dressing up as your boys. I've a photo of them that I'll email you, and you can tell me… The thing is: if they are your men, then they may have been bribed to kidnap one of our student applicants…Yes, Inspector…No, this is a second attempt…There are some bad fellows trying to get at his father's money…If they are yours, and it follows usual form, they will deny it, of course, and plead a case of mistaken identity. So, will you squeeze them hard, Inspector?…Yes…Quite so…I'll send it through now."

Dr. Chandra hung up, then leaned forward to pass Ravi his smartphone. "Mr. Panwar, give this to my secretary and work with her to forward your photo to the Chief Inspector."

"Yes sir. And thank you," said Ravi.

As Ravi closed the door behind him, Jayanti found herself speaking before she could stop herself. "Dr. Chandra, Ravi and I were educated together. He is a brilliant student and very much wants to be a doctor. I've seen him perform an emergency tracheotomy using nothing but a knife and pen. Can he please be allowed to sit the general knowledge exam again, perhaps this afternoon?"

Dr. Chandra looked severe. He folded his hands together and began tapping his thumbs together. "No, I'm afraid that won't be possible. We have a policy of not allowing re-sits under any circumstances. It's become necessary because students are always pleading extenuating circumstances."

"But please, sir…"

Dr. Chandra held up his hand.

Jayanti stopped talking.

Whump, whump, whump.

The doctor sighed. "I'm going to think about this for a day. Can you and Mr. Panwar come back and see me at 10am tomorrow?"

She nodded.

The principal continued. "In the meantime, I think it important that Mr. Panwar keep a low profile."

The principal's thumbs did some more tapping.

"I'll organize for you both to spend the rest of the day with our mobile clinic." Dr. Chandra looked at his watch. "If you hurry, you'll catch them out the front. It's a big white van." He reached for the phone. "I think you'll find that Sister Rosalind is also going along today."

Chapter 31

It seemed incongruous to Jayanti that a Christian medical van should pull up at a Hindu temple to run a clinic. The medical team had set up under the portico in front of the temple, in a space that evidently served as the village community hall. The nurses had set up stools beside a card table for the doctors and were now gathering the women of the village together for a lecture on postnatal care.

Jayanti loved the nurses. They seemed to exude cheerfulness wherever they went. Their uniform consisted of a white blouse and a sky-blue sari. She thought it a terrific blend of the medical and the distinctively Indian.

She was less sure of the young doctor. He was an intern. Jayanti watched him loop a stethoscope around his shoulders and open his sphygmomanometer case. He was soon taking the blood pressure of an old man sitting in front of him. The elderly man sat still on his stool, not daring to say anything.

She and Sister Rosalind had been detailed to help the young doctor in any way they could. The second doctor was being assisted by Ravi. He was none other than the man who had been with them in the principal's office. His name, she'd learned, was Jacobs.

When the old man being examined had left, Sister Rosalind leaned forward and whispered, "Doctor, may I have a quick word with you—perhaps in the van?"

The young doctor frowned. "I suppose so," he said.

The two of them climbed up into the back of the van.

Jayanti stood outside it, winding up a crepe bandage. She discovered that the privacy afforded by the van was probably not as good as Sister Rosalind had anticipated. Jayanti was able to hear a good deal of the conversation.

"...you will make a fine doctor, but may I make a suggestion that will help you?"

"Of course."

"The old man who sat in front of you just now: what was he thinking?"

"I...I don't know."

"From his facial expression. What was he saying?"

"He was respectful, perhaps a little intimidated."

"You are right. What did you want him to think of you?"

"I'm not sure..."

"Think."

"I wanted him to respect me."

"You were successful. Now tell me: what would Jesus want him to feel?"

There was a pause. "I...well...love, I suppose."

"Exactly, Daniel. You are the human face of Jesus now. So, will you lose your scowl and air of impatience so that others can see the love of Jesus?"

Jayanti made sure she was well away from the van when Sister Rosalind and the doctor returned.

The afternoon continued. Despite the dramas of the morning, Jayanti enjoyed what she was doing, although she felt frustrated at being able to do little more than help elderly people be seated and occasionally roll up a bandage for the doctor.

She glanced across at Ravi. He seemed to be absorbed in his work.

The portico was full of people wanting medical attention. They were crowded together, many leaning against the white posts of the portico. One elderly man, dressed in rags, sat by himself waiting to see Jacobs. No one went near him.

Eventually, it was the old man's turn to see the doctor. Jayanti watched as Jacobs unwrapped a long rag from the man's foot. She wished she could see what was happening. A few minutes later, she saw Ravi put on some latex gloves and begin bandaging the foot. When Ravi finished, he helped the old man to his feet, put an arm around his shoulders and give him a hug of encouragement.

Jayanti wished that she too might be allowed to do something more practical, like bandaging, as well.

It was quite late by the time they arrived back at the hospital in Vellore. The van had stopped by the college to drop off the young doctor and Sister Rosalind.

"What now?" asked Jayanti. "I'm tired, I'm starving, and I'm concerned for you."

Ravi took her hand and steered her past the long lines of motorbikes parked beside the hospital. There were hundreds of them. *How does anyone even find their bike, far less, get it out to ride it?* He led her across the road and into the first café they saw.

The smell inside was delicious. A man was taking fist-size balls of naan dough, rolling them flat, and slapping them on the inside wall of a clay tandoor oven. Jayanti peeked inside and saw the charcoal fire in its bottom. The man smiled at her but shooed her away so he could lower a wooden stick with a wire hook at its end. A second later, it emerged with a cooked piece of naan on its end.

They ordered some dahl and shared four pieces of garlic and coriander naan together.

As the tension of the day started to ease, Jayanti felt the cloying hands of despondency begin to grip her heart. She reached across to Ravi. "What are you going to do if they won't allow you to re-sit?"

Ravi took her hand and sandwiched it between his own. "I thought you were a woman of faith."

"Be serious," she said irritably. "What happened to you today was brutally unfair."

"I am serious," he said. "And I'm serious now about the need for us to do some shopping…" he squeezed her hand, "before we head over to the Fort and our new home.

"Of course," said Jayanti," slapping her forehead. "I'd quite forgotten. We need supplies for meals and…"

"Let's just get the bare essentials tonight. We'll do a big shop tomorrow." Ravi took a deep breath. "Now, let's see: what do we need?"

"Sheets," she said.

Jayanti gave Ravi's hand a small squeeze before letting it go.

Ravi knocked on the door.

"Come in."

Taking a deep breath, Ravi opened the door.

Chandra, principal of the college, was seated behind his desk. Jacobs, the senior doctor on yesterday's mobile clinic was seated to one side.

Ravi and Jayanti stood side by side in front of the desk. They were not offered a seat.

The principal leaned back, twisted sideways, and crossed his legs. Without preamble, he said, "Mr. Panwar, what do you know about leprosy?"

Jayanti saw the look of shock on Ravi's face. She reached for his hand.

Ravi swallowed. "Aah…leprosy has historically been a devastating disease for which there was no cure. Those who contracted it were socially stigmatized. It has been one of the most feared diseases of history." He paused.

"Go on."

"The bacillus causing the disease is actually a very weak pathogen which requires perfect conditions in order to survive. It only finds those conditions in humans and, for some reason, in the nine-banded armadillo that lives on the American continent."

"Did you know that the old man whose foot you bandaged yesterday had leprosy?"

Jayanti gave a small gasp.

"Yes sir," said Ravi. Jacobs told me."

"Yet you bandaged his foot."

Ravi said nothing.

"And I understand you gave him a hug."

The fan did its thing: *whump, whump, whump.*

Chandra leaned forward. "Why did you hug him, knowing he had leprosy?"

Jayanti was aware that her mouth was open. She closed it.

"He was lonely sir; starved of human contact." Ravi shrugged. "It was my way of showing he wasn't alone."

"The government says that leprosy has been eradicated in India," said Chandra. "But then again, they also say there is no longer any corruption in government." He sighed. "It may interest you to know that Jacobs has organized for the man…"

Ravi interrupted. "His name is Padmadhar, sir."

Chandra nodded, "Jacobs has organized for Padmadhar to go to Karigiri, our leprosy Hospital. It's about fourteen kilometers away."

"That's good, sir."

"Hmm." Chandra waved Ravi and Jayanti away. "You can go, now. The college will be in touch."

It was too much for Jayanti. "But please sir, what about Ravi. Can he re-sit his exam?"

"No he can not."

"But…"

The doctor held his hand up to forestall a further outburst from her. "However, he will be marked on the basis of the questions he was able to complete. Those he wasn't able to complete will not be counted against him."

Jayanti couldn't restrain herself; she flung herself at Ravi and gave him a hug.

Chandra leaned back and tapped the end of a pen on his desk. "Mr. Panwar, you can think yourself fortunate that you have such a ferocious advocate."

Ravi nodded. "I know sir. I'm very lucky."

The doctor continued. "But never doubt, Mr. Panwar; you have earned the right to continue being assessed by this college for training. If you had not hugged the beggar with leprosy, it would not be happening."

———

Rahul hated the dust of Vellore. He could only breathe through one nostril and knew he was inhaling too much of it. He pulled the tail of his headscarf across his face and continued his vigil outside the main gates of the hospital.

He'd actually gone inside the front entrance of the hospital earlier in the day as the workers had been streaming in and was surprised to discover that the foyer opened up directly into a chapel. The architect had put a large chapel at the very heart of the hospital. *Such a waste of space.*

He was back outside now, squatting against the wall, trying to make use of what little shade it afforded. His nose was broken. He knew it was. By rights, he should be in the hospital getting it attended to. As it was, Mr. Nāgá, the cobra, had given him a million reasons to delay.

He sighed. If there was one thing life had taught him: it was patience.

He contrived to look like a cycle-rickshaw wallah. There was a line of rickshaws in front of him. A driver was fast asleep on the passenger seat of one of them.

Rahul blew his nose with his left hand and flicked the phlegm onto the footpath.

A beggar was lying on his back, crabbing his way down the same footpath ringing a small bell. His leg had been amputated just below the knee. A begging bowl sat on his chest.

Rahul shook his head in distaste. Some beggars worked hard for their money.

He ignored the penetrating look of the beggar, sat back, and watched the comings and goings of the hospital.

And then, suddenly, there she was, with Ravi Panwar.

Rahul swallowed. She was looking fabulous—and she was holding Ravi's hand in a manner that suggested more than friendship.

Bloody jumped up rich kid.

He got to his feet and began tailing them down Gandhi Road, past shopkeepers threading flowers onto strings to make garlands. Some of them called after Jayanti. One of the men gyrated his pelvis after she'd passed.

Bastard.

Jayanti stopped just once to buy flowers.

Rahul knew why. She'd thread them into the plaits of her hair. He loved her hair—the way it swayed. It was so long.

The couple turned right down Main Bazaar Road and, not surprisingly, headed into the bazaar.

Rahul followed them, making his way through the narrow laneways, past shops selling spices, plastic bins, granite pestle and mortars, tin ware—everything you could imagine. It may have been his mood but the filth, newspapers, and rotting vegetation in the laneways were even worse than he'd seen in Delhi. Scraps of dirty canvas and hessian had been rigged overhead to keep most of the shops in shade; or perhaps it was to keep the filth underneath from being too obvious to the shoppers.

Ravi and Jayanti seemed to be shopping for everything: food, mosquito netting, laundry materials—all the requirements of home.

Rahul grunted. The whereabouts of that home was what he needed to discover.

The couple appeared to be in no rush and seemed to be enjoying themselves.

Rahul tried to keep himself from glowering as he made a pretense at shopping.

Eventually, Ravi and Jayanti emerged back on to Main Bazaar Road. They loaded all their shopping onto a cycle-rickshaw and headed off with the flow of the traffic.

Rahul followed in another rickshaw.

It was a surprise to Rahul to see the rickshaw ahead of him

continue west at the end of the road and cross the causeway into Vellore Fort. He began to pay more attention to the surroundings. Rahul noticed the presence of police and the fact that the causeway represented the only way in and out of the fort.

He nodded in admiration. Jayanti and Ravi had picked a good place to hide—but nonetheless, he had found them.

Twenty minutes later, he made a phone call.

"Mr. Nāgá, I have found Ravi Panwar. When can you fly down here?"

Chapter 32

J ayanti brushed away a persistent mosquito. "Mr. Panwar definitely said he was coming?"

"Yes," said Sister Rosalind.

Ravi came out of the house carrying two more chairs. He set them up on the patio area under the trees where they were seated.

"I wonder why he rang you and not Ravi?"

"There's no mystery there. I rang Mr. Panwar with some more information I remembered hearing from Rohit." Sister Rosalind smiled, "Just to add a bit more weight to Ravi's request for a meeting."

The imposing bulk of St John's church, just fifteen meters away, was silhouetted against the last of the twilight. Only a small shaft of light from the window of their house reached the patio.

Jayanti glanced back at her home. Setting it up in the last two days had been a joy. She'd put jars of flowers wherever she could and swept and cleaned the three small rooms until they were spotless. She and Ravi had enjoyed putting their stamp of ownership on the tiny house. Its main feature was its garden, a private space covered with sparse grass behind the church. The trees growing around its edge offered welcome shade during the day. But now, as twilight gave way to night, they began to look forbidding.

Jayanti reached for the soapstone pendant, the Peacock Stone, around her neck. It was heavy but its smoothness seemed to caress her skin and offer comfort. She liked the fact it was heavy: it made her aware she was wearing it. And wearing it reminded her she was married.

Ravi's phone rang.

He answered it, spoke briefly, and then got to his feet. "My father has just parked in front of St John's. I'll go and get him." He squared his shoulders. "Are you up for this?"

Sister Rosalind folded her scarf in front of her face. "Yes, Ravi."

Jayanti looked at her, seeking comfort. "I'm frightened," she said.

Sister Rosalind nodded.

It wasn't much solace.

Ravi returned a few minutes later out of the blackness followed closely by his father, Gokul Panwar, and the giant Sikh, Aakar Singh.

Jayanti and Sister Rosalind got to their feet.

No one said anything. Everyone stood still.

"Would you like to sit down?" said Ravi as he walked over to stand beside Jayanti.

Mr. Panwar ignored him. He did, however, walk forward to Sister Rosalind and move her scarf away from her face. Jayanti could see his eyes glitter.

"So it is you," he said, sneering. "I might have known."

Aakar Singh stood a few paces back. His right hand was tucked under the front fold of his jacket.

Ravi cleared his throat. "Father, you know the information we've got about the jewels you inherited from your great, great grandfather. We know about the three jewel cutters from Jaipur you hired—and the two who disappeared, doubtless murdered by you." Ravi gestured toward Sister Rosalind. "We have the testimony of the third jewel cutter whom Sister Rosalind and Jayanti have been close to over the last few years."

Jayanti felt a chill run through her.

Ravi sighed. "Father; it is time for this madness to stop. Too many people have been hurt. If you give the remainder of the jewels to charity and make reparation to the families of the jewel cutters, we will not go to the police. If you do not, we will." He shrugged. "We have placed copies of this information in safe places where it can be accessed, even if we are not present." He turned to Aakar. "So you can take your hand off your pistol, Aakar."

The Sikh did not move.

"So you plan to throw away my life along with your own," said Panwar.

"I don't think I'd call your way of living a life," said Ravi. "It's a meaningless existence built on the grief of others."

Ravi's father scoffed. "And what do you know about life? You're a fool who's never had to face its realities."

"I'm a married man who is a candidate applying for medical college." Ravi looked at his father levelly. "I'm no fool. In fact, since I've left you, I have discovered life."

Jayanti reached for Ravi's hand.

"What?" Mr. Panwar appeared incredulous. He pointed at Jayanti. "To that bitch: to the laundry maid?"

"Be very careful, Father. Jayanti is my wife, and she is also applying to study medicine. She is the finest woman I know."

Mr. Panwar snorted. Then, he bent over, put his hands on his knees, and began to laugh.

Jayanti felt his derision, but was untouched by it. She glanced at Ravi. He looked grim.

When she looked back at Mr. Panwar, he was holding a gun in his hand. It had a silencer attached. His laughter had been a ruse.

Somewhere in the distance, a night owl screeched.

For a moment, no one said anything.

"Use the bitch for sex. Why not, she's pretty enough, but marriage..." Panwar shook his head. "That is out of the question. That would bring me shame." He aimed the gun at Jayanti.

Ravi stepped in front of her and stared at his father.

Jayanti tightened her grip on Ravi's hand.

This was now an appalling game of brinkmanship.

Aakar Singh removed his hand from the flaps of his coat. Sure enough, he held a gun. No silencer.

Panwar did not change his aim. "I've never known quite what to do with you, Ravi. At times, you've been a nuisance. But now that you've married some servant slut and are threatening to expose me to the police, you've become a threat."

"Put the gun down, father," said Ravi.

Mr. Panwar shook his head. "No, I don't think so."

Jayanti watched in horror as Mr. Panwar moved the gun and aimed it at Sister Rosalind.

"One way or another, Ravi, I'll kill these two bitches. Whether you die with them is up to you. You have three seconds to decide."

"Gokul, put the gun down. This is not good for anyone, least of all, yourself." Sister Rosalind's voice, amazingly, was perfectly calm.

Mr. Panwar straightened his arm, "Two…"

There was a faint rustle—and then a voice, a silky voice that Jayanti had never heard before, said, "No one move."

She glanced around, bewildered.

Shadows moved in different parts of the garden.

The silky voice continued. "Stay quite still. Can you imagine what a twenty gram bullet will do if it hits your belly at two-thousand feet per second?"

The black balaclava made Rahul's face itch. He didn't like it. But Mr. Nágá had insisted. All four of them were hooded, Mr. Nágá, Walker, Kumar, and himself.

They had been in the garden for some minutes listening to the drama playing out before them.

Rahul had been deeply disturbed. He looked at Jayanti, wanting to reach out to her. Seeing her beauty and her courage was disturbing. The light from the house highlighted the profile of her face, the face that had once laughed with him, scolded him, and taught him.

He was conscious of an ache deep within him, a very disturbing ache.

The balaclava was making him sweat. Even his trigger finger felt wet. His gun had been aimed at Mr. Panwar's head. The trigger had been depressed past its first stage of resistance and hovered over the hair-trigger second stage—the merest flinch from dispensing death. Mr. Panwar was very lucky to be alive. Rahul gritted his teeth. No one would ever threaten Jayanti as long as he lived.

Had he heard rightly? Jayanti was married. *Married!* Rahul clenched his fist and held it against his solar plexus. His mind was in turmoil. What had he hoped? He'd planned nothing. He shook his head. Jayanti had always been there, but out of reach: too perfect to attain.

Bile churned within him.

Mr. Nāgá's voice cut through the silence. It was a voice that was soft but had the steel of authority. It was a frightening voice—and Rahul didn't frighten easily. "Let's play a game," Mr. Nāgá said.

Rahul checked his line of fire and where everyone was standing. Kumar was behind him on his flank, just where he'd expect him to be. He was the only one without a gun. Walker was behind the Sikh. He had his gun aimed at the back of the giant in front of him.

Mr. Nāgá continued. "You may keep your gun aimed, Mr. Panwar. I may require you to kill those in front of you." Mr. Nāgá moved forward and stepped into the light. He was holding an old fashioned Luger pistol with the ease of someone who was very familiar with it. Mr Nāgá aimed his gun at Ravi's Father.

Rahul saw Mr. Panwar begin to lower his gun.

"Don't move," Mr. Nāgá's voice was like a whip.

Mr. Panwar froze.

"Well, this is interesting; very interesting." The silky voice continued. "I came here tonight to snatch Ravi Panwar, but it appears that would have been foolish." He gave a soft laugh. "It seems that the father has no great regard for his son, and would not offer up his wealth to get him back. It was fortunate, indeed, to learn that."

"Who are you?" said Ravi, stiffly.

"That is no business of yours. And you should be grateful, for the instant you learn it, I shall kill you. But for convenience, you can call me Mr. Nāgá."

Jayanti whispered, "The cobra."

"Yes."

"And who are you?"

There was a small pause before Jayanti said quietly. "I am the mongoose."

Mr. Nāgá laughed. "Very good. I like your spirit." He shook his head. "It will get you killed, but I like your spirit." The muzzle of the Luger swept around. "It seems as if all of you, except Mr. Panwar, are surplus to my requirements. I will need to take him, of course, to persuade him to contribute his fortunes…to a more worthy cause." He smiled.

Rahul wasn't sure he liked the direction things were going.

Mr. Nāgá continued. "But to convince him to co-operate, I will need to kill someone. The question is: who should it be?"

Mr. Nāgá appeared to be enjoying himself.

Rahul was not. He looked at Jayanti and saw fire smoldering in her eyes. Rahul shook his head. Jayanti never knew when to be afraid and run. She was clueless. Even now she was trying to edge around Ravi so she could protect him.

But Ravi held her back.

She responded by stepping back and then moving two steps to the side. "Then shoot me," she said. "Don't hurt Ravi or Sister Rosalind."

Mr. Nāgá shook his head. The muzzle of the Luger lowered so that it was pointed to Mr. Panwar's knees. "Panwar, I will shoot you in the knee and cripple you for life if you do not kill your son. Is that clear?"

Rahul was horrified. In a fleeting second, he knew what he had to do. He had to protect Ravi, for there was no doubt that Jayanti had lost her heart to him. Protecting him would be the greatest gift he could ever give her. He anguished for a moment at the irony of life. Then, tucking the pistol behind his back, he walked into the circle of light.

"Now, now," he said. "Let's cool things down a bit. I think there's a better solution." He stopped in front of Ravi, blocking Mr. Nāgá's view of him—and put his hands on hips. As he did, he lifted the back of his shirt, exposing the Glock tucked into his waistband.

Take it, you bastard, take it.

He felt a tug.

Good.

Rahul continued to speak. "I think we only need to take Mr. Panwar."

Jayanti took a step toward him. "Rahul: it's you. I recognize your voice. What are you doing?"

Without turning around, Rahul said, "I'm sorry, Jayanti."

Mr. Nāgá's voice cut across her. "I will not tell you again, Panwar."

Ravi's father lifted his pistol and trained on his son—he had a clear line of sight. His trigger finger flinched.

Rahul dived in front of Ravi.

Panwar's gun fired.

Rahul spun around from the punch in his chest.

Another shot was fired.

Rahul saw a gun in the Sikh's hand, and Mr. Panwar falling to the ground.

Almost simultaneously, Ravi fired twice. Tap tap on the trigger. *Very professional.*

Light-headed.

He had the impression of Mr. Nāgá falling.

Walker was already on the ground. Why? Kumar was standing over him with a short piece of hosepipe in his hand.

The Sikh swung the gun toward Kumar.

"Friend," yelled Kumar, holding his hands up to signify submission.

The Sikh moved the muzzle of his gun and shot Mr. Walker twice.

It was an execution. *Good.*

And then the pain hit.

"Aargh," Rahul grunted. He tried to scream but found he

couldn't breathe properly. He moved his hand to his chest. It was wet. Then the searing pain hit. He gasped, staggered, and fell to the ground. Rahul writhed for a moment begging for oblivion, but also wanting to stay its hand. He had to check: had to see. Rahul arched his head back, the tendons standing out like steel rods—desperately looking…and then he saw:

Jayanti was still alive.

———

"Ravi!" screamed Jayanti.

"I'm all right," he yelled.

Jayanti then spun around and dropped to her knees beside Rahul. "Rahul…" she ripped open his shirt and saw the oozing blood. Immediately, she took her scarf, bunched it up, and pressed it against the wound.

Rahul's face was in a rictus of agony.

"Rahul, Rahul. It's okay. We'll get help." She pushed down on the padding. "Why? Why?" she yelled at him.

Rahul coughed. "Scolding again," he said weakly. He tried to smile.

Sister Rosalind knelt on the other side of Rahul, bent over to remove his mask, and cradled his head.

Rahul tried to smile at her. "The gods don't like me."

"One of them does."

"Which one?"

"The one who came to earth to rescue you back to himself."

Rahul coughed. "Why would he do that?"

"So you could be with him."

Sister Rosalind wiped the sweat from Rahul's forehead with the end of her scarf.

Rahul arched his back in another spasm of pain. Then he relaxed. "I would like to meet such a God," he wheezed.

"Then tell him so."

Rahul coughed again, and spluttered, "Hello…God."

"Rahul, don't you dare die," said Jayanti, shaking his arm.

Rahul looked at her weakly. "I…I…"

Jayanti bent over so she could hear.

"…love…," he whispered.

"What?" she said, frowning.

He closed his eyes and smiled tiredly. "Clueless."

Jayanti watched in horror as Rahul's life slipped away.

"The police are on their way," said Ravi.

Jayanti managed a small nod as she curled herself up and leaned against his chest. She desperately wanted to feel his love and security in a violent world of death and grief.

Ravi stroked her hair.

"It's over, Jayanti. It's all over. We'll be okay." He rocked her gently against himself.

Jayanti sobbed. "Rahul. Rahul…Why?" His loss was more than she could bear. He'd been a brother to her. Yes, he'd teased; but he'd always cared for her. She moaned like a stricken child.

"Kumar, can you rustle up some hot sweet tea for us?" Ravi pointed to the house. You'll see it all on the kitchen bench.

Kumar had been hanging back, as if not daring to come near. On hearing Ravi's words, he stepped forward and squatted down beside the body of his friend. It was as if Ravi's words had given him permission. Kumar put a hand on Rahul's feet, then he rocked forward and kissed them.

Sister Rosalind put a hand on his shoulder.

"I'm sorry, Kumar," she said.

Kumar sniffed.

Sister Rosalind continued. "Kumar, Rahul had a woman…"

Kumar nodded. Tears rolled down his cheeks. He wiped his nose and said, "Durgamma will become my woman."

He said it simply—as a fact.

"Thank you, Kumar." Sister Rosalind squeezed his shoulder. "You stay here. I'll get some tea for us all."

Aakar Singh had been standing in the background with his arms folded. As Sister Rosalind left for the house, he came forward and picked up Rahul's mask. He then held out his hand to Kumar. "Give me your mask," he growled.

Kumar did so.

The giant nodded his thanks, turned, and followed Sister Rosalind into the house.

Jayanti didn't understand. "What...?"

Ravi hugged her and kissed her forehead. "I suspect he is going to burn them."

"But I don't understand. Why? Your father...?"

"Aakar would never hurt me," he replied.

Jayanti wasn't sure she understood much more.

Some minutes later, they were seated in the patio chairs drinking tea.

A gentle evening breeze began to stir the leaves above them.

It seemed surreal to Jayanti. Four dead bodies lay on the grass just meters away. Each was covered with a sheet.

The sheets were new. She would need to buy more.

Stupid thoughts. *Stupid, stupid, stupid.*

She turned to Ravi. "Ravi, I'm so sorry about your father. I'm sure he didn't mean what he said and that he was actually very proud..." her voice faltered. She knew it was a lie, but she didn't know what else to say.

Ravi nodded, acknowledging her attempt. He put his head in his hands and massaged his temples. "I suppose that I am technically an orphan now."

No one said anything.

A zephyr of wind set the smallest branches into motion.

Sister Rosalind broke the silence. "My dear Ravi," she said. "That is not quite true." She reached out a hand toward him. "I'm afraid there's no easy way to say this." She cleared her throat.

What on earth....?

With a clear voice, Sister Rosalind said, "I am your mother, Ravi."

The leaves whispered the scandal they had just overheard. *Sphshh, sphshh.*

Jayanti felt her mind spinning. Nothing made sense.

"I beg your pardon?" said Ravi, formally.

"I am your mother, Ravi." Sister Rosalind tried to smile, but her lip began to tremble.

Jayanti had never before seen Sister Rosalind anything but composed.

"Please forgive me, Ravi. I never wanted to leave you."

She put a hand over her mouth as if the telling of her story was an affront to everyone, particularly to herself.

"You were just nine months old when your father brutalized me particularly savagely. At that time, I desperately wanted to leave the marriage because I feared for your safety as well as mine. I was also very uneasy about what might be going on in the cellar of the house." She shrugged. "Your father was very secretive about it and used to beat me when I inquired about it. He told me to mind my own business."

Jayanti was beginning to recover from the shock of what she'd heard. She reached out toward the sister. "How on earth did you come to be married to such a man?"

Sister Rosalind smiled sadly. "I married quite young. It was an arranged marriage organized by my parents. He'd seen me when I was a young Kodambakkam film actress in Chennai." She shrugged. "My parents were beguiled by his wealth."

"What happened when I was nine months old?" asked Ravi.

"I tried to run away with you but your father caught me and took you from me. He said you could have no life without him. He would ensure that was the case. Then he banished me from the home."

"And so you left me, just like that." Jayanti could hear the bitterness in his voice.

Sister Rosalind shook her head. "No, I never left you."

"You did. I never saw you."

"I never left you, Ravi. I left my good friend Aakar Singh behind to protect you. He came with me as my servant from my parent's home."

The giant Sikh was standing behind her chair, looking stolid and immovable.

She continued. "I was with you in every gesture of care he gave you. Aakar used to report to me each fortnight. Sometimes we'd meet in the city to discuss how you were going."

Ravi looked up at the Sikh.

Aakar nodded. "Memsahib has been a good mother to you, Ravi."

Sister Rosalind continued, "It was Aakar who voiced his concerns over the two missing gem cutters. That's why we conspired together to help Rohit escape."

Jayanti gasped. "It was you…?"

Sister Rosalind nodded.

"But you left me," said Ravi again.

"No Ravi, I not only gave you Aakar, but someone very special to me. I gave you Jayanti."

Jayanti opened her mouth.

As she did, an appalling thought crossed her mind. "Does this mean that your becoming a nun was…all a sham, simply a way of staying close to Ravi?"

The sister shook her head. "Oh no, dear: nothing of the sort. Along with you two, my faith in Jesus Christ is the most special thing in my life." She smiled. "Believe me when I say that I'm very much where I ought to be. The Sisters of Charity took me in knowing I was an abandoned wife. I had no intention of marrying again."

Ravi was frowning. Jayanti recognized it as the expression he wore when he'd retreated to a very private place. He was thinking deeply.

After a few minutes of silence he looked up at Sister Rosalind and shook his head, as if bewildered. "A mother," he said.

Sister Rosalind stayed still.

Jayanti held her breath. She was a wise woman who knew Ravi needed time.

No one drank the tea that had been poured.

In the distance, Jayanti could hear the whoops of police cars and ambulances coming closer.

Their sound seemed to stir Ravi from his contemplation. He got up from his seat, crossed over to Sister Rosalind, knelt down, and took her hand. Ravi sniffed. "I used to think that if I ever had a mother, I'd want her to be someone just like you." He lowered his head. "The fact that you are my mother..." his voice faltered.

Sister Rosalind put her hands either side of his face and gathered him to herself. Then she cradled her son to her bosom.

Jayanti put her hand on her chest, feeling as if she'd just run a marathon. As she caught her breath, she felt a sharp edge dig into her.

She must have chipped Rohit's stone pendant when Rahul pushed her over. Jayanti fished the pendant out and looked at it.

One third of its edge had broken off.

It had broken away to reveal the end of what looked to be a gemstone secreted inside it. The stone flashed a blue color, so intense that it shocked her.

Chapter 33

"Why did he do it?" asked Ravi.

Jayanti took hold of his arm and hugged it. She'd heard Ravi ask this question a number of times in the days since the shootings. It wasn't a question that needed an answer: the question was a symptom of his difficulty in digesting it.

She kept quiet.

Jayanti was walking with Ravi through the grounds of Vellore Fort toward the tall, wedge-shaped gate of the Jalakandeswara temple complex.

Ravi was wrestling with the burden of knowing that Rahul had leaped in front of him to protect him from the bullet from his father's gun. Jayanti acknowledged to herself that it would be hard to digest. Ravi's father had tried to kill him—and someone he barely knew had died in his place.

Rahul's death was no easier for her to come to terms with. She'd cried a lot.

Sister Rosalind sought to comfort her.

"Rahul loved you, Jayanti, but I suspect he was a conflicted man. He threw in his lot with Mr. Nāgá, probably because of money. The trouble was, he was inherently good. So, when he saw your love for Ravi, he tried to protect him. His action was his gift to you." She'd smiled sadly. "Remember him well."

Jayanti knew it would take her a long time to fully understand the significance of what had happened. It would also take considerable time for Ravi to come to terms with the fact that his father had thought so little of him. She shook her head. It was a terrible thing for any son to bear. Ravi had spoken only once of his grief over what could have been—and hadn't mentioned it since.

She gazed up at the tall sloping walls of the Hindu temple gate. It was intricately carved into myriads of pillared porticos and gods.

Why is life so harsh and complicated?

Jayanti felt the need for solid certainty and simplicity. "Let's walk over to the walls of the fort and see the moat," she said.

Ravi nodded and looked at his watch. "We've got fifty minutes before we have to be back at the police station."

Jayanti groaned inwardly.

An investigation into multiple murders was always going to be a long and protracted affair, but reliving it for the police time and time again, forced her to continually confront the horror of what happened.

They'd all agreed to tell the police exactly what had occurred. The only thing they agreed to change was the reason Rahul and Kumar were present. They were described as friends who had come to help keep Ravi safe.

Eventually, the police had established the sequence of events.

Gokul Panwar had been confronting Ravi and Jayanti over Ravi's secret marriage. He'd pulled a gun and threatened to kill Jayanti to bring the 'shameful' marriage to an end.

At that moment, the drama had been gate-crashed by two would-be kidnappers who threatened them with guns.

Ravi had shot one of the men with a gun that Rahul had managed to give him, whilst Kumar had fought with the other. Kumar managed to hit his man over the head as Aakar Sing fired two shots into the kidnapper.

Mr. Panwar had seized the opportunity afforded by the mêlée to shoot Jayanti, but Rahul leaped in front to protect her—and was mortally wounded.

Aakar Singh had then shot Mr. Panwar to stop him killing again. Simple.

Jayanti shook her head. It hadn't been simple at all.

Further questioning established that both Aakar Singh and Ravi had current firearms licenses.

Eventually, the investigating officers expressed themselves pleased at solving both the kidnap reported to them earlier in the week by Chandra of CMC, as well as a multiple murder. However, they still required all those involved in the drama to stay in Vellore until investigations were completed.

Sister Rosalind secured lodgings for Aakar and Kumar in the servants' quarters at Big Bungalow.

Jayanti looked at the stolid walls of the fort and was amazed at the size of the stones used to build it. Many were more than twelve feet long. Despite the stones being irregular in shape, she doubted she would be able to squeeze a postcard between the cracks. It was extraordinary workmanship.

They strolled on to the outer walls above the moat. Ornate stone cubicles clung to the outside of them, overhanging the water. Jayanti presumed they'd been built to protect people needing to draw water.

"I took...my mother for a walk here yesterday," said Ravi. He leaned his back against the parapet and put his hands in his pockets.

"What's it been like getting to know each other..." she fought for the right words, "...in a whole new way?"

"Weird."

"Bad?"

He took a moment to reply. "No. It was a bit rough in the beginning...until I found out..."

"What?"

He sniffed. "Do you know she kept a notebook on me?"

Jayanti shook her head.

"Yeah. She showed it to me. Evidently, she's got sixteen of them. She started a new book each year and wrote down everything I was doing." He turned to her. "There are things she's done in my life that I had no idea she was responsible for." Ravi tried to laugh, but it sounded more like a sob.

Jayanti put a hand on his shoulder.

"She divided each page into four columns and headed them: 'Date'; 'Activity'; 'Joys'; and 'Items for Prayer'. My...my mother managed to catch up with Aakar almost every fortnight."

"It doesn't surprise me. Sister Rosalind is...a very remarkable woman...and very organized. Sister Elizabeth says she pretty much runs the convent in Delhi." Jayanti stared out from the parapets across the city, barely seeing any of it. Its impatience and noise seemed to be held at bay by the moat, allowing her to relive the experience of the past few days.

She recalled the conversation she'd had with Sister Rosalind yesterday. It began with her asking the nun why she'd thought to place her in the house of Gokul Panwar.

"You needed a place to be safe." She'd smiled.

"You didn't just use me to..."

"To reach my son?" She'd shaken her head. "No, I didn't connive in that way. I just knew that you were the sort of person I would want to influence my son. He was becoming someone...er, who was a little too much like his father." She smiled. "But I never dreamed I would be as successful as I was."

"It must have been hard for you, as a mother."

"It was. Ravi's father made it clear that things would not go well for Ravi if I interfered. That was the threat he continually held over me. I had to be careful."

"I'm not sure I was very careful."

Sister Rosalind had kissed her on her head. "You were a gift of God."

———

Jayanti had been in turmoil over what to do with the gemstone still mostly encased in its soapstone shell. She wanted to shelter Ravi from yet another issue, thinking that he had quite enough to cope with as it was.

She glanced up at him seated at the tiny kitchen table. Their evening meal had become one of her favorite times. It was when they talked best. She'd put a jar of flowers on the table, and he'd lit the four cotton wicks of a brass sacramental oil lamp. Its warm shadows encouraged intimacy and reflection.

"Ravi, how much do you know about gemstones?"

"A bit. My father taught me a little."

"If I showed you a gemstone, could you tell me what it was?"

Ravi leaned back and looked at her. "Jayanti, what's on your mind?"

Wordlessly, she got up and fetched her bag from the sideboard. Jayanti took out the chipped soapstone pendant and laid it in front of Ravi. As she did, the lamplight flashed through the brilliant blue of the gem.

Ravi looked at it. "Isn't that the pendant Sister...er, my mother gave you?"

She nodded. "But it actually came from Rohit, the beggar. He asked her to give it to me."

Ravi picked it up from the table, held it in front of the nearest flame, and gave a low whistle. "Wow!" He turned it round in the light. "Do you mind if I break it free of the soapstone?"

"No."

Ravi picked up a fork and levered off small chips of stone until he could pull the gem free. He again held it up to the light.

"Do you know what it is?" asked Jayanti.

For a moment, Ravi did not answer. Eventually he said, "This is a sapphire. It's the best sapphire I've ever seen." He continued to inspect it. "In fact, this is the best sapphire anyone would ever expect to see in a life-time."

"Really?"

Ravi handed the gem to her. "Hold it in front of the light."

She did. The intense blue again flashed its brilliance at her.

"That deep cornflower blue indicates that it comes from Burma. The best sapphires come from either Kashmir or Burma."

"It's beautiful," said Jayanti, as she turned it around in her fingers. Staring into its glinting blue depths was hypnotic. "Do you suppose it's very valuable?"

Ravi shook his head. "I can't say for sure because I don't know whether it's been heat-treated."

"What?"

"Some people heat-treat sapphires to give them a deeper blue color. Proper gemologists can tell." He reached over, took the sapphire from Jayanti and held it against the flame. "But something tells me this is the real deal."

"Wow! Maybe it could help with our college fees…" she lowered her head, "if we get in."

Ravi laughed.

"What are you laughing at," she said, sitting up.

"Well, my darling, I very much suspect that what you have here is a pretty generous dowry."

"Have I?" she said, brightening.

"Hmm," he smiled. "I don't think you have any idea of what you have."

"Then tell me."

Ravi drew a deep breath. "Well, the only sapphire I've seen that looks anything like this is the Bismarck sapphire. I've only seen pictures of it. Cartier actually put it into a necklace." He turned the gem in his fingers. "This, like the Bismarck sapphire, looks to be a bit over sixty carats. And it has the same color—a deep cornflower blue." He nodded. "It really is fabulous."

"How fabulous?"

Ravi leaned back in his chair. "Well, a top quality Kashmir sapphire would fetch twenty five thousand American dollars per carat. And this, as far as I can judge, is at least that good."

Jayanti furrowed her brow in disbelief. "How can you tell?"

"Gemologists talk of the three Cs: clarity, color, and carats."

"Carat; that's the measure of a gem's weight, isn't it?"

Ravi nodded.

She did some mental arithmetic. "What!" Jayanti reared her head up. "If what you say is true, then this sapphire is worth over a million American dollars."

He grinned. "I told you that you had a good dowry. But we'd need to get it checked by a real expert. I can only give you a rough guide."

"But even if it were a tenth of that value, that would still be more than I could possibly imagine..." Her voice trailed off.

Ravi reached across the table and held her fingertips. "My darling, there is a very good chance that this sapphire will be worth a good deal more than I've said."

Jayanti was speechless. She picked up the gem and examined it. "It looks so...alive."

"Hmm, not surprising. It's considered to be the ultimate blue gemstone. The ancient Persians believed that the earth rested on a giant sapphire which gave its blue color to the sky."

"Oh, that's beautiful imagery. Gosh, if I'd known it was so special, I'd have urged you to be more cautious breaking it free with your fork."

Ravi shook his head. "I wasn't worried. Sapphire is the third hardest mineral that exists. It's part of the corundum family—along with the ruby."

"Really?"

"Hmm." He reached over and reclaimed her hand. "You understand, of course, that a sapphire symbolizes faith, remembrance, and commitment." Ravi played with her fingers. "Prince Charles gave Princess Diana a sapphire engagement ring."

Jayanti got up from her seat and carried the dirty plates to the sink. "Then let's pray that this symbolizes a rather more enduring commitment for us."

"Oh, it will."

She walked back to him and rested a hand on its shoulder. "Why?"

"It's bigger."

She punched his arm.

Chapter 34

The old house in Delhi, with its dark secrets, seemed to wake up as if from a deep sleep. Jayanti reflected that whilst she may not be able to open its eyes, she could certainly open its doors. She was sitting on the grand curving steps that led up to the landing. The paneling in the entrance hall, decorated with swords and muskets, was bathed in the light that streamed in through the open front door.

It felt strange to be back; strange to sleep with Ravi in his room rather than the cellar; and strange to have Sister Rosalind sleeping in the house. She was sleeping in her old bedroom—the one that had previously been hidden behind a door Jayanti had never seen open. The only door that remained shut was that leading to Gokul Panwar's suite. That door remained closed, as if in shame.

The funeral of Ravi's father had taken place at St John's in Vellore. It had been a double funeral shared with Rahul. Ravi had asked for it to be that way as he said he would be able to say nothing at a funeral just for his father. As it was, Rev. Thomas was able to speak of Rahul, about a self-sacrifice that reflected Christ's sacrifice for all of humankind.

Greater love has no one than that they lay down their life for a friend.

Ravi came out of the library carrying a box. Seeing Jayanti, he put it down on a hall table, climbed up a few steps, and sat beside her. "You have no idea how much I loved sitting next to you on these steps."

Jayanti leaned against him. "How's it going?"

"Slowly. I've talked with mother. She's had permission to take two months off from her work with the Missionaries of Charity to stay here and help sort things out." He dropped his head. "It's weird isn't it? I've organized her to have power of attorney over my financial affairs so she can act on our behalf. She now has total control over the finances that my father worked so hard to cut her off from."

"She'll be very good at it."

He nodded, "She's trying to obtain probate from the judge of the District Court. It's pretty straightforward, evidently, so she isn't expecting any problems."

Jayanti looked around the entrance hall. Dust motes hung in the shafts of sunlight. "What will you do with the house?"

"What will *we* do with our house?" he corrected. "Do you want to keep it?"

"Honestly?"

"Hmm."

"No."

"Whew. I'm so relieved to hear you say that," he smiled.

"Then what shall...*we* do with it?"

Ravi shrugged.

"Why not give it to the Missionaries of Charity as another home for the destitute? Their old home is overcrowded."

"I'm not sure they would allow that in this suburb. It's zoned for consular housing and expensive private dwellings."

"Couldn't they sell it and buy a suitable property elsewhere?"

Ravi put an arm around her. "Let's do that."

Sister Rosalind came into the hallway from the study. For a moment, she looked at the two of them sitting on the stairs together and said nothing. The beginnings of a smile played on her face. "I've found something that you should both see," she said.

Jayanti and Ravi followed her into the study and stood around the ornate desk.

Sister Rosalind picked up a small wooden box and handed it to Ravi. "I found this at the back of one of the desk drawers."

Jayanti looked over Ravi's shoulder as he opened it. The velvet nest inside was empty. However, it did contain a piece of paper. Ravi picked it up and unfolded it.

Jayanti caught her breath as he opened it. Two things had been drawn on the paper: a six pronged star, and a stylized drawing of a peacock.

"That has to be the box in which our sapphire was originally housed," she said.

Ravi nodded. "I agree. Rohit must have seen it when he was asked to re-cut the stone inside."

"And wanted to record what he'd seen on the pendant in which he hid the peacock stone," added Jayanti.

Ravi raised an eyebrow. "The peacock stone?"

"It's the name I gave it." She shrugged. "It sounded right."

He nodded. "The question is: what does it all mean? It appears as if the sapphire and these hieroglyphs point to a significance that lies beyond the existence of the gem alone."

"Zurich!" said Jayanti in surprise.

Sister Rosalind nodded. "That's where Gokul had his overseas bank account. He has two accounts in Delhi and one overseas in Zurich."

"So you have to go to Zurich?"

The nun nodded. "Someone has to take a copy of the probate certificate in order to access the strong boxes and accounts he has there. I rang the bank yesterday, and they made that very clear."

"Well, that clears up the mystery of where father's jewels are located," said Ravi as he mopped up the last of his chicken tikka and yogurt.

Since they had returned to Delhi, the kitchen staff had consistently over-catered for their meals. It was as if they were relieved to finally be doing their job.

"What on earth will we do with the jewels if we find them?" asked Jayanti.

"Good question." Sister Rosalind turned to Ravi. "Have you come to a final decision about this, Ravi?"

Ravi nodded. "Yes. I'd like to persist with Sister Elizabeth's plan: sell the jewels and give the proceeds to charity."

Jayanti smiled. "Fabulous."

"If you do that, Ravi, you will have to be very careful." Sister Rosalind lifted her chin. Jayanti could see in that simple action the film actress she'd once been. The nun continued. "Money does strange things to people and to organizations, even philanthropic organizations. Too much money can cause as many problems as too little. It can turn people's heads and result in waste."

"Could you oversee it, mother?" asked Ravi.

Sister Rosalind looked at her son in silence. Eventually she nodded. "Yes."

Ravi continued. "Taking things slowly would probably give us the best returns as well. If we dump a large number of jewels on the market in Antwerp, it would depress the market."

"I agree," said Sister Rosalind. "If the sum of money involved is as much as we suspect, then it may take up to ten years to disburse —if we do it wisely."

Jayanti grinned. "I'd give a lot to see the faces of the Swiss bankers as they hand over the strongbox keys to a nun dressed like Mother Teresa."

"One thing has been bothering me," said Ravi, rubbing his forehead.

Jayanti and Sister Rosalind looked at him.

"Why didn't Rohit sell the sapphire when he became destitute? It would have given him and his family a life of luxury. What is it that we don't know? It doesn't make sense."

"I've wondered about that too," said Sister Rosalind. "It may have a simple explanation. I think Rohit knew the value of the stone and understood that it was simply too expensive for him to sell and remain anonymous." She shrugged. "Alternatively, he was a craftsman, a master gem cutter, who may not have had the heart to cut up such a beautiful stone."

"But, why didn't he sell it when he contracted cancer?" Asked Ravi. "He needed help and had nothing to lose."

Sister Rosalind shook her head. "By that stage, he was under our care. I'm not sure he wanted to be anywhere else."

Everyone remained quiet for a moment.

"There may also be another reason," said Jayanti slowly.

Ravi looked at her questioningly.

"Rohit went to great lengths to hide the stone in a place that featured the two pictures of a star and a peacock. I think he knew, or at least suspected, that the combination was a key to something special…"

"Such as the key to Gokul's fortune," finished Sister Rosalind. She sighed. "We may find out later this afternoon. I've been asked to ring Zurich at 3:30 pm so they can give me further information on the protocol for accessing Gokul's account."

A servant came in from the kitchen and poured each of them a glass of chai.

Jayanti toyed with her glass. She was thinking about Aakar Singh. He'd been asked to travel to Jaipur to make inquiries about the identities of the missing gem cutters. "Has Aakar managed to find out anything in Jaipur?" she asked.

Sister Rosalind nodded. "Yes he has. He's pretty sure about the identity of two of them and he's now checking on the third. The fact that all were master gem-cutters who went missing at the same time has made his investigations fairly straightforward."

"What will we be able to do for the families?" asked Jayanti.

"Well, again, we need to be careful. The very worst thing to do would be to dump a load of conscience money onto struggling families ill-equipped to handle it." She folded her hands in front of her. "Ravi and I have thought of starting a trust that will enable them to meet any housing, educational, dowry and health needs they have."

"That's a wonderful idea."

"I wish we could do more," said Ravi. "But we may at least be able to bring some hope and healing."

Chapter 35

Jayanti didn't know what to do with herself. Sister Rosalind was away in Switzerland and Ravi was deep into some administrative project in the study. She looked at her watch. It would be two hours before Elizabeth joined them for dinner. It was ages since she they had had a good chat, and she was looking forward to catching up with her. Jayanti loved the unpretentious ways of the Australian nun and the way she could laugh with her.

She re-entered the house through the kitchen door from the laundry area. Quite why she had gone outside to finger the stone plinth against which the washing was bashed, she couldn't say. She nodded to the kitchen staff and made her way along the corridor into the entrance hall.

That morning, Aakar Singh had come back from Jaipur and given his report to Ravi. Jayanti suspected that Ravi was working on it now. Aakar was now seated at the desk in his office. She could see him through the internal window. Jayanti knocked on the door.

Aakar's deep voice growled. "Come in."

When he saw Jayanti, he stood up and bowed his apologies. "Memsahib, I did not know it was you." He waved to a chair. "Please…to sit down."

As she did so, she was slightly alarmed to see a disassembled pistol laid out on newspaper in front of the Sikh. Aakar had obviously been cleaning it.

"It's good to have you back, Aakar."

The desk chair squeaked as it took the weight of the giant. "Memsahib," he said. "I have wanted to talk with you."

"Please do."

"All those years you were with us here…" he paused as if finding it difficult to continue.

"Yes…"

"I hope you didn't think me a bad man. I had orders not to make things too comfortable for you."

"Oh no, Aakar. It was your name alone that kept me safe. No one hurt me."

The giant nodded and then flashed a smile that showed his white teeth. "You are very beautiful. Sometimes I needed to talk to some rascal fellows with naughty thoughts."

"Thank you Aakar."

"I show Mr. Panwar where you live in the cellar." He grinned. "But I do not show him your bathroom."

Jayanti laughed. "I think that bathroom kept me sane."

Aakar picked up a soft wire brush and began brushing the slide of the pistol.

"What will you do when we sell this house, Aakar?"

"No problems. I will manage your house in Delhi and talk with the people in Jaipur…maybe four months."

"And then?"

"When you and Sahib Ravi are safe being doctors in Vellore, my job here will be done."

"Aakar, it is very unlikely that either of us will be accepted to CMC."

The Sikh waved the brush dismissively and continued with his cleaning.

"Where will you go then?" she asked.

"To Amritsar."

"To your home?"

"To my spiritual home; I am Sikh."

"What will you do there?"

"I have a position, a post, as one of the guards at the temple."

"Oh: what: the Golden Temple?"

He nodded. "Yes. It is very beautiful. Have you been there?"

"No. Tell me about it."

Aakar sat back and adopted a faraway look. "You enter through a white marbled portico, down steps to a beautiful lake. It is square...and everywhere is marble. Is very beautiful." He paused. "And then...a causeway to an island in the middle of the lake." He furrowed his brow as if calling the image to mind. "And on the island, a temple covered in gold—the most beautiful temple. You must see it at night when the lights shine. Aah," he tapped his heart.

"I would love to see it."

Aakar opened a drawer and produced a photo of a Sikh dressed in a long yellow chola, white pants and a blue turban. He was holding a spear. "This is what I will look like."

"You will also hold a ceremonial spear?"

He looked up at her. "It is not ceremonial."

"Hmm." She couldn't resist adding, "And perhaps this pistol?"

He smiled. "Perhaps."

Jayanti pictured Aakar holding a spear and suspected that the mere sight of him would make the need for a pistol redundant.

"I just wanted to say, 'thank you', Aakar—for everything."

Aakar stopped brushing. "Memsahib, It has been an honor. You are very good for Ravi...and good for my heart."

"No!" laughed Jayanti, "It wasn't me who gave you the chili."

"I reckon it was," insisted Elizabeth.

Jayanti, Elizabeth, and Ravi were seated at the dining table. They'd finished their first course and were enjoying the stories of Elizabeth's harrowing introduction to India.

Before the banter could continue, Ravi's phone rang. He'd left it on the table as they were all expecting a call from Sister Rosalind in Zurich.

Jayanti put a hand over her mouth, half afraid of what she might learn.

Ravi picked it up, paused, and then said, "One moment, Mother, I'll put you on speaker phone so Jayanti and Elizabeth can hear."

Both Elizabeth and Jayanti got up and stood beside Ravi at the end of the dining table.

"Hello, my dears." Sister Rosalind's voice could be heard clearly.

They all called out their greetings.

"What have you managed to discover?" asked Jayanti.

"Well, I have managed to gain access to Gokul's accounts here, as well as his strong box. It's very big."

Ravi rubbed his forehead. "Have you looked inside?"

"That's where we have a problem. Inside the bank's strongbox… is another strongbox. It seems as though Gokul wanted to make doubly sure that the contents would be secure."

"But surely…" began Jayanti, squeezing her fingers into a fist.

"I'm afraid that the bank can be of no use. They have given me access to their strongbox, but have no jurisdiction or responsibility beyond that."

Jayanti groaned.

"Do we know anything else? What do we need to get inside the second strong box?" asked Ravi.

"There is a combination lock, a big one. The bank says it needs a thirteen figure code comprising six digits between one and twenty, interspersed with seven letters of the English alphabet."

"Whew! That's huge," said Ravi.

"Yes, the bank could tell me that, because they require customers to register the existence of the second strong box. They also require the nature of the second box to be registered—at least, they need to be told what it's not. Evidently it's part of the requirement that ensures the strong boxes contain no explosives. It's a terrorist security thing. Sadly, they can't tell us anything more."

"Nothing at all?" asked Jayanti.

"No. The staff here tell me that owners usually choose to register the existence of the safe by using the first letter of the combination lock to remind them which code they must use."

"And what is that letter," asked Ravi.

"K."

"Where are you now, Mother?" asked Ravi.

"I'm in the bank. The staff here have been very helpful. They tell me I can stay as long as I like. They close at five, however, so I've only got two hours. Tomorrow morning I need to catch my flight home."

"So we've got two hours?"

"Yes."

Ravi nodded. "Thanks, Mother. We'll get back to you."

"God bless you."

Ravi leaned back and rubbed his hair. "Would anyone like to suggest what a thirteen letter code might be that begins with the letter K?"

Jayanti and Elizabeth resumed their seats.

Jayanti let her gaze wander to the jar of wildflowers she'd put in the center of the table and watched the light dance through the glass vase. "I think we've got a good starting point," she said, slowly.

Ravi looked at her with a puzzled frown.

"Rohit's star, peacock, and sapphire—don't you see. That has to be the key that unlocks the strong box." She reached out and placed a hand on Ravi's arm. "You're great with numbers and logic, Ravi —you do Sudoku puzzles all the time. What numbers do a star, a peacock, and a sapphire suggest?"

"What sapphire are you talking about?" asked Elizabeth.

Ravi got up from the table and returned moments later with the tiny satinwood box she'd last seen in the study. He opened it, picked out the sapphire, and showed it to Elizabeth.

"Wow, she exclaimed. "Is…is that real?"

"It's definitely a sapphire. Jayanti and I scratched the study window with it." He smiled. "We actually scratched our initials."

Elizabeth feigned shock. "Am I having dinner with a pair of graffiti vandals?"

Jayanti reached over and took the piece of paper out of the box, smoothed it out and placed it on the table.

Ravi put the giant sapphire next to it. "Ladies," he said. "We have two hours."

The next hour passed slowly.

Jayanti had fetched a pad of paper, and there were now pages with diagrams, digits and letters scrawled all over them.

Elizabeth sat back and sighed. "Look, I know that I'm a rather unsubtle antipodean, but wouldn't it be a whole lot simpler to hire a security firm to take the strong box to an engineer's workshop, get them to open it, and then bring it back?"

Ravi nodded. "I'll fly to Zurich, if necessary and organize for something like that to happen, but it would be a lot nicer and simpler if we didn't have to."

The beginnings of a possibility began to swim in and out of focus in Jayanti's mind. "Ravi, what numbers are associated with a cut gem?" she asked.

"Well, a cut gem usually consists of the table, the flat top bit, and the crown, which is the faceted bit around it. The tapered part of the gem under the crown is called the pavilion."

"Could numbers be associated with it?" asked Elizabeth.

Ravi, bit his lip. "Sort of. Gem cutters write down the number of facets in each layer."

Jayanti couldn't restrain herself from bobbing up and down in her seat. "Well, how would you write down the sequence for the peacock stone?"

"Peacock stone?" queried Elizabeth.

"That's what I call it."

"Well, let's see." He picked it up. "There's one facet comprising the table, obviously." He counted the next layer of facets. "There's eight star facets; eight main facets and sixteen break facets. Those are the ones on the bottom of the crown." Ravi turned the sapphire upside down. "And the pavilion has sixteen break facets and eight main facets." He looked up. "What does that look like?"

Jayanti pushed a piece of paper over to him. It showed the numbers 1 8 8 16 16 8. "There's your six numbers," said Jayani, quietly.

"But are they in the right order?" asked Elizabeth.

Ravi drew three intersecting lines, making a six-pronged star. Then, starting at the top he labeled the end of each arm with each of the numbers, beginning at the top and going clockwise.

"The only reason I see for a star is to use it to reverse the numbers." Ravi pointed to the top number at the end of the first arm. "So the first number is not the one on the top, but actually the one on the other end of the line at the bottom. If we do that, what does it look like?

Elizabeth quickly scribbled down the numbers: 16 16 8 1 8 8, and pushed the piece of paper in the middle for them all to see.

"So now we need seven alphabet letters that begin with K," said Ravi. "What sequence can we think of that begins with K."

Jayanti suddenly knew. She put a hand over her mouth. "I've got it," she said.

Ravi and Elizabeth looked at her.

"It doesn't begin with K, it ends with K. The word is backward, like the numbers."

"And what word is that?" asked Elizabeth.

"Peacock."

Everyone was silent. Time itself seemed to stand still.

"Could…could it possibly be?" asked Elizabeth tentatively.

Ravi nodded. "I think it has to be." He turned to Jayanti. "Well done, my darling." He reached for his phone. "Shall I ring?"

Jayanti nodded.

"Yes Ravi." Sister Rosalind's voice came through clearly.

"Mother, I've been sitting with a couple of geniuses here and we've come up with a number-letter sequence we think might work."

"What is it, dear?"

Jayanti wanted to scream. She sounded so controlled, as if she were asking what the cricket score was.

Ravi read out the sequence.

There was a long pause.

The lamp guttered causing light to flicker across the walls.

"Well, well." Sister Rosalind's voice brought them all to attention. "My goodness. The front flap of the box opens to reveal about ten shallow drawers."

"What's in them?" squealed Jayanti.

"Aah, Jayanti, my dear: rather a lot of jewels, hundreds in fact… in each tray."

Jayanti found herself hugging Elizabeth's neck.

An instant later she flung herself at Ravi. He was trying to speak to his mother. "Fabulous, Mum. Enjoy your trip home. We'll sort it out later."

He put the phone on the table and hugged her.

Eventually, order was restored.

They made such a noise that Aakar Singh burst through the dining room door to check that all was well.

"Aakar, my good friend," said Ravi, could you tell kitchen we are ready for dessert. I think they've prepared some kheer." He grinned. "Then come and join us in eating it. We're celebrating."

It was only later when Jayanti was eating her flavored rice porridge that she realized that Ravi had called his mother, 'Mum.' She approved. It was better than 'Mother'. He was slowly getting used to his status as son.

After the plates had been cleared away, Ravi excused himself and left the room.

Jayanti stretched. The tensions of the day were beginning to catch up on her. She yawned.

"Well, my lovely Jayanti," said Elizabeth. "I'd better get back to the convent or they will think I've absconded."

"Must you?" said Jayanti holding out a hand.

"Sadly, yes."

Aakar stood up from the table. "I will drive Miss Elizabeth home."

"Thank you Aakar." Elizabeth got up from the table. "Please don't bother Ravi. Just thank him for a wonderful night."

Jayanti hugged her and walked her to the door.

Ravi came out from the study and also said his farewells.

As the giant wooden door of the house closed, Jayanti and Ravi walked to the grand curving staircase and sat together on the fifth step—their favorite step. Outside, the madness of Delhi had died to a faint hum.

Ravi put his arm around her. "It's been quite a night," he said.

"Hmm," she said.

The stillness of the house began to settle around them allowing its secrets to stir into life.

Jayanti stroked the white marble step beside her. Sister Rosalind must have trodden on this step countless times, sometimes carrying Ravi. It was a pleasing thought. The peace of her memory seemed to dispel the grimness of the military hardware displayed on the paneled walls. Perhaps something of her had always been here. Jayanti pulled Ravi's arm around her tighter.

"It's been a good day," she said.

Ravi nodded. "It has, but I've been looking forward to getting you to myself." He sighed. "And this is the perfect spot."

"Perfect for what?"

"It's the right spot for me to share some news."

Jayanti put her head on his shoulders.

"What's that?" she said sleepily.

"You've won a place to study at CMC."

"What!" She pulled away from him. "When did you find out?"

"This morning." He grinned. "But I thought I'd hold onto the news until I unearthed some more information."

Her mouth dropped open "But, but...what about you? What...?" She couldn't finish the sentence, appalled at the thought that Ravi had not been accepted.

"And I've been accepted too."

She flung herself into his arms.

Eventually, Jayanti got herself under control and rested her head against his chest.

The house again began to settle for the night with its mysterious creaks and clunks. A moth circled the chandelier above them determined to learn the secret of its light.

"Just one more thing," said Ravi, eventually.

"Hmm," she said, yawning.

"I've just rung CMC, and they've told me they make no provision for a husband and wife to live together at the college. There are separate men's and women's dormitories."

"What!"

"But when I said the Panwar estate would fund the new wing of their hospital, they thought they might be able to find us suitable accommodation."

Notes

Chapter 1

1. Okay

Chapter 2

1. Asshole
2. Brown sugar heroin.
3. Opium

About the Author

Nick Hawkes has lived in several countries of the world, and collected many an adventure. Along the way, he has earned degrees in both science and theology—and has written books on both. Since then, he has turned his hand to novels, writing romantic thrillers that feed the heart, mind, and soul.

His seven full-length novels are known as, 'The Stone Collection.'

Nick Hawkes' first novel, *The Celtic Stone,* won the Australian Caleb Award in 2014.

Also by Nick Hawkes

The Atlantis Stone

Benjamin is part Aborigine, but nightmares from the past cause him to disown his heritage. Unfortunately, he feels no more at home in the Western world and so struggles to know his identity. Benjamin seeks to hide from both worlds in his workshop where he ekes out a living as a wood-turner. However, an attempt on his life propels him into a mysterious affair surrounding the fabled "mahogany ship" sighted by early white settlers near Warrnambool in Australia.

Felicity, a historian, is seeking to rebuild her life in the nearby town of Port Fairy after a messy divorce. The discovery of the "Atlantis stone" whilst scuba diving results in her joining Benjamin in an adventure that takes them overseas to the ancient city of Cagliari in Sardinia.

An anthropologist dying of cancer and an ex-SAS soldier with post-traumatic stress, join Benjamin and Felicity in an adventure that centres on a medieval treaty, a hunger for gold... and, of course, the Atlantis stone.

More details at www.author-nick.com

(See next page for more)

The Fire Stone

Sebastian, a young farm hand living in the Australian mallee, is being watched by Val, a fugitive hiding in the forests on the banks of the River Murray. Val has an official document that confirms his death fourteen years ago. There is no official document that confirms his particular skill: assassin.

Pip divides her life between her musical studies at the Adelaide Conservatorium and her work as a barista. Her ordered life is shattered when bullets fired through the window of her home reduce her cello to matchwood. The violence appears all the more bewildering given that she lives with her father David an Anglican cleric and retired missionary.

A web of violence draws all four of them together.

Everything in Sebastian's life begins to change when he is given the gift of a Koroit opal—*The Fire Stone*. It begins a journey in which he is challenged by David's wisdom and confronted by Pip's love.

The four of them seek to escape the violence that pursues them by sailing across the Pacific to the islands of Vanuatu. There, in the village community of Lamap, the final drama is played out…

…before *The Fire Stone* makes an unexpected return.

More details at www.author-nick.com

Made in the USA
Coppell, TX
02 April 2020

18214987R00180